DIRTY
LETTERS

OTHER TITLES BY VI KEELAND & PENELOPE WARD

Hate Notes

Rebel Heir

Rebel Heart

Cocky Bastard

Stuck-Up Suit

Playboy Pilot

Mister Moneybags

British Bedmate

Other books by Vi Keeland

All Grown Up

We Shouldn't

The Naked Truth

Sex, Not Love

Beautiful Mistake

Egomaniac

Bossman

The Baller

Left Behind (cowritten with Dylan Scott)

Beat

Throb

Worth the Fight

Worth the Chance

Worth Forgiving

Belong to You

Made for You

Other books by Penelope Ward

When August Ends

Love Online

Gentleman Nine

Drunk Dial

Mack Daddy

Stepbrother Dearest

Neighbor Dearest

RoomHate

Sins of Sevin

Jake Undone (Jake #1)

Jake Understood (Jake #2)

My Skylar

Gemini

DIRTY LETTERS

New York Times Bestselling Authors
VI KEELAND
PENELOPE WARD

Montlake
Romance

Published by Montlake Romance, Seattle

www.apub.com

Amazon, the Amazon logo, and Montlake Romance are trademarks of Amazon.com, Inc., or its affiliates.

ISBN-13: 9781542016797
ISBN-10: 1542016797

Cover design by Perfect Pear Creative Covers

Cover photography by Stefanie Renoma

Printed in the United States of America

To anyone suffering from anxiety, you're not alone.

CHAPTER 1

LUCA

Oh boy, here we go again.

I pushed my shopping cart forward rather than turning to walk down the aisle I'd originally planned. But after taking a step or two, I couldn't help myself. I backed up enough to hide my body behind the endcap and peeked my head out to watch the action.

A woman with the frizziest, most unnatural color of red hair placed a deodorant back on the shelf and grabbed a new one. She opened the top of the stick and sniffed it, then proceeded to lift one side of her shirt and wipe the deodorant under her armpit, then moved on to the other. Replacing the cap, she examined the shelf for a moment before picking another brand. Again, she plucked the top off, sniffed, then swiped under each of her pits. I watched, fascinated by how serious she was, while she sampled six different deodorants before a store employee finally noticed what she was doing. When they both ran down the aisle yelling, I figured that was my cue to move my ass and finish up my shopping trip.

A few months back, I'd seen a man *sample* a dozen whole rotisserie chickens. He removed the plastic cover off each one, ripped off a leg, took a big bite, jammed the leg back inside the cavity of the chicken, and replaced the cover of each. When I'd told the manager, he'd sighed and yelled to a stock boy to go fetch Mr. Hammond. Food shopping at two in the morning in a twenty-four-hour supermarket tended to bring out a unique brand of shoppers. *I fit right in.*

"How are you doing today, Luca?" Doris, the cashier, asked as I loaded my groceries onto the conveyor belt. She'd been working at this supermarket since I started coming here about five years ago—really nice lady. I knew she was a grandmother of nine and number ten was on the way. She babysat a few of them during the day, which was why she worked the graveyard shift. Doris was also one of the few people who I ever told the truth about why I shopped forty miles away from my home in the middle of the night.

"I'm doing good." She scanned a package of black licorice followed by two canisters of Pringles and two boxes of packaged brownies. Not my usual grocery items, so I explained. "I'm stocking up for a road trip, not pregnant."

Doris's brows rose. "A road trip? Must be something special if you're boxing yourself into a little car for a long haul."

"I have to clean out my dad's apartment in Manhattan."

"He passed away last year, right?"

I nodded. "I've been avoiding it. I'd rather be water-boarded than step foot onto a tiny island with a population of eight and a half million people. Not to mention hours stuck in a car with traffic jams to get there—pure torture."

Doris frowned. "Can't you hire someone to do it?"

I *had* hired someone. Then a combination of my own guilt and Dr. Maxwell, my therapist, made me decide to do it on my own. But eventually the stress of thinking about all those people in New York City gave me trouble sleeping, and I hired the company again. Then I canceled. *Again.* Then I'd hired a new company because I was too embarrassed to hire the same company a third time. And again I canceled. *Wash. Rinse. Repeat.* Until I was out of time, and, well, now it's tomorrow.

"It's just something I need to do myself."

Doris looked genuinely concerned. "You going to be okay? I'm a good copilot if you need a friend to tag along."

I smiled. "Thanks, Doris. That's really generous of you. But I have someone coming. We're leaving tomorrow evening to avoid traffic as much as possible."

Doris finished scanning my groceries, and I swiped my card. Before leaving, I reached into my cart and grabbed the bag containing bing cherries and a package of dark-chocolate Milano cookies. I put it at the end of her checkout counter, like always. "The cherries are for your grandkids. Hide the Milanos from the little monsters."

She thanked me. "Have a safe trip, sweetheart. Can't wait to hear all about it."

Yeah, me too. This was going to be one hell of an interesting road trip.

"You could focus on relaxing more if you'd let me drive my car. Maybe listen to some of those breathing technique recordings I gave you."

I looked over at Dr. Maxwell's dented-up Cadillac parked in my driveway. The man shouldn't be driving at all. In fact, he was a prime example of why people over a certain age should be retested to keep their driving privileges. *Relaxing* would be the last thing I would be able to do with him behind the wheel. Plus, he knew I needed to be in control as much as humanly possible.

I started the ignition, and my bow-tie-wearing copilot lifted binoculars up to his eyes, peering out his window. I needed a new therapist for thinking it was a good idea to go on this trip with my current therapist.

"You ready, Doc?"

He nodded and didn't lower his binoculars. "Never been to the Big Apple. Can't wait to see what birds we'll encounter."

I shook my head. "Pigeons, Doc. Rats with wings. That's what we'll encounter."

We set off on our seven-hour trip from Vermont to Manhattan. The first few hours were uneventful until we hit a traffic jam. I started to sweat—literally—and my fingers began to tingle at the tips. *Oh no. Not while I'm driving.* The fear of the looming panic attack was sometimes almost as bad as the actual attack. My heart started to race and my head felt light. I sometimes vomited during a severe episode and did *not* want that to happen while on the highway. I made the rash decision to drive up the shoulder so I could escape the feeling of being boxed in between immovable cars. The rumble strip on the road jarred Dr. Maxwell from his nap. He woke and grabbed on to the *oh shit* bar above his door. "What's happening? What's going on?"

"Nothing. We just hit some traffic. My heart started to race, and I needed to take a detour."

Only Doc would look relieved by what I'd just said. He released his death grip on the car and spoke in a calming voice. "Relax your grip on the wheel, Luca."

I looked down. My knuckles were white, and the surrounding lengths of my fingers were bright red. I did as instructed, because while I might not trust the nutty doc to drive a car, he knew how to steer me away from panic attacks. Nodding, I said, "I tried a breathing technique. It obviously didn't work."

"Tell me what you're doing right now."

My eyes flashed to him and back to the road as I continued on the service road. "What I'm doing? I'm driving."

"No. Tell me what you were just able to do when you felt the feeling of panic set in."

"I got off at the exit?" I wasn't sure what he was getting at.

"That's right. You steered the car from one road to another road, which made you feel safer. You can do that. And you can also pull over at any time and get out of the car if you feel like it."

I nodded. Of course, he was right. But he wasn't merely stating the obvious. He was reminding me that *I* was in control of the situation and had exerted that control when I felt I needed to. The biggest part of my anxiety disorder was the overwhelming fear of being trapped. It was why I didn't do crowds, traffic, public transportation, or small spaces—yet I could be okay walking outside in a busy city. Exercising control to remove myself from the situation helped alleviate the anxiety.

"Take a nice deep breath, Luca."

I inhaled through my nose and blew out a deep breath through my mouth. A chill hit my skin, which actually comforted me. My body became clammy when it headed into a panic attack; a coating of sweat often permeated my entire face with the rise of my body temperature. A chill meant my body was cooling back off.

"Tell me about that date you had Saturday night."

I knew he was trying to distract me, to keep my mind focused on something other than the panic attack brewing, but I was okay with that. "He brought . . . *his mother*."

Doc's brows drew together. "His mother?"

"Yup. To a picnic lunch I'd made." Picnic lunches at the park were my go-to first date regardless of the weather. They allowed me to avoid crowded restaurants, yet keep it casual. It was that or my place, and the last guy I'd invited over to my house for dinner assumed that meant I'd invited him for first-date sex.

"Why on earth would he bring his mother?"

I shrugged. "He said he'd mentioned our plans to her, and she had said she'd never been to that park." This is what I got for being up front with men about my issues before we met—I got *weirdos*. But it wasn't fair to hide the fact that I couldn't go out on dates like a normal twenty-five-year-old woman. Not so shockingly, men tended to disappear fast when telling them about yourself and using words like *agoraphobic* and *anxiety*. Which in turn meant the remaining dating pool needed a bucket of chlorine.

Realizing our conversation had distracted me and helped quell the looming full-fledged panic attack I'd felt coming on, I said, "Thank you for that, by the way. I feel a lot better already. I'm just going to pull over in that empty parking lot up ahead and get out and do some stretches."

Doc smiled, knowing yoga was one of my own self-calming techniques. "Atta girl."

The rest of the trip was almost peaceful—sans a few extra detours and Doc talking to his *lady friend* on his cell with the volume turned up so loud that I heard her remind him to fill his Viagra prescription. I'd timed it so we'd arrive in Manhattan in the middle of the night to avoid as much traffic as possible, and we were lucky to nab a parking spot on the street, since a garage was out of the question for me. My trusty therapist was staying at a hotel, which was only half a block from my dad's apartment.

"Doc. Wake up. We're here."

He woke looking confused, and I felt bad for having to interrupt his sleep at all. "What? Huh? Oh. Okay. Here. Yes. Okay."

I walked him to his hotel and waited out front to make sure he checked in with no issues. "Thanks again for taking the ride with me, Doc. Give me a call if you feel up to breakfast in the morning. I know it's late so, if not, maybe lunch."

Doc patted my shoulder. "You call me if you need me. Anytime, Luca. And you did well today. Really well. I'm proud of you." I knew he meant it.

Even though I'd been tired for the last few hours of the drive, when I let myself into Dad's place, I was suddenly wide awake. It was the oddest feeling to walk into my father's living space without him there. He'd been gone for a year now—although you wouldn't know it from looking at his apartment. Mrs. Cascio, Dad's neighbor, had been checking on the place every few days, bringing in the mail, and generally keeping the cobwebs at bay.

I walked around and opened all the windows, because fresh air always helped me feel less trapped. Dad's bookshelves were still lined with framed photos, none of which had been updated in the five years since Mom died. I lifted a small silver double frame. The left side had a photo of me in my Girl Scouts uniform, and the right had one of me sitting on Dad's lap while leaning forward and blowing out the candles on a birthday cake. I must've been six. A large ivory frame displayed my parents' wedding photo. I traced my finger along the length of Mom's veil. Everyone always told me I looked just like her, but growing up, I didn't see the resemblance. Now, though, I was the spitting image of her. It was hard to believe they were both gone.

The small dining room table had a pile of mail. I'd had Dad's mail forwarded to my house, so mostly it was just catalogs and junk. Once a month, Mrs. Cascio sent me everything that arrived, even though I'd told her it wasn't necessary. I mindlessly fingered through the pile, not expecting to see anything worth keeping. But I stopped at an envelope addressed to me—well, not me, but *Luca Ryan*. That was a name I hadn't heard in a long time. In second grade, my teacher, Mrs. Ryan, started a pen pal writing program with a small town in England. We weren't allowed to use our real last names for safety reasons, so the entire class used her last name—hence I was Luca Ryan.

I checked out the return address for the sender's name.

G. Quinn

Wow, really? It couldn't be.

I squinted at the postmark. It was from a PO box in California, not England, but I didn't know any other Quinn other than Griffin. And

7

the handwriting did look pretty familiar. But it had been close to eight years since we'd exchanged letters. Why would he write now?

Curious, I ripped it open and scanned right to the bottom of the letter for the name. Sure enough, it was from Griffin. I started at the beginning.

Dear Luca,

Do you like scotch? I remember you said you didn't like the taste of beer. But we never did get around to comparing our taste in hard liquor. Why is that, you might ask? Let me remind you—because you stopped *answering* my letters eight damn years ago.

I wanted to let you know, I'm still pissed off about that. My mum used to say I hold grudges. But I prefer to think of it as *I remember the facts*. And the fact of the matter is, *you suck*. There, I've said it. I've been holding that shit in for a long time.

Don't get me wrong—I'm not obsessive or anything. I don't sit in my house thinking about you all day long. In fact, there have been months that go by when thoughts of you don't even enter my brain. But then some random thing will pop into my head out of the blue. Like I'll see some kid in a pram eating black licorice, and I'll think of you. Side note—I've tried it again as an adult, and I still think it tastes like the bottom of my shoe, so perhaps it's that *you* just have no taste. You probably don't even like scotch.

Anyway, I'm sure this letter won't find its way to you. Or if by some miracle it does, you won't answer. But if you're reading this, you should know two things.

1. The Macallan 1926 is worth the extra cash. Goes down smooth.
2. You *SUCK.*

    Later, traitor,

    Griffin

What in the hell?

CHAPTER 2

LUCA

You suck.
   You suck.
   You suck.
   I couldn't concentrate on anything else ever since opening that letter.

As I packed more of my father's stuff, thoughts of a boy—well, now a man—who had once been near and dear to my heart flooded my mind.

A text from Doc interrupted my mental trip down memory lane.

Doc: I could have sworn I just saw a tit in Central Park.

A tit?

Luca: What?

Doc: A Eurasian blue tit. One of the most exquisite birds in the tit family.

Luca: Ah. Bird peeping. I should have known.

Doc: It's a nonmigratory bird found overseas, so it couldn't possibly be one. But if not a tit, then what is it? Last time I saw one, I was in England!

The fact that he'd mentioned England was strange—almost like a sign from the universe, given the letter from Griffin. Although technically the letter came from California. I really needed to take a breather and talk to Doc about this. I'd never mentioned Griffin to him before.

Luca: I need to talk to you about something. Can you come to me?

Doc: I think it would be good for you to try to venture out.

Sighing, I knew he was right. I needed to make sure he wasn't in a congested spot, though.

Luca: Is the park crowded right now?

Doc: No. Not where I'm sitting anyway.

Luca: Okay. Can you let me know exactly where to find you?

Doc was sitting on a bench surrounded by pigeons when I arrived at The Falconer statue in Central Park. His binoculars were facing up toward the sky, and when he lowered them down to eye level, he jumped like I'd startled him.

"Well, looks like they found their spirit animal," I teased. "I guess word got out that the biggest bird lover to ever visit New York City was in town."

"I wish. It was the bread. Doesn't take much to get their attention. The problem is, they don't understand once you run out. The next thing you know, you're in an Alfred Hitchcock movie." He turned to me and examined my expression. "What's going on, Luca? You seem a little anxious. Is being out and about bothering you?"

"No, that's not it."

"Is the packing stressing you out? Do you need my help?"

"No. I've actually been pretty productive in that regard." I carefully opened the coffee I'd just bought from the food truck around the corner and blew on it. "Something else has come up, though."

"Oh?"

Taking a sip, I nodded. "I received an unexpected letter from an old pen pal. His name is Griffin. The letter was in the pile of mail that's normally forwarded to me in Vermont."

"What's bothering you about the letter?"

"It was the first time I'd heard from him in many years, and it was . . . a little bit abrasive . . . taunting. Basically, he told me I sucked. It hurt because . . . he's right in a way. I never really properly explained to him why I'd stopped responding to his letters eight years ago."

Doc briefly closed his eyes in understanding, seeming to know exactly where I was going with this. "Eight years ago . . . the fire."

I simply nodded.

Eight years ago, my entire life changed.

At seventeen, I'd been a normal teenager. Friday nights were spent sitting in the packed bleachers watching my *captain of the football team* boyfriend throw touchdown passes, going to the mall with my friends, and attending concerts. I couldn't have even told you what agoraphobia was back then. I didn't have a fear in the world.

My life as I knew it ended on the Fourth of July, senior year. It was supposed to be the summer of my dreams, but instead it became my worst nightmare.

My best friend, Isabella, and I had gone to see our favorite band, The Steel Brothers, in concert in New Jersey when some nearby fireworks landed on the roof of the venue, igniting a fire that engulfed the building. More than a hundred people died, including Isabella. My life had been spared only because I happened to be waiting in line in the concession area, which was downstairs and away from the site of the explosion.

"Well, you know how long I've spent feeling like I didn't deserve to live when Izzy had to die," I said. "If she had just been the one who'd gone to get the sodas, she'd still be alive. My mental state back then was so bad that for a while, I didn't allow myself to enjoy any of the things that brought me happiness. One of those things was writing to Griffin.

He lived in England, and we'd been writing to each other since second grade—a decade. Over the years, we became more than just pen pals. We were trusted confidantes to each other. When the accident happened . . . I just stopped writing to him, Doc. I fell into my own world and stopped responding. I let our friendship die along with all the other parts of me I felt were dead."

Soon after that time, I'd also started to avoid crowded places, and over the years, my fears had only grown worse. Now at twenty-five, my list of phobias was long. The only good thing to come out of being an antisocial recluse was that it afforded me endless hours of solitude to write. My very first self-published novel ended up going viral a couple of years ago, and before I knew it, I had penned three bestselling thrillers under the pen name of Ryan Griffin and landed a deal with a major publishing house.

"Did you say his name is Griffin? Isn't that your—"

"Yes. Ryan was the last name I used in my letters to him—it was my teacher's last name. And the Griffin comes from *that* Griffin."

He was intrigued. "That's so interesting, Luca." It had been a long time since I'd given Doc new material to ponder and analyze.

Around the time my books started doing well, I realized I wanted to take charge of not just my career but my life. That was when I'd found Dr. Maxwell, who was semiretired and the only shrink in Vermont who made house calls for the agoraphobic. What I didn't know at the time was that Doc was even more peculiar than I was—which of course meant he eventually became my new best friend. Totally odd patient-client relationship, I know, but it worked for us. It helped that my tree-lined property was a bird lover's haven.

"When was the last time before this that Griffin wrote to you?" he asked.

"He wrote a few times that first year after I stopped responding before he finally gave up on getting another letter from me. I was just numb back then. And by the time I realized what I'd done—that

I'd sabotaged one of the most precious things in my life—I was too ashamed to write him back." I sighed and admitted the painful truth. "In many ways, losing Griffin was my self-punishment for surviving the fire."

He stared off for a bit to absorb everything. "Well, your pen name is certainly evidence that you've clung to Griffin in some capacity."

"Absolutely. I've never forgotten him. I just didn't think I'd ever hear from him again. I'm shocked. I can't even blame him for having an attitude, though. In his eyes, I deserved it. He doesn't know what really happened."

"What's to stop you from explaining now? Writing him back would surely be therapeutic and long overdue."

"He hates me, Doc."

"He doesn't *hate* you. He wouldn't have written to you all these years later if he did. Clearly, you're still on his mind. He might be angry. But you don't let anger get to you like that unless on some level you care."

I knew Griffin had cared about me at one time. I'd cared about him deeply, too. Stopping our communication was probably one of my biggest regrets in life. Well, aside from offering to get the sodas at the concert.

As I recalled some of my memories of Griffin, I managed a chuckle. "He was so funny. I always felt like I could tell him anything. But the weird thing is, while he didn't know my identity and vice versa, he probably knew the real me better than anyone at that time. Well, he knew the person I *was*."

"You're still her, Luca. Just a bit more . . ." He hesitated.

"Extra?"

"No."

"Nuts?"

"I was going to say vulnerable."

Doc turned his attention to a bird that had landed on the bench across from us. He immediately brought the binoculars to his eyes. "A northern cardinal!" He turned to me. "Do you know what they say about cardinals?"

"What?"

"They're messengers from our loved ones who have passed. Perhaps you might want to ponder what our little red friend might be trying to tell you at this very moment, Luca."

◆ ◆ ◆

We stayed in New York for five days before the long ride back to Vermont.

Walking into my precious house—my safe haven—after being away for so long brought me a great deal of comfort.

I'd picked up my pet pig, Hortencia, from a local farmer who agreed to watch her. How does a homebound girl end up with a pet pig, you ask? Well, a couple of years ago, there was a fire at a farm down the road from my house. When I'd heard about some of the animals dying, naturally it triggered me. Doc thought it would be a good exposure exercise to visit the site of the blaze. When I had, I learned that not all the animals had died. Some of them were still there, housed in a temporary barn. When I looked into my pig's eyes, I basically saw myself: a sad, lonely being. She'd probably lost her best friend, too. So I did what any person who'd found her soul mate would do: I took her home. Ever since, she'd been like my child, definitely spoiled. Since I never planned to have kids, I figured I could get away with treating her as such.

As I tried to get back in the routine of being home, I continued to be haunted by Griffin's letter.

You suck.

You suck.

You suck.

He was never one to mince words, but after all this time—that was harsh.

It felt like I should want to cry over this, but I couldn't actually cry anymore. In fact, Doc and I often joked about the fact that I was incapable of shedding tears. He'd urged me to try to cry, to let everything out, but I never could—not since the accident. Not even when my father died.

Venturing down to my basement, I went in search of the plastic-covered container that I'd put Griffin's old letters in—I'd kept them all.

Maybe if I could somehow reconnect with him by rereading one or two, that would help me decide whether or not I should write him back. Responding to his abrasive letter could be opening a massive can of worms. It might be better to let sleeping dogs lie, to let my memories of him remain mostly positive. I supposed responding could also bring me some much-needed closure, even if he never wrote me back again.

Opening the container, I closed my eyes while selecting one. I didn't want to manipulate fate by choosing a particular letter to read. I just picked one at random.

Upon recognition of the date, I realized it was one of the older ones, from when we were probably about ten.

Dear Luca,

How have you been?

I feel sad because my mum and dad told me that they are getting a divorce. They said it's not my fault.

How was your dance recital? Did you get flowers after, like you wanted? I would send you some if I had money. It costs a lot to send things to America.

I wrote you a song. It starts like this:

Luca. Luca. Luca.

I want to buy you a bazooka.

I'm not done yet. Looking for more words that
rhyme with Luca.

Later, gator,
Griff

Clutching the letter to my chest, I thought about the image of
him I had in my head. Somewhere in the box was the one picture of
himself he'd ever sent me. When we were around twelve, we broke the
unofficial "rules" and finally exchanged photos. I'd chosen one where I
was dressed up for a dance competition, wearing makeup and with tap
shoes on. He'd sent me a photo of himself standing in front of some
building in London. At that age, I was just starting to be boy crazy. It
definitely surprised me to learn that Griffin, with his big brown eyes
and dark hair, was quite the cutie.

I'll never forget what he'd written back to me after receiving my
photo.

Turn this letter around for my reaction to your photo on the back.

And then when I did, it said:

Wow, Luca. You're really pretty!

I don't think I had ever blushed so much in my life. That was the
first moment it hit me that maybe my feelings for Griffin could be more
than just platonic. Of course, I'd kept that thought deep inside because
it wasn't like anything could have happened given the distance between
us. Neither of us had the money to fly to see each other. The distance
only made it easier, though, for us to open up to each other.

Remembering the words of that sweet young version of Griffin and
comparing them to the harsh ones I'd received a week ago was a tough
pill to swallow. Still no clearer on whether to contact him, I pulled out
another letter.

This one, according to the date, was from when we were probably
around fifteen or sixteen.

Dear Luca,

I'm gonna tell you a secret. Don't trust boys. Like ever. We'll tell you anything to get into your pants. And then when we do, we'll blow it—literally—in like two seconds.

Okay . . . you can trust me, but no other guys. (And that's only because I'm far away and can't try anything anyway, otherwise I might not trust me, either.)

Anyway . . . I had sex. I guess maybe you figured that out already.

It was good, but not as great as I thought it was going to be. It was a little awkward, really. Mostly fast. You haven't done it yet, right? I hope the answer is no. It better be no, Luca. If it's yes, don't tell me. I couldn't handle knowing. (Actually, no, I do want you to tell me. I just might need to steal some of my father's scotch first before you do.)

My mum is doing better. Thank you for asking. They said the cancer hasn't spread beyond her ovaries. So that is good. (That's good, right?) Do you know anything about ovarian cancer? I need you to tell me it's going to be okay. I would trust that if it came from you. I guess I just need to hear it. Because I can't lose my mum.

Don't take too long to write back. Hearing from you always puts me in a good mood.

Later, gator,
Griff

I sighed and put that letter back into its rightful envelope. So many feels.

Okay maybe just one more.

Taking another one out, I opened it and read.

Dear Luca,

Listen to me. If there's one thing I ever tell you that you actually believe, believe this: once a cheater, always a cheater. How do I know this? Because my fucking father is one, that's how! I come from cheating stock.

So if you're looking to get cheated on again, stay with that bloody loser you're dating.

Did you hear that? That's me fucking yelling from England! Do NOT give that fucker a second chance. I don't care how sorry he says he is.

He doesn't deserve you, Luca. He doesn't.

He's lucky there's an ocean between us, because I would have broken his face for hurting you the way he did. I'd be in jail, and then my letters would come with a disclaimer that they're being sent to you from a correctional facility.

Can you tell I'm mad? Because I'm fucking mad.

Anyway . . . (now that I've gotten that out) what else is new with you?

I have some news, actually. I joined a band. It's with these guys from school. Don't laugh, but it's sort of like—a boy band. Except I'm much cuter than Harry Styles. But you wouldn't know that because you haven't seen me recently. Should we change that soon? *Show me yours and I'll show you mine* kind of thing? Just kidding. No pressure. Just food for thought. I know you like to remain a mystery. And I sort of like that, too. (But for the record, if given a choice, I would like to see what you look like now.)

Write back soon.

Later, gator,

Griff

P.S. Still cracking my knuckles over here.

I shut my eyes and smiled.

There was only one letter I'd never read. It was the last one that had arrived almost a year after I'd stopped responding. By that time, I was so ashamed for not writing back in so long that I couldn't even bear to read them anymore. I didn't know at the time it would be the final letter.

I broke my rule and sifted through the pile looking for that one unopened letter until I found it. I knew it wasn't going to be pretty, but I opened it anyway.

Nothing could have prepared me for what I actually discovered inside, though. *Nothing.*

Luca,

Did you notice I left out the "Dear"? You're not dear to me anymore. Because you fucking stopped responding to my letters. You'd better be dead. That's all I have to say.

Wait. I don't mean that. I would never wish you were dead. Ever. I'm just so fucking confused. I'm writing to tell you that this is the last letter you're ever going to receive from me.

That's a damn shame, because I could really use a friend right now, Luca.

My mother died.

I can't believe I'm even writing that.

We found out two months ago that her cancer returned and that it spread. Everything happened so fast after that.

My mother DIED, Luca.

She's gone.

I couldn't read what else the letter said because the ink was stained from his tears.

And now, without warning, my own tears were pouring out in an endless stream—tears I didn't even know I had the capacity to make anymore.

An hour must have passed before I finally stopped crying my eyes out.

I hadn't cried since Isabella died in the fire. I'd thought my tears were all dried up. Apparently it was just that nothing had affected me enough to make me cry since.

He'd lost his mother, and I didn't even know.

I was certain now beyond a shadow of a doubt that I had to write to him. I owed him a full explanation of what happened to me and why I'd stopped responding.

Even if he continued to hate me after, at the very least he deserved an apology.

This couldn't wait anymore.

I knew that I'd be up all night pouring my soul out to him.

I only hoped he could forgive me.

CHAPTER 3

LUCA

It had been two weeks since I'd mailed the letter. Well, it was more like a book—several pages long. I'd explained all the details about the fire and my emotional state after and apologized for never having acknowledged his mother's death, making sure he knew that I'd only opened the final letter recently after losing my dad. I told him about my anxiety issues—explaining agoraphobia in detail and how it wasn't a one-size-fits-all mental health disorder. I wanted him to understand I wasn't a total shut-in, that I loved the outdoors and could have intimate relationships. Honestly? I couldn't even say what else I'd written. I'd stayed up that entire night until my heart was empty. In my head, I wasn't writing to the guy who'd told me I sucked. I was writing to the Griffin I hoped was the same person I'd cared for so much.

I normally went to the post office twice a week during their slow hours to check my PO box that I used for reader mail. A week after sending the letter, though, I found myself checking it every single afternoon.

For several days, there had been no letter from Griffin. On the fourteenth day, a bright-red envelope stood out from the rest of the mail. The name on the return address: Griffin Quinn.

My hand was shaking. *Do I rip it open and read it here?* Could I even wait long enough to drive home?

I decided that it wouldn't be a good idea to potentially receive upsetting news in a public place. God forbid I pass out and wake up with a swarm of people huddling over me or something. The thought of that made me shiver.

So I decided to race home.

Once I arrived back at the house, I fed Hortencia really quickly so that she'd be content and pacified while I read the letter.

Sitting down in a comfortable spot on my couch as my heart pounded, I carefully opened the envelope.

> Dear Luca,
> I suck.
> Do you still look up a word in the dictionary to memorize every day like you used to? Well, just in case you hadn't reached this one yet, let me do the honors.
> Self-ab*sorbed
> /self-əbˈzôrbd/
> *adjective*

1. preoccupied with one's own feelings, interests, or situation.
2. a friend who shits on you because he never stopped for a minute to think maybe there was a reason his best friend stopped writing.

I smiled and looked over at the old beat-up Merriam-Webster dictionary sitting on the corner of my desk. My copy was from 1993 and had 470,000 words. The spine had multiple layers of duct tape holding it together from all my years of use. Ever since I was four and learned to read, each morning I flipped open to a random page, closed my eyes, and pointed to a word on the page to memorize. I'd highlighted the ones I'd committed to memory, which meant the old book had a ton of yellow in it now. Although by my calculations, I'd have to live to be 1,288 years old in order to finish. But that never discouraged me any.

I loved that Griffin remembered my little hobby. Only four people knew about it. It made my chest heavy to realize that he was the only one left now—Mom, Dad, and Izzy were all gone. Not even Doc knew. Not that I'd hidden it or anything. There'd just never been a reason to bring it up.

I went back to reading, anxious to see what he'd written.

> I'm so sorry for everything you went through, Luca. Even sorrier that I wasn't there for you when it happened. I lost my mum, and she was too young to die, but we're *supposed* to lose our parents. We're not supposed to bury our friends as teenagers. Especially not the way you lost Izzy. Jesus, my letter was pretty damn insensitive. It's not an excuse, but I'd had a little too much to drink when I wrote it. Do you think we can start over? How about if we try. Yes? That's nice of you. Okay. I'll go first.

> Dear Luca,
> Hey! It's been too long. I've thought about you a lot over the years and wondered what you were doing. For some reason, those thoughts have been more frequent lately. It's too bad we lost touch. That was probably my fault. Anyway, I'll catch you up on my life. Moved to the States four years ago. Still strumming my guitar— my music career has been . . . interesting. It didn't exactly turn out the way I thought it would. But it pays the bills. Not married, no kids. Had a girl for a while. Now I don't. Love the Pacific Ocean. Bought a

surfboard. I suck at it but paddle out to escape life as often as I can.

So . . . agoraphobic, huh?

It's kind of a cool word. Wonder how many points that gets you in Scrabble? The B, P, H, and C are each worth at least three. But wait . . . I don't want you to think I'm a weirdo and sit around and play Scrabble all the time. Then again, you wouldn't think that's weird—you memorize the damn dictionary. A quiet game might be just up your alley. Maybe a two-person game? Would three people in a room freak you out? Or is there a set number that pushes you over the edge? Seventeen maybe? That's a lot. Way more than can play Scrabble at once, that's for sure.

It's too bad you don't have agrizoophobia. (Fear of wild animals, just in case you haven't hit that in the dictionary yet, either, slowpoke.) That would get you ten points just for the Z.

Maybe next time. I mean, some wild animals are pretty damn scary.

Later, gator,

Griff

P.S. Your letter told me everything wrong with you . . . or at least everything you *think* is wrong with you. Tell me three things that you're proud of in your next one.

P.P.S. I lied. You were never not dear to me.

P.P.P.S. I'm so very sorry for your loss, Luca.

"So let me get this straight, he poked fun at your condition, and that's one of the things you like about him?" Doc stopped and held his pointer finger up to his lips to shush me, even though he'd just asked me a question. We definitely didn't have traditional therapy sessions. Twice a week, we walked in the woods for a few hours and talked while he looked for birds. He brought a notebook, but half the time he was jotting down notes on the breeds of bird he saw, not anything that I said.

"Yeah. I know it's odd. But he wasn't really poking fun at me. I mean, he was, but he wasn't. It's one of the things I'd always loved about our relationship. He was always honest, and his joking around was never mean-spirited. It was more like his way of showing me that whatever I was obsessing over wasn't such a big deal. Like when I was seventeen and still a virgin—I'd told him I was nervous that by the time I did it, everyone else was going to be more experienced, and I'd seem like an awkward amateur. So he made up this crazy song called 'Urgin' the Virgin.' He just has a way of making it okay to laugh at my fears."

"Hmm," Doc said. I assumed his response was related to a bird sighting and not what I'd babbled on about. But when I looked over, his trusty binoculars weren't even up.

"Hmm, what?"

"Well, you fired your old agent because she made a few jokes about your condition, even though she'd always said she was joking. You were never fully convinced of the nature of her ribbing. Yet with Griffin, a man you've never even met, you're able to accept his poking fun as harmless and almost comforting. It seems that you've placed a lot of trust with this pen pal of yours."

I thought about it. "I *do* trust him. I might not have ever met him, but I considered him one of the closest friends I ever had. We shared a lot over the years. He lived in England, so there wasn't a chance we were going to walk into each other in the halls at school, which helped break down the normal walls that kids put up to protect themselves. We were really close. Even about some pretty intimate stuff."

"And yet you broke off all contact with him after the fire."

"I told you, I was very self-destructive back then. It felt so unfair that I was still alive and Izzy wasn't. I didn't allow anything that might cause me happiness to stay in my life. And I think a part of me was ashamed to tell him what had happened. I know now it doesn't make sense, but I was ashamed I didn't save Izzy."

Doc and I walked in silence for a while. Eventually he stopped to peer through his binoculars. He spoke to me while looking off into the distance. "Allowing him back into your life can be good for a number of reasons. One, your relationship with him is intertwined with the period of your life that has caused you the most sadness and grief. You've permanently eliminated almost everything from that time of your life—leaving New York, not listening to music, crowds, gatherings, sadly even your parents have passed. So on a daily basis it's very easy for you to pretend that part of your life didn't exist. But it did, and while we can push things we don't want to think about into the recesses of our mind, the only way to truly put them behind us is to deal with them. Griffin is part of your old life that you've tried to bury. Dealing with that relationship is a step toward moving forward."

I nodded. That made sense. "What are the other reasons?"

Doc adjusted his binoculars. "Hmm?"

"You said allowing Griffin back into my life could be good for a number of reasons. But you only told me one."

"Oh. Yes. Acceptance. The more people you open up to about your condition, the less you'll fear the reactions of others and the better your support system."

"I guess . . ."

"Plus, then there's the coitus."

I assumed I'd heard him wrong. "The what?"

"Coitus—you know, the unison of the male and female genitalia. It's been a while since you've been with a man."

Oh God. "Um. Yeah. I got it. Let's just take it one step at a time."

◆ ◆ ◆

Once, I'd written 14,331 words in a day. It was the most productive writing day I'd ever had. Although my average daily word count was more like two thousand. Yet it took me half a day to write a few hundred words in a letter to Griffin. It wasn't so easy answering the question he'd asked.

> Dear Griffin,
> The ten pages of tragedy and heartbreak that I wrote to you about bled from my fingers. Yet you asked me a simple question—what three things am I most proud of—and I've been staring at an empty page for the better part of an hour. The first one is easy.
> My work. I'm proud of the books I've written. I guess in my depressing first letter, I failed to mention that my dream came true—I'm a writer, Griff! Four years ago, my debut crime-fiction novel became a *New York Times* bestseller. I've published three additional books since, and I'm currently in the thick of the editing process of my fifth.
> The other two things I'm proud of aren't so easy to come up with. But I guess something I'm very proud of is asking for help after Izzy died. It took me a while longer than it probably should've, but I found myself a therapist, and I'm working on facing my fears. One of the hardest things I've ever done was to pick up the phone and make that first appointment. It may sound silly, but even explaining my issue over the phone the very first time was difficult. I'm not better yet, but I'm working toward it these days, and for that, I'm proud.

God this is tough. Why did you have to ask for three things? I'm realizing I'm not very good at tooting my own horn. But the last thing I'm proud of is something I do as often as I can—I guess I'd describe it as random acts of kindness. For example, a few times I paid for the groceries of a stranger behind me. Or on a really cold day, I sometimes pick up hot chocolate for the school crossing guards—they're stuck outside in the cold. I know it's not earth-shattering, but I enjoy doing it. Once a month, I spend the day cooking a bunch of different meals and then drop them off at Mr. Fenley's house—he's my neighbor who lost his wife last year, and he really misses her home cooking.

Okay, enough about me. Now it's my turn to pick a question for you to answer:

Tell me three things you're afraid of.

Your favorite pen pal,
Luca

P.S. I love handwritten letters, but if you feel more comfortable on e-mail, we can exchange messages that way.

P.P.S. I'd love to exchange more recent photos. I'll show you mine if you show me yours? ;)

P.P.P.S. Agrizoophobia is thirty points without bonus spaces. But logizomechanophobia—fear of computers—is forty-three points.

I thought about including my photo in the envelope, but in the end I decided against it. We weren't kids anymore. Mrs. Ryan's rules didn't apply. But swapping adult photos felt like a big step for some reason.

Especially now that Griffin lived here in the States. Once we took that first step, what was stopping us from taking a second? That thought was pretty scary but also pretty exciting.

I folded the letter into an envelope and addressed it to his PO box in California. When I was done, I slapped on a stamp and looked down at the name. It was pretty damn crazy.

Griffin Quinn.

After all these years.

CHAPTER 4

GRIFFIN

"What's the total?"

My lawyer shook his head. "Just under a hundred and nineteen thousand."

I raked my fingers through my hair. "Jesus. How could I be so fucking blind?"

"It was over a period of two and a half years. Don't be so hard on yourself. Unfortunately, I see this type of thing happening all the time. I've had cases where it's in the millions, Griff. You were on the road a lot. Big money was rolling in and rolling out. You had to trust someone."

"Yeah. Apparently my childhood best friend was the wrong fucking choice."

The first thing I did when I signed my first record deal was bring over my buddy Will from England and hire him as my manager. I was traveling all over for gigs to promote my album. My record label was pushing me to get back into the studio and start my next one, and overnight, the day my single dropped, I gained two hundred thousand followers on Instagram. And that was before the shit *really* hit the fan. I needed someone to keep me organized, someone I could trust to deal with my finances on a day-to-day basis. My lawyer, Aaron, had warned me not to hire a friend. I told him he was nuts—no way was I hiring some firm over my buddy.

I held out my hand to Aaron. "Thanks for not saying *I told you so*, man."

He smiled. "Never. That's not part of my job. Did you decide how we're handling this? You know where I stand. Let the police deal with it. If he did this to his buddy, what's he going to do to strangers?"

I knew he was right, but I just couldn't press charges. Deep down, I felt partly responsible for Will's issues. I'd brought him to the parties that got him hooked on drugs. And when I realized how out of control his habit had gotten, what did I do? I took off for a three-month tour and left him alone in my big house with access to all the cash he needed to dig his own grave. Maybe if I'd canceled a few shows and pushed him into rehab, none of this shit would've happened.

"He borrowed the money from his family to pay it all back. As long as that check clears by the end of the week, I just want to put this shit behind me."

Aaron nodded. "Your call. What about his G-Wagen in the driveway?"

"I told him that was interest. Donate it somewhere. I don't want it."

"You sure? That's an expensive two-year-old car."

"I don't want his money. I'll take back what he stole. But that's it."

"You got it." Aaron stood. "Any particular charity?"

"No. You pick one." I walked him to the door and opened it. "On second thought, see if there's a legit charity for people suffering from agoraphobia."

My lawyer's brows drew together. "You serious?"

"Absolutely."

He chuckled. "Whatever you say, boss."

I watched as Aaron pulled out in his Audi R8. He had to navigate past Will's G-Wagen and my Tesla Roadster. The damn excesses in

California. Shit was definitely easier back in Yorkshire. Not that I didn't appreciate the fortune and fame, but some days I questioned if the price of it all was worth it—friends stealing from friends, women who use you for an introduction to record industry people, endless paparazzi, the inability to walk into a record store and spend a little quiet time perusing the aisles. I missed the simple things in life, and right now was a lull in the crazy times. Pretty soon, I'd be on tour again. Then Cole would swallow up Griffin completely.

Which reminded me. Instead of going back into the house, I walked down to the end of my driveway to check the mailbox. It had been a week since I wrote back to Luca, and I'd hoped that my first letter hadn't scared her off. Hell, I actually didn't think she'd even get my letter. I certainly never expected the shit she'd told me when she wrote back.

Losing a friend in a fire—at a crowded concert of all places. That was pretty fucked up.

I sifted through a two-inch stack of mail as I walked back to the house and smiled seeing Luca's familiar handwriting.

Settling into the couch, I tore it open and read every word. Twice.

When was the last time someone was that honest with me? My mum probably. It definitely hadn't been in the last three years since my star had risen in the music world. My life was filled with two kinds of people now—people who yessed me because they worked for me or my label, and people who wanted something from me.

Luca was neither—and unless she was totally full of shit, she also had no idea who the hell I was. She either didn't know who Cole Archer was or did and didn't recognize me from the one picture we'd exchanged more than ten years ago. Either way, being Griffin again felt good. Talking to Luca felt even better.

I read her letter twice more and then grabbed one of the half dozen notepads I kept lying around the house for when lyrics or music came to me.

Dear Luca,

Three things I'm afraid of? How am I supposed to answer that and still sound like a tough guy? I sure as shit can't tell you I'm afraid of the dark, or spiders, or heights. That would ruin my street cred. So I'm going to have to go with some real scary shit. Like failure.

If you want to know the truth, which I'm pretty sure you do, I'm afraid of failing. Letting others down, letting myself down, letting the . . .

I was just about to say *letting the fans down*. But Griffin didn't have any fans. I didn't want to start lying to Luca, so I'd just have to be careful how I phrased things.

. . . letting the life I've built out here in California fall apart.

What else am I afraid of? Death. Fearing something that is inescapable might not be the most productive use of time. Maybe it isn't even death that I fear but more the fear of the unknown. Do we really go to heaven? I think anyone who has a healthy fear of death must be skeptical of that answer—because if I was certain that I'd go to a place where there's no pain and no sickness and everyone gets cool wings and meets up with their old chums, I'm pretty sure I wouldn't fear death.

The last fear was a new one, one that I debated back and forth about sharing before eventually deciding to be honest. I mean, she'd shared some damn scary shit with me. It was the least I could do.

The last one is a relatively new fear, but that doesn't make it any less real. I'm afraid I'll fuck something up

34

and scare you away again. So let's make a pact, okay? If I screw up, you'll let me know and not just stop answering my letters.

I think at this point, we've exchanged enough heavy stuff to hold us for a while. So let's move on to the lighter portion of Luca and Griffin, Part Deux. I've got eight years' worth of unanswered questions:

1. Did you finally have sex? If so, you owe me your first-time story, since I shared mine and you promised to share yours. (Is it fucked up that I sort of wish you *haven't* had sex yet?)

2. How do you feel about bacon? I mean, you mentioned you have a pet pig, so I'm wondering if this means you don't eat bacon. Or maybe you're a vegetarian like half the people out here in healthy California.

3. If you were going to sing karaoke, what song would you choose and why?

> Later, gator,
> Griff
> P.S. While the thought of you showing me yours is extremely enticing, I'd like to hold off on exchanging photos for a while. Let's keep the mystery going.
> P.P.S. Hippopotomonstrosesquipedaliophobia—fear of long words—sixty-five points. Makes your little nineteen-point agoraphobia seem like child's play now, doesn't it? Get a real fear, Ryan.
> P.P.P.S. Do you have genophobia? I definitely don't.

CHAPTER 5

LUCA

I ran to the dictionary to look up the word *genophobia*: *The psychological fear of sexual relations or sexual intercourse.*

Great.

Well, he definitely wasted no time speaking his mind. In that sense, it was like no time had passed.

His questions certainly gave me a lot to ponder. The funny thing? I knew how I wanted to answer them, aside from one: how I felt about bacon. That was a dilemma I'd often struggled with. *Gah!* Why did he have to ask that?

I knew I wouldn't be writing him back until tonight anyway; I was late for an appointment with Doc. While we normally took walks in the woods, the weather wasn't cooperating today. So we planned to meet at Doc's house.

It was a good thing I had agoraphobia and not claustrophobia, because Dr. Maxwell had a tiny house—literally—like the kind you see on those shows featured on HGTV. Until Doc, I hadn't ever met anyone who actually lived in one.

Doc pointed to his favorite bird painting hanging on the wall. "This one still has to be my favorite, Luca. The hummingbird."

About a year ago, Doc decided that he was going to strive toward a life of minimalism—thus, the tiny house. Apparently all he needed were air and birds. He also concluded that he no longer wished for me to pay for my therapy in dollars, because he had enough money. He insisted that I instead choose another way to compensate him and asked that I come up with something I felt was suitable.

What do you get the man who doesn't apparently want or need anything? I knew it had to have something to do with birds.

Besides my writing, I'd always dabbled in art, just simple oil paintings. One afternoon, I Googled how to paint a bird. Over several months, I perfected the craft from the feather details down to the beak formation. I taught myself how to sketch and paint several types of birds but only presented him with the very best ones. The rest I kept in my basement. It was like a mortuary of birds down there. The one commonality among all the birds I'd painted? They all looked stoic, never flying, just posed. And their beaks were never open. We'd dubbed my art "The Stoic Bird Collection." Doc theorized that the birds' expressions were a reflection of how I felt inside. That's some heavy shit. Anyway, my framed artwork now graced every small corner of Doc's house, and I sort of cracked up every time I looked around at my creations.

Doc took a seat across from me. "So tell me, Luca, how has your correspondence with Griffin been going?"

The mere mention of Griffin's name had me feeling all giddy inside. "It's been really amazing. It feels like we sort of took up where we left off, which is pretty unbelievable, considering all we've both been through and the time that has passed."

"What does he do in California exactly?"

"You know . . . he doesn't go into the specifics of his job, but I know he works in the music industry and is an aspiring musician. I assume he must have taken any position to get his foot in the door."

"Ah. Smart."

"Something interesting, though . . . When I suggested that we exchange photos, he actually said he preferred that we keep the mystery going. I thought that was a little strange. In the past, he was always the one pushing to see what I looked like."

"Are you thinking that maybe he's ashamed of how he looks?"

"I'm not sure. Either that or he just enjoys the suspense." I sighed. "Is it weird to not care at all what he looks like now? I mean . . . there's a part of me that definitely imagines him as good-looking, like he was in the one photo I received from him when we were twelve. But at the same time, it just doesn't matter to me."

"I am actually a little surprised you were so eager to send him a photo of yourself. That's not like you. You tend to be a bit more guarded than that."

"Not with him. I think it's a selfish need to let him know that I'm not unattractive—or at least I don't think I am. I guess I kind of want him to want me. As awkward as I can be around other people, I'm pretty comfortable in my own skin. People have told me that I'm attractive enough times to believe it, even if some of those people were probably just trying to get into my pants."

"I'm glad you see yourself as beautiful, Luca—as you should, both inside and out. Of course, it doesn't matter what others think, only what you think."

While I knew he was theoretically right—it shouldn't matter what anyone else thinks—I definitely cared what Griff thought. Maybe a bit more than I should so soon.

"Sometimes at night when I'm bored, I put on makeup and get dressed up for no reason."

"I would say that's odd, but I spend half my life having one-sided philosophical conversations with birds."

"Yeah. You really can't talk, Doc." I laughed. "Anyway . . . I get all dressed up with nowhere to go. It's pretty pathetic. But I get to see what

I'd look like if I actually left the house. I take a few photos. I clean up nicely."

"You know you're giving me a great idea for one of your next exposure exercises, right?"

"Let me guess. You're gonna make me get dressed up and actually go out and be around people, aren't you?"

"Yes. And I know just the place we'll go."

I should probably be concerned. "Great."

Finally, nestled into my comfy spot on the couch with a hot cup of tea by my side, I began to write back to Griffin.

> Dear Griffin,
> I actually had to look up what genophobia is. At first, I thought you were referring to being a germophobe, which I certainly am not, considering I live with a pig! (I do keep her as clean as possible, although show her a pile of mud and all bets are off. Her true piggish tendencies come out.)
> Am I a genophobe? No. I love the idea of sex, of opening myself up to someone like that—I guess opening myself up literally and figuratively. :-) It can be a little scary, but not to the point of a phobia. My sexual experiences haven't exactly lived up to the potential I believe possible with the right partner, though. In other words, I haven't had the mind-blowing sex that probably exists. At least, I hope it exists. I'm still waiting to experience it.
> That leads me to answer your first question, which I basically just did. Did I finally have sex? Yes—but

not until I was twenty. It took me a while to start dating after the fire. I ended up losing my virginity to a guy I'd met through a support group for people affected by the fire. Michael had lost his cousin. After one of the sessions, we ended up going to his car to talk and one thing led to another. He hadn't a clue I was a virgin. Anyway, it was quick and painful. And incidentally, leather against a bare ass is not the most comfortable feeling. He stopped going to the meetings soon after and that was the end of him. Not exactly the "first time" story that dreams are made of. Then again, neither was yours. I've had two other partners since then who were nothing to write home about—or nothing to write my pen pal about. It wasn't all their fault. It takes two to tango, and I just don't think I let myself go to that place of vulnerability you probably need to in order to get lost in someone else. Do you have any pointers for me in that arena?

So karaoke . . . I've only done karaoke once but found it to be way more enjoyable than I'd ever imagined, even though I was alone in my living room with only Hortencia watching. I might have been a little drunk, sort of like you were when you first reached out to me again. (That was the best drunken decision anyone has ever made, by the way.) Okay, see? I'm stalling because I'm a little hesitant to tell you that my all-time favorite song to sing karaoke to is: (Drumroll) "Fernando" by ABBA! Then again, you might have guessed I would have chosen an ABBA song if you remembered anything I ever said in our dozens of letters.

I saved the hardest of your questions for last. It seriously took me all day to figure out how to answer this because it's honestly a huge moral dilemma for me. While I no longer eat it, I LOVE bacon. I spent many years proclaiming it my favorite food: eggs and bacon, bacon bits, bacon-wrapped scallops. The craving just doesn't go away overnight because you become the adoptive mother to a pig. The fact that my mouth is salivating now kind of sickens me. So I feel about bacon sort of how I feel about a lot of things in life. I stay away from it, but I can't help the fact that I like it. (Sort of like porn, maybe?) Of course, as I write this, Hortencia is staring at me and I feel like Hannibal Lecter.

On that weird note, I hope you write back soon. I'm enjoying our reconnection so much. It's really starting to feel like old times.

Do you still believe in God?

Your favorite pen pal,

Luca

P.S. Since you don't want to exchange photos, I thought I would tell you a little about myself now. I'm five foot six, 125 pounds, and clean up nicely when I have to. When I don't have to, I can be found most nights wrapped in a fleece blanket and looking like a potato.

P.P.S. That was your cue to tell me more about what you look like now.

The wait to receive a letter was always torture. I was never guaranteed that he'd write back. I just had to have blind faith each time. So while I waited, I'd pass the time moving on with my life: meeting my daily word count, attending sessions with Doc, caring for Hortencia. But the anticipation of more correspondence was ever present.

It took more than a week, but finally the bright-red envelope showed up in my PO box. The "letter days" were always something to celebrate. I'd drive home, get Hortencia settled, and relax into my chair to savor every single word.

Dear Luca,

Bacon and porn go awesomely together, by the way.

In my next life, I want to come back as a pig and be adopted by you. Is that weird?

I love your answers to my questions and how honest you are. I wouldn't mind rolling around in the mud with you and Hortencia. Ironically, I had bacon for breakfast this morning, and I have to say, I found myself overanalyzing that decision, so thanks a lot for that.

I think if you're going to choose an ABBA song, "Fernando" is a good choice. You could have chosen "Dancing Queen," and that would have been too obviously basic and boring—two things you most definitely are not, Luca.

You asked me whether I still believe in God. I feel like God's presence waxes and wanes in our lives, but yes, I do believe He or She exists. The times we feel more distanced from God are the times when we're suffering or in pain. Despite the lack of strength during those times, God makes us work our way back to Him again. Then He rewards us for our faith and perseverance. I sometimes feel like reconnecting with you is an example of a reward, of the way God works His magic sometimes. Faith isn't easy. I don't think we're supposed to have all the answers or to understand why bad things happen. We don't know, for example, whether our loved ones are in a better place. Maybe we just think they were punished when they died, but maybe they were spared. Maybe we're the ones in hell. We just don't have all the answers, and we weren't meant to know. You know? Note to Luca: don't get Griffin started on philosophical speak, or he may never stop rambling.

Thank you for the visual you provided in describing what you look like. Now I can't get it out of my mind. Me? I sort of look like the photo I sent you years back except a bit brawnier (thank God) with some facial hair now. I hope you don't think I'm being shady in not wanting to share photos. This anonymity with you affords me a certain level of comfort that I can't get anywhere else.

I've reread the section of your letter where you answered my question about sex a few times, but I haven't figured something out. Have you never actually HAD an orgasm? Could I BE more intrusive? (Yes, I sound like Chandler from *Friends*.) Please tell me you came at least once during those times. I do get what you're saying about needing to trust someone to truly let go. That's the difference between sheer fucking and actually having a true sexual connection with someone. The latter is rare. I've had a lot of sex, but most of the time it's a means to an end, and when it's over, there is nothing worth clinging on to. I'm not proud of that, but women (at least out here) make it too easy for men. For the most part, we'll take what you offer up, but it's nice to have to fight for it sometimes. I get the impression you don't make it easy and that's hot, Luca. Believe me. I don't want to be with someone who's okay with me just sticking my dick inside her and going home. I want someone who understands that she's worth more than that and who wants more than that. You wouldn't believe how many shallow women I come across each day who are just perfectly fine with—as Americans say—"wham bam thank you ma'am." I want to feel something more, too. I think you are the type of person who wants more and expects more, but that you weren't in the place in your life to make wise choices when you had sex with those few lucky blokes. I think the person you are now is a lot wiser and more selective. That's good, because you deserve more. For the record, I'd be perfectly fine if you decided never to have sex again. ;-) Kidding. Although I was jealous as all bloody hell of that football player boyfriend you had in high school. It killed me whenever you'd talk about the possibility of having sex with him. So I'm kind of glad it wasn't him, even if you did waste your first time with an "alleged" cousin in mourning, who might have just been trolling that meeting for a vulnerable person. Anyway, that cheater you dated in high school wasn't worthy. I love that I can admit my jealousy to you now. Or maybe I just think I can, but in reality I'm making you uncomfortable and you're currently installing an ADP security system at your house. Tell me which it is. Also, has anyone ever gone down on you?

Later, gator,

Griff

P.S. You don't have to answer that, but if you do, I might take it as a hint that you want to talk a bit more about sex. Now that we're adults, I think it might be kind of fun to explore our options—and our fantasies.

P.P.S. In your letter, you stated that you hadn't had "the mind-blowing sex that PROBABLY exists." It most definitely exists, Luca.

P.P.P.S. Spring for the alarm system with the video camera.

I read that letter at least five times. God, he made me laugh and smile. And holy crap, he hadn't even touched me, yet I found myself totally turned on by his words. It didn't matter that I knew nothing about his looks. Our chemistry had never been based on physical things, but always the intense mental and emotional connection we had. I trusted him more than almost anyone, and that meant I most definitely wanted to explore wherever our words would take us. So much had happened to me since we were teenagers. The one good thing to come out of it was that I no longer believed in holding things inside. If you have something to say, say it, and if there's something you want, do it. I'd yet to get over my agoraphobia, but from within the confines of my house, I felt like I could rule the world. At least, Griffin made me feel that way.

CHAPTER 6

GRIFFIN

It had been a long and arduous day in the recording studio. My band-mates had all left when the production coordinator snuck up behind me as I was getting ready to leave.

"Hey, Griffin."

"Hey, Melinda."

The last time I saw Melinda a few months ago, I was backing her up against the wall as we fucked in the sound booth. She was as attractive as anyone else I'd messed around with, in a bottled-blonde, silicone kind of way. But I most definitely wasn't looking for a repeat. Lately, I'd had a hard time focusing on anything other than Luca's letters, which was completely fucked up.

"A bunch of us are going to The Roxy tonight to celebrate wrapping up," Melinda said. "You coming with?"

"Ah . . . not sure what my plans are yet."

"I was really hoping you'd be there."

"Yeah, I'll let you know."

"If not . . . maybe I could just come over to your place and we can hang out."

My place? Um, no.

"I'll have to see."

Not really.

"Okay . . . well, maybe I'll hear from you later."

"Yeah. See ya," I said as I moved past her and exited the building.

After I entered my car, I hesitated to start it. Thoughts of Luca were flooding my mind along with some pretty strong feelings of guilt. We'd always prided ourselves on being completely honest with one another, and yet I was hiding the biggest part of myself from her. I hadn't even asked her about the books she wrote, even though I was really curious. That's because I didn't think it was fair that she should have to talk about her career when I was being vague about mine. But honestly, what choice did I have? If I wanted to experience things exactly as they once were with her, then I couldn't exactly tell her that her trusty friend Griffin was now Cole Archer, lead singer of the band Archer, well-known to legions of fans around the world. Luca would freak the fuck out. My life was the antithesis of hers. She couldn't even go shopping during the day, for heaven's sake, let alone deal with the onslaught of people who would inevitably follow her around if word ever got out about us. I felt like I was backed into a corner here. If I didn't tell her, she was going to find out someday and be angry that I hid this. If I did tell her, there would be no chance in hell she would ever want to meet me. At the same time, I honestly felt like I couldn't go on without knowing who *she* really was. This woman was one of the most important people in my life. As these weeks went on, I needed to know more and more about what the faceless woman I dreamed about looked like. With the tour looming in a couple of months, I felt like I needed a little peace of mind before I'd be working nonstop.

After scrolling on my phone to find the name of a private investigator who'd once helped me before, I dialed the number.

"Julian . . . Cole Archer here."

"Cole . . . it's been a while."

"Yeah, yeah it has."

"What can I do for you?"

"Well, I have a bit of a different need this time. Are you able to travel right now?"

"How far are we talking?"

"Vermont."

"What's going on up there?"

"I have a friend I want you to locate. I don't want you to talk to her or approach her. I just want you to take some photos and follow her around for a couple of days, give me a feel for her routine, and also let me know if you feel she's safe up there."

"I assume you have her name and address?"

"That's the complicated part. This girl . . . she's an old friend, but we don't actually know each other's real names."

"Some freaky shit going on?"

"Nah. Nothing like that. We met as pen pals when we were kids. Started using fake last names from the get-go, because those were the rules back then. We recently reconnected and simply never changed that habit. She doesn't even know I'm Cole Archer."

"Hmm. Okay. Well, what information do I have to go on?"

"I have her PO box. You'd need to hang out at the local post office until she checks it and then follow her home. I can't guarantee how long it will take before she shows up, but I'll pay whatever you want for your time."

"It's cold as balls up there, you know."

"Buy out L.L.Bean and add it to the invoice. I'll send you the address. How soon do you think you can do it?"

"I can probably head up there this weekend."

I sighed, feeling a mix of dread and excitement. "Perfect."

After I hung up, guilt started to really creep in. I hated having to do things this way, but I really needed to know more before I decided how to move forward. Truthfully, it was her last letter that finally did me in, where things started to feel like they were veering into another territory with us.

I pulled it out and reread it.

Dear Griffin,

I've started this letter five different times. Each time resulted in me tossing a crumpled-up piece of stationery into the wastebasket next to my desk. Actually, that was sort of a lie—not all of the five made it *into* the wastebasket. I have pretty shitty aim. But anyway . . . the reason it's taken me a few tries to pen this letter is because I'd been trying to hold back on answering some of your questions so you don't think I'm a nutjob. Though I've already told you about all my fears, my struggle with bacon, and that I talk to a pet pig on occasion. Alas, perhaps that ship has already sailed anyway. So here goes . . . the naked truth on oral sex, orgasm, and masturbation . . .

I have had an orgasm before. Unfortunately, not with a partner. I'm not sure if my inability to climax during sexual activities with a man is partner related—meaning the men just didn't do it for me—or it's a physical issue with me. But I *can* orgasm, just not while in the presence of any of the men I've been with. In fact, I find bringing myself to climax to be pretty easy. I have a nice collection of vibrators—the LELO INA Wave rabbit being my favorite. It gives dual internal and external stimulation. But honestly, I can get there with my hand in a pinch.

My head fell back against the headrest, and I shut my eyes. Jesus Christ, the vision of Luca touching herself made me fucking nuts. For a quick second, I thought about unzipping my pants and rubbing one out right here in the car. But the last thing I needed was to get arrested jerking off in front of the recording studio. Or worse, a fan to come by and video me while I whacked off—that shit would go viral in a heartbeat. My jeans were getting snug. I needed to remember not to read Luca's letters anywhere but in the privacy of my house in the future.

I took a few deep, cleansing breaths and opened my eyes. There was no way I could drive at the moment, so I figured I might as well enjoy myself and finish the letter for the sixth damn time.

Oddly, the paragraph I just wrote wasn't the one that I debated on writing. The next one is . . .

I never told you, but I have a secret nickname for you: Mee-Mee. The story behind it is pretty embarrassing. But screw it . . . here goes nothing. I was almost thirteen when you sent me your one and only photo. I spent a good deal of time looking at it. In case you weren't aware, you were really, really handsome. I had a big crush on you to begin with—and that was before you'd sent that picture. But once I got a look at how gorgeous you were—it took things to a new level for me. Remember, I was a teenager with raging hormones. Anyway, one night I was lying in my bed staring at the photo you'd sent when I slipped my hand into my panties for the very first time. It felt so good, but I didn't own a vibrator yet, obviously, and I needed more stimulation. So I had to improvise. This is the part that gets embarrassing. Do you remember those little Furby key chains? The vibrating ones that McDonald's gave out in their Happy Meals years ago? I'm sure you can see where this story is headed now. Anyway . . . I had a few of one little Furby in particular. Yep, you guessed it . . . his name was Mee-Mee.

Well, I got the bright idea to give Mee-Mee a try inside my underwear. I held him against my privates and let the vibration stimulate my clit. I'm pretty sure I had no idea what I was doing—but boy did I hit the jackpot. That night I had my first orgasm ever—one hand holding your photo up to look at and the other pressing Mee-Mee against my body. So basically you were a big part of my first orgasm.

Was that TMI? I hope not. By the way, my dad never did figure out why I'd suddenly become obsessed with going to McDonald's. Needless to say, *Happy* Meals made me pretty damn happy for a while after that.

Incidentally, I suddenly crave some chicken nuggets, apple slices, and a milk box. How about you? ;)

Okay, last question—oral sex. Yes, I've both given and received. While it was pleasant on the receiving end, it didn't end with an orgasm. Maybe the guy wasn't that good at it? I'm not sure. But I can tell you, I studied for my first giving event—did you know there is a whole For Dummies porn series? *Blowjobs for Dummies* cost me $29.99 for the fifteen-minute video. But I've been told it was a very good investment.

Think I answered all your questions. My turn! Tell me your darkest fantasy.

Your favorite pen pal,
Luca
P.S. Pretty sure I still have one Mee-Mee somewhere in a box in my closet. If you'd send me an updated picture, I might dig him out . . .
P.P.S. Pretty sure LELO will be needing new batteries after these last few letters.

CHAPTER 7

LUCA

"Luca?" Cecily, the lady who worked the front desk at my little post office, yelled to me. Luckily, the building was empty today. I locked up my PO box, feeling a bit disappointed that I still hadn't received a return letter from Griffin. It had been more than a week since my last letter to him, and I began to grow concerned that maybe I'd been too honest sharing my sexual escapades—namely my masturbating with a Furby—and scared him away. Walking into the main office adjoining the PO box room, Cecily held up a finger. "I have a package for you. It didn't fit into your box. Let me go grab it."

"Oh. Okay." I'd been expecting my publisher to send advance review copies of my latest completed book, but when Cecily walked out carrying an enormous *red* box, my heart started to race. *Did Griff send me something?*

She set the package down on the counter. "Usually your boxes are fairly heavy; this one is pretty light for its size."

I had to push up on my toes to see the return address. An ear-to-ear smile spread across my face seeing Griff's familiar handwriting. Cecily noticed.

"Looks like it's something you're happy arrived safely."

"Yeah. I wasn't expecting a box, just a letter."

She smiled warmly. "Well, I hope it's something fun."

I carried the package out to my car, barely able to stop myself from ripping it open right there in the parking lot. Normally, I waited until I got home to read Griff's letters, but I was way too excited to do that with this package. So I put it on the front passenger seat, went around to the driver's side, and got into the car, then proceeded to tear into the large box.

There was a red envelope with my name on top of red tissue paper. I took it out and debated reading it, but my curiosity got the best of me, and I did the rude thing and opened the gift before even reading the card.

Unfolding the tissue paper, my eyes grew wide.

Oh my God!

I started to crack up. There had to be more than a hundred vibrating Furby key chains inside. I couldn't even imagine where the heck he'd gotten them, since they'd stopped putting them inside Happy Meals more than a decade ago. I picked one up, looked at the bottom, and slid the on-off switch to "On." Sure enough, it started to vibrate in the palm of my hand. It made me squeal like I was thirteen again.

There was no way I could wait until I got home to read his letter now. I tore into the envelope like an addict needing her next fix.

Dear Luca,

If you'd asked me my darkest fantasy a month ago, I'd probably have told you I might have fantasized a time or two about a little BDSM action. Depriving a woman of all her senses—her eyes blindfolded and ears covered with headphones. She'd have on a pair of assless leather chaps and some spiky heels. Her hands would be tied behind her back while she was bent over a spanking horse, and her ass cheeks would flame red with my handprint. I'm sure you get the picture—considering your bacon and porn obsession and all.

But things have changed for me as of late. These days, my deepest, darkest fantasy borders on depraved. *Depraved, Luca.* I can't stop thinking about a certain five-foot-six woman lying in my bed, legs spread-eagled, with a fucking Furby pressed to her pussy.

Sadly, I'm dead serious. I even thought about going to a self-help group—maybe one for furries? I think maybe they'd understand.

Luca, Luca, Luca. What have you done to me?

Love,
Mee-Mee

P.S. You know what to do with these. Think of me while you're doing it.

P.P.S. Are you a screamer? A moaner? Ever done it in public?

P.P.P.S. They shut off my eBay account due to possible fraud activity because of multiple successive purchases. No sellers had heavy inventory of vibrating Mee-Mee—but seventy-seven people had a hundred combined!

Hortencia thought they were chew toys. I chased her around the house, trying to get the Furby out of her mouth, but that only made her think it was a game. By the time I wrestled it from her, she ran back into my office and grabbed another from the box. I needed to find a safer place to put my new little collection before Doc arrived for our session today. So I grabbed a plastic storage bin from the basement, one with a lid that latched closed, and started to transfer the little toys into it. Underneath all the Furbys, on the bottom of the box, sticking half under one of the cardboard flaps, was a piece of paper folded in half. I opened it, thinking maybe Griffin had written a second note. But instead it was an eBay receipt for one of the vibrating key chains. He must've accidentally tossed it in when he was packing up the toys. The top left-hand corner had the shipping information:

Marchese Music

12 Via Cerritos

Palos Verdes Estates, CA 00274

Wow. That must be where Griffin works. Marchese Music.

And I now had his address, or at least a place I could find him. My mind immediately started racing. Imagine if I showed up at the door of his work? He likely wouldn't even recognize me. I could probably get to see him in person, and he would have no idea it was even me. That would be crazy.

I laughed at the thought and finished packing up the Furbys. But instead of throwing away the address, I tucked it into my desk drawer.

A few minutes later, Hortencia started to go nuts. She grunted and ran back and forth between my office and the front door. I'd always thought pigs made an *oink* sound, but mine made more of a *groink* sound. At least she did that whenever Doc pulled into the driveway.

"Change of plans for today, Luca," he yelled as he opened my screen door.

I tugged on Hortencia's collar to make her back away from the door. "Come on, girl, leave the doctor alone. He only wants to play with you if you grow wings."

Doc bent and gave Hortencia a treat from his pocket. The man carried peanut butter crunch pig treats in one pocket and dog biscuits in the other—even though he didn't have a dog. "Get ready, Luca, dear. We're going to the pet store today."

I froze. "No we're not. You said we were walking today."

"I said that because when I tell you we're going to do any type of exposure therapy, you stress on the days leading up to the outing. This way, you have less time to stress in advance."

"Except now five days' worth of stress will get jammed into a fifteen-minute car ride to the store, and my head might explode."

Doc frowned. "I don't think it works that way."

"Don't you remember the last time we went to the pet store?" We'd tried some exposure therapy a few months back, the weekend before Easter. Unbeknownst to either Doc or me, it happened to be the same day the store had an Easter Bunny dressed up to take pictures with pets. We'd entered through a side door, so we didn't see the packed parking lot. The place was a madhouse of people and their animals. Halfway down the first aisle, I'd gotten so dizzy and nauseous that I had to sit on the ground while I hyperventilated. Unfortunately, I'd accidentally sat in a small puddle of dog urine. When I finally got enough courage to get up and leave the store, every dog thought I was a fire hydrant and wanted to sniff me—or rather sniff my wet ass.

"We're going to a smaller store this time. And I went by this morning on my way over here and made sure there are no events being held today."

That didn't make me feel any better. "Why don't we go to the store in our next session, and today we can just take a nice walk. It's beautiful out."

He shook his head. "I need to get a new bird feeder. A squirrel knocked down my hummingbird one."

"You have at least twenty different feeders in your yard. The hummingbirds can eat something else for a few days."

Doc walked over and put both his hands on my shoulders. "Trust me, Luca. Our therapy visits are not about going to the store and not having panic attacks. Having a panic attack while we're there is perfectly expected. Exposure is about entering a feared situation and dealing with the panic when it comes. We will get through this together."

I shut my eyes. "Fine."

"That's my girl."

◆ ◆ ◆

"So tell me what's new with your pen-pal friend." Doc and I had parked in the pet-store parking lot, but I needed a few minutes to calm myself enough to walk in. So we took a walk around the block. I knew he was bringing up Griff to distract me, but honestly, if thoughts of Griff couldn't bring my mind someplace else, I wasn't sure anything could.

"He sent me a gift."

"Oh?"

I wasn't about to tell Doc my Furby masturbation story, so I sidestepped the truth. "Just some toys that I'd been sort of obsessed with back when we were kids. It wasn't like he sent me diamonds or anything."

"I'm sure him remembering something you liked meant more to you than a piece of jewelry anyway."

I smiled. Doc really did know me well. "We've been exchanging letters once a week for a while now, and things have sort of . . . gotten personal. Like we talk openly about dating and our sex lives, or my lack of a sex life might be more like it."

"And you two still haven't exchanged current photos or spoken on the telephone?"

"I tried. But Griff said he liked the mystery of things the way they are."

Doc was quiet for a moment. "Do you believe he's telling you the truth?"

That was something I'd thought about a lot lately. I got the feeling that maybe Griff wasn't as confident as he was when we were kids. He didn't really want to talk about his job—other than saying things hadn't worked out as planned. And he'd been dodgy on even his physical description. It made me think that maybe Griff was embarrassed about not having done as well as he'd liked in the music industry, and maybe that had shaken his confidence overall. It probably hadn't helped that I'd gone and bragged that my debut novel hit the *New York Times* best-seller list.

"I'm not sure. But I do have a theory that maybe he's a little ashamed of his job, and his confidence has deteriorated. It's funny because neither of those things matters. I don't care what he looks like or if he works in a grocery store stocking shelves. Whenever I've done online dating in the past, I didn't give a man a chance if he wasn't physically attractive to me. Yet I honestly don't care if Griffin hasn't aged well and has a huge scar running down his face. I like the guy he is inside and his sense of humor."

"That's very mature. It sounds like you're really growing feelings for this man."

I sighed. "I think I am. But I'm not sure how to let Griffin know that I like him for who he is and that it doesn't matter what he looks like. It's a hard subject to discuss via letters. But I think I'm going to try and push it a little more."

"Good. I'm definitely curious to meet the man who has captured your interest."

"You and me both, Doc. Funny enough, we could do that. I found a receipt in the bottom of the box he sent me, and it had an address where he'd had my gift shipped. I think it might be where he works. Technically, the two of us could show up there, and he wouldn't even know who we were. I've changed a lot in the last decade, appearance-wise. It's too bad he doesn't live closer, or I might actually do it, because I'm so curious."

We arrived back at the front of the pet store after our walk around the block. The parking lot had a few cars but nothing like the last time we'd done a pet-store outing. Doc looked at me. "Think of today as another step toward seeing Griffin. You never know—today we are visiting a pet store . . . next month you could be getting on a plane to California."

If only it were that easy. I took a deep breath and tugged at the collar of my T-shirt. I felt a little warm and confined already, just looking at the door. "Let's get this over with."

"You did very well today, Luca," Doc said as I pulled into my driveway. He reached down between his legs and grabbed his bag from the pet store from the floor of the car.

"I think *very well* might be a stretch."

"You're underestimating yourself. You stayed inside for almost a full ten minutes."

"I stood at the door for nine and a half of that."

"That's okay. It doesn't matter how far inside the building you were. What matters is that you felt panic and dealt with it. You could have very easily run out that door. But instead, you stood your ground and toughed it out. That's progress."

Doc might have felt like I'd made some headway today, but I just felt deflated. What did it matter what Griff even looked like? There was no way I'd ever be getting on a plane. I forced a sad smile. "Thanks, Doc. I appreciate what you tried to do today."

"Progress takes time, Luca. Don't feel down. You might not be where you want to be, but you're also not where you were yesterday. Each day is a baby step. You just keep looking forward and taking them, and I promise one day you're going to look back and be surprised how far those tiny little steps have taken you."

"Wonder how many baby steps there are between here and California," I joked. "At least I won't have to worry what Griff will look like by the time I get there, because I won't be able to see him with my cataracts by then anyway."

Doc's pep talk didn't work to cheer me up too much. I was tired of longing to do normal-people things and frustrated that I couldn't seem to conquer my fears. That night, I didn't write back to Griff, not wanting him to feel the wrath of my foul mood. I couldn't seem to fall asleep, either. I tossed and turned for hours until I finally got out of bed and took a sleeping pill—something I didn't like to do too often. Those things really knocked me out.

So it wasn't a surprise that I slept in the next day. I woke to the sound of a loud horn—not a car horn, more like a train or tractor-trailer horn. The first few times I heard it, I pulled the blanket over my head and attempted to ignore it. But after the third time, Hortencia was going crazy *groink*ing, so I got out of bed to see what was going on.

What in the hell?

I rubbed my eyes and moved the blinds on the front window to get a better look. Sure enough, my eyes hadn't been playing tricks on me. A giant seventies-era-looking RV with wood paneling was parked in front of my house. Seeing me, the driver rolled down his window.

Oh my God. I'm terrified.

It was Doc. He leaned half his body out the window, flailing his arms around as if I could miss him.

"Look what my sister, Louise, has! Bet we can see plenty of birds on our trip."

I opened the front door and shielded my eyes from the sun with my hand. "Our trip where?" There was no way in the world I was getting in that damn thing with Doc driving.

"To California, silly girl!"

CHAPTER 8

GRIFFIN

Bloody hell. I couldn't stop staring at her.

Julian had sent the photos of Luca nearly two hours ago, and yet I hadn't moved from my spot. She was far more beautiful than I'd ever imagined. To be honest, given her peculiarities, I'd almost expected her to be a bit more average-looking. Average would have been absolutely fine, because looks aside, our chemistry was otherwise off the charts. But now? Now that I'd actually discovered Luca was a knockout? That just added so much fuel to the fire, and I doubted it could ever be extinguished.

She had the same long brown hair I remembered from that one photo she'd sent me years ago. Her green eyes were gigantic and glowing like beautiful orbs that let you see into her soul. I wanted to stare into them for hours.

Wow.

She looked like a better version of . . . what were those dolls named . . . the ones the sick girl in the hospital requested. I'd sent her a dozen of them. *Blythe dolls!* That's right. With her gorgeous eyes, Luca was a real-life Blythe doll.

The guilt felt ten times worse now that I'd seen her. Not only that, Julian had snapped photos from the post office at the exact moment she'd received my gift. The joy on her face when she'd opened that box of Furbys was not something I would ever soon forget. *Oh, beautiful girl. How great it is to see your smile, to see you happy.*

Julian had sent over several photos along with an e-mailed report of his initial findings from Vermont.

Greetings from Montpelier!

Attached are all the photos I've taken since arriving up here.

Here is what I know so far. As you can see, your friend is quite the looker. That's the good news. The rest is a little fucking bizarro, if you ask me, so hang on for the ride.

First off, she walks a pig on a leash. Yes, I said . . . PIG. A freaking pig. Not sure what that's all about. Other than when she ventures out to do that, she mostly seems to just go from the house to the post office, then home again. So it's been pretty easy to keep tabs on her.

Here's the really odd part. There's this old dude who picked her up once, and they went out together. I followed them to a pet store and back. That was it. Not sure if he's her grandfather or a sugar daddy or what. I think he's a Peeping Tom, though, because I saw him using these binoculars outside her house.

A real perv. Strange shit, man. If you want me to look into him more, let me know.

The story gets even weirder. The next day, the same guy shows up at her house driving an old RV. She gets in, stays inside for a few minutes, then runs back inside her house. No clue what that was all about.

That's pretty much all I've got for now. Couldn't put this all together into something that makes sense if you paid me double or my life depended on it. Not sure how much more information you need.

Anyway, off topic, I sort of found a little side piece at a bar here last night. Name's Vanessa. I'm thinking of sticking around in town for a bit if you want me to continue the job. That old dude is up to something. I just know it.

Let me know!

Julian

As strange as Luca's lifestyle may have seemed to him, everything made perfect sense to me. I knew that guy was her eccentric therapist whom she often ventured out with, because she'd mentioned him in her first letter. And of course, I'd already known about Hortencia. So, oddly, none of this alarmed me at all.

I wrote back, telling Julian to hang out there until I let him know otherwise. I didn't think he was going to find anything more of value, but he clearly had nothing else better to do—besides "Vanessa"—at the moment, so I figured I'd keep him there a little longer.

"Mr. Archer?"

Shit. Apparently my cap and sunglasses did nothing to hide my identity as I attempted to venture incognito to the post office.

"Yes."

"Can I have your autograph?"

"Sure," I said, quickly scribbling my signature onto a piece of some girl's mail.

"I'm a huge fan," she squeaked. "You have no idea. 'Luca' is like my favorite song ever."

Ugh. She had to remind me.

"Thanks," I said before rushing away.

That was going to be another thing I'd have to contend with. How exactly was I supposed to explain to Luca that I'd written my most successful song—more like a rant—in honor of her while I was drunk and pissed one night? Who knew that thing was going to fly up the charts the way it did? I'd certainly never imagined when I wrote it that Luca and I would end up reconnecting.

I sighed. I supposed the song was the least of my problems right now.

Throwing my hood over my head, I picked up the pace so no one else would recognize me. After all, I had Luca's letter in my hands and couldn't get back to my car fast enough.

Ripping the envelope open, I eagerly began to read it.

> Dear Griffin,
>
> I've officially burned out three Furbys. It's a good thing you got me so many, even if your eBay account was sacrificed in the process. I'm sorry about that, but it did make me laugh out loud for some reason when

you told me it got shut down. Seriously, thank you for that surprise gift. I don't think I smiled or laughed in years like I did when I opened it. And yes, I'm serious when I said I burned three of them out already. (Whoops.) I thought of you every second, by the way. ;-) I considered sending you a video to prove how much I appreciate your gift, but I thought that might freak you out. Would you want something like that from me? A video? That, of course, would require us to exchange numbers/e-mails. And that also could lead to—GASP—talking on the phone. And talking on the phone could lead to—GASP—seeing each other. And seeing each other could lead to . . . well, you get the point. I know you said you like the dynamic we have going right now and the mystery of it all. Don't get me wrong, I LOVE what we have. But I don't know . . . don't you sometimes want more?

I had to stop reading the letter for a moment.
Shit.
Fuck.
Shit.
A feeling of dread filled me. Not to mention, I was hard as a rock. Strange combo. I knew where this was going, and it was messing me up inside. I took a deep breath in and continued.

I'm sorry if I'm crossing a line in even bringing this up. But it's been weighing heavily on me lately. I really would love for what we have to be about more than just the letters. I'm crazy about you. There, I said it. Feel free to pretend I didn't. I'll just take your lack of acknowledgment as a hint to not bring any of this up again. (Who's the one installing the security cameras now, huh?)

Okay, now that I have gotten all that off my chest, I'll answer your questions. You wanted to know if I am a screamer or a moaner. Both, actually—but mostly when I am pleasuring myself, because that's when I am most comfortable and not worrying about what others think. I also live in a very secluded spot, so no one except Hortencia is going to hear me scream. That works out if you want some privacy, but it's not exactly convenient if you're being ax murdered or attacked by a grizzly bear.

In answer to your other question, I've actually never done it in a public place, but I think if I did, it would be in California. ;-) By the way, that's the second winky face I've drawn in this letter, and I'm starting to creep myself out a little. No more winky faces.

Please tell me I haven't scared you off with my video suggestion above.

Your favorite pen pal,

Luca

P.S. Do you prefer shaved, runway strip, or full carpet? Asking for a friend.

P.P.S. That friend might be named Luca.

I let out a deep breath and rested my head on the seat. *Fuuuuck.* What now?

My spying on her was goddamn unfair. I couldn't seem to go on without seeing her, and yet I wasn't even affording her the same opportunity with me? What I'd done felt like stealing.

I have to tell her the truth.

But when she found out who I was, it was going to ruin what we had. I lived for her letters, for her nonjudgment. Luca was literally the only person left in this world who truly saw me for me. The thought of that ever changing . . . well, I couldn't fathom it. At the same time, now that I'd seen her, I wanted nothing more than to smell her, taste her, *be* with her in the flesh. Although it was never about the physical with us, I couldn't exactly just forget her image now. *Luca, Luca, Luca. What am I going to do with you?* I needed just a bit more time to figure it all out.

It took me a few days to decide how I wanted to respond to her.

After returning from the studio one afternoon, I bit the bullet and ultimately attempted to buy myself a bit more time.

> Dear Luca,
> If this letter arrives a little later than the others . . . it's because I've been locked in my room for days wanking off to thoughts of this little porn video you'd like to send me. Which begs the question: Are you trying to kill me? There are other ways to kill people besides axes and grizzly bears, you know. Proposing such a thing when I can't exactly touch you would be one of them. Pretty sure that's a crime of torture. I'm glad you've been putting the Furbys to good use, even if three were sacrificed in the process. They clearly weren't designed for long-term usage.
> I'm definitely skirting around the issue, aren't I?
> Okay.
> Here goes.

One of the things that has always defined our relationship, I think, is blind faith. Would you agree? Do you have blind faith in me? I can honestly say I have blind faith in you. Even though we haven't met, I trust you with my life. I don't think I can say that about anyone else on this earth. So, that said, I need to ask you a favor. I need you to trust me when I say that the best thing for right now is for us to continue things as we have been. You're very special to me, Luca. And I want to be able to be the right man for you. I'm sad to say that currently I'm not. Sometimes when you follow your dreams, you realize they aren't free, and the cost is far greater than you'd ever anticipated.

But I'm trying to figure out how to change things, sooner rather than later. I do desperately want to meet you, touch you, and do many other things with you (and to you). When the time is right to take the next step, I promise to let you know. And I hope it will all make sense.

Can you do that for me? Can you put blind faith in me on this? Don't answer that question now. Take time to think about it. Think about ME and ask yourself if you really believe that I would ever intentionally hurt you or steer you wrong.

On to another pressing matter, specifically your vagina and my preferences as far as it's concerned. Believe me when I tell you that I will take you any way you give yourself to me, whether bald or hairier than the aforementioned grizzly bear. I will love every second of going down on you and giving you the best orgasm of your life, better than any Furby ever could. I dream about it every day, Luca.

Later, gator,
Griff

P.S. Do you prefer Cavalier or Roundhead? (Uncut or other.) Asking for a friend.

P.P.S. That friend might be named Mee-Mee.

CHAPTER 9

LUCA

Doc was seriously nuts. He'd parked the RV at his house and basically told me it was ready to go anytime I decided to take him up on his offer to drive us to California. The damn thing was bigger than his actual residence.

He would have taken off with me the day he'd first brought it to my house if I'd agreed. I told him I really needed some time to think about it.

A part of me wanted to take him up on his crazy idea, but actually moving forward would mean having to face the potential of finding something out I really didn't want to know. Griffin was hiding something. That I was certain of. The realization hurt. His most recent letter had asked me to have blind faith in him, but how could you do that when someone has given you every reason to suspect something is awry? A battle was waging inside me as to how to handle things moving forward.

A knock at the door startled me. I knew it was Doc, but I was nowhere near ready to go to wherever he was threatening to take me tonight.

I opened the door. Doc was wearing a suit. *Oh no.*

"You haven't gotten dressed yet?" he asked.

"No. Because you won't tell me where we're going."

"Luca . . . that's the point. I promise it won't be anything you can't handle."

◆ ◆ ◆

A couple of hours later, having donned my fanciest black dress, I shivered in Doc's car as we drove along.

He glanced over at me. "You look splendid."

"Thank you. Now, will you tell me where we're going, please?"

"We'll be there soon enough."

We ended up pulling up in front of an old brick building. Outside, the sign read: VERMONT AUDUBON SOCIETY.

"You're taking me to meet a bunch of your bird nerds?"

"It's the annual gala. It's packed full of people and the perfect opportunity to practice your panic skills. Don't worry. It's out back in the courtyard, not inside."

I sunk down into my seat. "I still can't handle that."

"That's where you're wrong. You can do anything you put your mind to or, in this case, *don't* put your mind to. Keep your mind out of it and go with the flow, moment by moment. Sit there and experience all the feelings of panic without fleeing."

I wanted to flee this car, never mind the gala. "I can't."

"You can. True freedom awaits if you can just learn to sit through the feelings without escaping. Once panic subsides, you'll realize there was never anything to fear at all. Have you learned nothing from our studies of Dr. Claire Weekes's teachings?"

My tone was abrasive. "Why are you doing this tonight?"

"Because, Luca, it's time. Your life is passing you by. We need to get you to a point where you can be functional around people again. That means being able to handle being around them."

When I said nothing, he continued.

"I'll tell you what . . . if you can just get through fifteen minutes at the gala, we can leave. I won't bother you for the rest of the night. Then I'll take you right home."

Letting out a shaky breath, I said, "I don't know . . ."

"If you won't do it for me, do it for your Griffin."

My Griffin.

I thought a lot about what that statement really meant—doing it for Griffin.

I thought about the many miles between us.

I thought about the lifestyle he must live as a single man in California, how different it must be from mine.

If I truly ever wanted a chance to meet him, I had to at least *try* to face my fears. I suppose if I made a fool of myself in front of a bunch of bird people, that would be better than doing it in front of Griff.

I surrendered and began to exit the car. "Fifteen minutes."

A wave of nausea hit me upon joining the crowd gathered in the society's courtyard. The adrenaline immediately started pumping within me, and I was in full-fledged panic mode almost immediately. The sound of all these people talking mixed together into one loud, jumbled mess. The sky above seemed to be swaying.

When we got to a table, I sat down and trembled in my seat.

"You're doing great, Luca."

Doc started a conversation with the woman in the next seat over, leaving me to suffer in silence right next to him. Sweat permeated my body as the torturous minutes passed while I gripped the linen tablecloth.

Do it for Griffin, I kept telling myself.

At one point, something interesting happened. The dizzying hot flashes of panic seemed to dissipate after they had gotten to the worst point. My heart rate slowed. Relief washed over me. I wanted to cry because it felt like I'd survived a near-death experience. I didn't recall this ever happening before because I typically never stuck anything out long enough to really see it through to the end.

Before I knew it, Doc announced, "Time is up, Luca. How are you feeling?"

"Still alive. Can we leave now? I feel a bit exhausted from this."

"You did a good job. I'm very proud of you. We can absolutely leave."

Once we returned to his car, I broke down, and tears started to fall. It was the first time I'd cried since reading the letter about Griffin's mom passing. It seemed that once I'd allowed the floodgates to open, tears were going to be a regular thing for me. *Great. Just great.*

He was shocked. "You're crying . . ."

"This is only the second time I've cried in a very long time."

"I know. It's not because of what happened in there, is it?"

"No. It's because I'm . . . scared."

"Okay . . . tell me why."

"It's Griffin. His last letter. He basically implied that there is some reason why he hasn't wanted to take things further with me. He asked me to have blind faith in him, that it's the right decision to keep going as we are for now, without talking to or seeing each other. A part of me really wants to believe in him, and the other part of me is terrified that I'm going to get hurt."

"You don't think he's married, do you?"

"No. I don't think it's anything like that. Griffin has always been very unforgiving toward cheaters. So that never even crossed my mind."

"Are you thinking some other ominous thing is going on?"

I'd memorized the part of his last letter that had bothered me most. *Sometimes when you follow your dreams, you realize they aren't free, and the cost is far greater than you'd ever anticipated.* "I'm not certain, but I think he may struggle financially. He's mentioned before that his career hasn't gone as planned. And then in his last letter, he said his dreams were far more costly than he'd thought. I don't know if he means that

73

literally or figuratively. But I don't care if he lives a simple life or has gone through some tough times. I *have* money—between what my dad left me and the success of my books—and look how much it's helped my personal life. Money and things don't buy happiness—a beautiful heart is far more valuable than anything that can be bought."

Doc smiled. "You're very wise for a person of your age, Luca."

"Nah. I just had a smart mom. She used to say, *Money impresses the lazy girls. Smart girls are rich when they have something they can't buy.*"

"Wise mother, wise daughter." He nodded. "So what are your plans, then? Will you broach the subject with Griffin and see if that changes his mind-set on taking the next step together?"

"I honestly have no idea what to do, Doc. None. A part of me wants to take you up on your offer to drive with me to California, show him that I don't care if he lives in a one-room apartment or sings for tips outside the bus depot. But the other part of me feels like that would be a terrible violation of his trust."

"I can tell you from personal experience that sometimes we men need a little push. I remember when I met my Geraldine. I was in medical school and on day eight of eating ramen noodles. My water bill was two months late, and I held my breath each evening when I turned on the faucet, hoping they wouldn't turn off my water because I'd lose half the ingredients of my nightly meal. Geraldine had a job and always dressed so nicely. She worked at the library I frequented, and I had the biggest crush on her. But what was I going to do, ask her to split a bag of ramen noodles and skip eating on Friday the following week?"

"Did you wait until after you graduated to ask her out?"

Doc looked out the window for a moment, and I watched the fondness of the memory he recalled play out on his face. He shook his head. "My Geraldine was a straight shooter. One day she marched over to the table I was studying at and said, 'Every night before you leave, you spend ten minutes hanging around my desk and talking. You *are* flirting with me, right?' I said that I had indeed been flirting, or at least attempting to do so, and her response was to blurt out, 'Well, why haven't you asked me out yet?'" Doc chuckled. "She'd caught me so off guard, I didn't have time to make up an excuse. So I told her the truth—that I'd like nothing more than to take her out, but I was too broke because my books and rent drained every last cent from my bank account."

"What did she say?"

"Nothing. Not a damn word. She just walked away. I thought I'd blown it with her. But the next night when I showed up, I found a magazine on the desk I normally sat at. It was opened to an article titled 'Fifty Dream First Dates That Are Free.'"

I laughed. "Did it work?"

"I ripped the pages from the magazine and took her on one of those fifty dates every single week for fifty consecutive weeks. By the time I got to the last one, I'd just graduated and secured my first job. I proposed on our fiftieth free date—inside a tent I'd made out of sheets in the backyard."

"I love that story! How come you never shared it with me before?"

Doc shrugged. "Guess the right time just hadn't come. Unlike now."

I sighed. "I suppose we could take the trip to California and play it by ear. I mean, Griffin wouldn't have to find out we were even there if I decided against letting him know who I am. We could go simply to uncover what we need to and then leave. He doesn't know what I look like. But what about the whole blind-faith thing? I'd be violating his trust."

"Well, my dear, you need to determine if you can be patient with him or if you need to know what's really going on now. I do think a trip out west would be beneficial in more ways than one. It could not only satisfy your curiosity about Griffin but also serve as an excellent exposure exercise in tackling the unknowns of travel."

My heart was racing. "So you're thinking we should go to California . . ."

"I'm thinking that no harm can come from discovering the truth and venturing out of your comfort zone. I am a bit biased, as I've already mapped out some fantastic bird-watching locations on the way, but I digress. Don't let that influence your decision. This needs to be your call."

Later that evening, I was pacing in my living room.

"Give me a sign, Hortencia. I need to know the right thing to do here."

Groink.

The truth was, I knew that the right answer for me was to take Doc up on his offer. When else in my life would I have access to an RV and a willing road-trip partner? But it might also be the wrong answer for moving things forward between Griff and me. *Blind faith.* That's what he'd asked me for. I wouldn't exactly be honoring his wishes if I found him working the front desk at a music studio and walked in pretending to be someone else. I'd be violating his trust. But at the same time, wouldn't I be having blind faith in *us*? It felt like maybe he didn't have blind faith in *me*—to trust that I'd like him for the person he was inside, regardless of whatever his issues were. Maybe I had to have enough faith for both of us? Sort of like Geraldine did with Doc. I wouldn't be disrespecting his wishes; I'd be taking a leap of blind faith for two.

Oh my God.

I'm going to do it, aren't I?

I looked over at Hortencia, who had been lying next to my desk. "What do you think, girl? Should I take a road trip?"

My faithful companion sat up and perked an ear.

"Should I go and take a blind leap of faith or not?"

Hortencia answered by running out of the room. For a second, I thought she was rushing to the front door—showing me that she was ready to go, too. But she came back a minute later. And laid her answer at my feet.

Mee-Mee. I hadn't even realized that she'd swiped another Furby. But the timing couldn't have been more perfect.

I picked up the wet furry key chain and patted Hortencia on her head. "Okay . . . whatever you say. Road trip it is!"

CHAPTER 10

LUCA

"You take a left here."

I'd pulled over at a stop sign, which was also the end of the road we'd been traveling on for the last half hour. We basically had two choices. Turn left or turn around. "Ummm . . . Doc. There's no more paved road. To the left is only dirt."

"Well, then I guess we drive on dirt for a little while."

I sighed. "Can I see the map, please?"

Doc had been flipping back and forth between a half dozen foldable maps over the last three days. He also had a giant Hagstrom book. I hadn't seen one of those since I was a kid—*for a damn good reason, apparently*. I took the map from Doc and traced the route he'd highlighted in yellow. "I don't see why we can't use Waze. It tells you when to turn and how to avoid traffic jams, too."

"Those applicators are tracking devices."

"You mean apps."

"Whatever. The government already knows too much about us. Our forefathers fought for freedom, and the young people today give it all back."

I leaned forward in my seat and looked down the dirt road Doc wanted me to turn onto. It looked pretty sketchy. Our RV didn't have four-wheel drive, and the path was really narrow. "I don't think we should go this way. I'm afraid we might get stuck."

"Okay. So let's walk, then."

"Walk?" My brows drew together. "Where are you taking us?"

"Just a short little diversion. It shouldn't be more than a half mile up the road."

I shook my head. "I thought we were done with detours yesterday, when you made us drive two hundred miles off our path to see a Blackburnian warbler."

"A detour means going off our path. This little visit is right on our way."

I glanced down the dirt path once again. "I think the interstate is more like right on our way."

Doc unbuckled and started to get out of the RV. *I guess we're taking another detour.*

"The baya weaver builds the most beautiful nests. He builds it for the female, and if she approves, she'll mate with him. They've never been spotted in this country before the last month."

I turned off the RV and unbuckled. I supposed the man had taken two weeks off from his life to do this crazy trip with me, the least I could do was indulge him on his excitement over a few birds. It wasn't like anyone was waiting for us in California. I hopped down from the driver's seat and stretched my arms over my head and then twisted from side to side. A walk would do me some good anyway. Since I wouldn't let Doc drive, I'd been behind that big wheel for the better part of eight hours already today.

"Imagine if humans did that?" I mused. "If men had to build an entire house to try and attract a woman?"

"I'm afraid I'd have been in trouble. I never was too handy swinging a hammer."

Doc and I started to walk down the dirt road. I wasn't even sure where we were heading—a park again, I assumed. "Are you sure this is the way? It seems pretty residential, and I can't imagine that a national park doesn't have a paved road leading up to the entrance."

"I think this is right. Martha said when we arrived at her street, to go about another half to three quarters of a mile and look for the painted garbage cans."

"Martha?"

"The woman we're going to visit from my online bird club. The baya weaver built his nest in her backyard."

I stopped in place. "We're going to someone's house? How do we know she's not a crazy serial killer?"

Doc pushed his glasses up his nose. "I could say the same about Griffin, couldn't I?"

Great. Another thing for me to worry about. Griffin being a serial killer might've been the *only* thing that hadn't crossed my mind in three days of driving. I'd already panicked he might be married, gay, a gigolo, a hoarder . . . There'd even been a hundred-mile stretch through Illinois when I'd considered maybe Griff was really a woman—one who'd been playing me for eighteen years and had sent me a photo of her little brother. That insane thought had led to a few hours of internal debate over whether I could ever be physically attracted to a woman for him— her—him . . . whatever. I was seriously considering turning into a lesbian for a man I'd never met who turned out to be a woman. Now I'd have to contend with thoughts about Griffin the serial killer through at least the rest of Nebraska and half of Colorado.

Great. Just great.

Martha was the most colorful person I'd ever seen. *Literally*, not figuratively. She'd told Doc to look out for her painted garbage cans to identify her house but had failed to mention *everything* she owned was painted. The exterior of her small dollhouse-like home was painted in three shades of pink, with yellow and teal trim, and each room of the interior was painted a different neon color. Her clothes were also just as bright—she wore a bright-yellow blouse with even brighter red pants, and her glasses were a glossy shade of violet. If Doc was surprised by the shock of color, he'd done a damn good job of hiding it. He and Martha seemed pretty excited to finally meet. Apparently they'd been part of the same group and chatting for a few years now. This trip was making me realize there was a lot about Doc I didn't know.

The three of us walked around Martha's property for a while. She gave us a tour that ended at a tree next to a wide flowing stream. She pointed up to the coveted nest, and although it was way cooler looking than I'd expected, I still didn't fully get Doc's reverence. He stayed outside to nest sit and wait for the baya weaver to return, while Martha and I went into the house to make some tea.

"So . . . you and Chester . . . are you . . . a couple?"

It took me a few seconds to realize she was talking about Doc. I forgot he had an actual first name. "Oh God, no."

She filled the kettle and turned to me with it in her hands. "*Are you sure?* It's just the two of you in that RV together, and you also took a trip to New York City last month, right?"

"Um. Yeah. I'm positive. Doc is my . . . doc."

Her brows drew together, so I clarified.

"He's my shrink. I'm his patient."

A look of relief washed across her face. She seriously thought my seventy-something-year-old doctor was my boyfriend?

She patted me on my shoulder. "He refers to you as his *special* friend."

I smiled. "He probably didn't want to mention anything because of doctor-patient confidentiality and all."

Martha seemed pleased by that. Apparently the old bird was interested in showing Doc more than her nest. "Oh! Well, that makes sense. So what's wrong with you?"

I blinked a few times. No one had ever asked me such a direct question about my mental health. "Um. I have a fear of crowds and confined places."

She set the kettle down on the stove and lit the burner. "That's okay. I don't like clowns."

Not exactly the same, but *okeydoke*. "So . . . you and Doc have been friends for a while, I take it?"

"Has to be three or four years now."

"Have you always been a bird lover?"

"My mother used to have a pet bird when I was little. Her name was Kelly. She had the brightest colors on her wings, and I could watch her flutter around for hours. But it wasn't until I joined the group that Doc and I are part of that I realized the true magic of bird-watching."

She'd been frank asking me about my issues, so I figured candor was fine. "Which is . . . ?"

Martha smiled. "Bird-watching is about the journey. You never know where the hobby will take you. I've spent months trying out different foods and feeders to see how changing the habitat can attract different species. Feeding the birds also attracts other wildlife, like butterflies, dragonflies, even chipmunks. Then there are the friendships that hiking and festivals bring, not to mention the online clubs. Heck, I've visited friends in Alaska to watch birds—friends I'd never have met if I hadn't started on this journey." She tilted her head and studied me. "That's why Doc is such a natural. You know how he is—it's always about the trip, not the final destination."

That *was* Doc's philosophy. He'd been pushing me to take little steps, to learn to feel happiness *here*, instead of waiting to get *there*. But I'd been so focused on finding a cure for my fears that I hadn't stopped to realize he'd been trying to teach me to accept who I am every step of the way. Two years ago, I never would have taken this road trip. It was way too outside my comfort zone. And I definitely wouldn't have gone in pursuit of a relationship that was equally as terrifying as it was exciting. While Griffin had always been one of the few people I'd been truly comfortable with, there was a huge difference between accepting your pen pal for who she was and a real-life relationship. And he'd just come back into my life. I wasn't ready to lose him. It was a big risk, but something told me the potential reward might make it worth it. So I took a giant scary leap. Yet for the first time in a long time, I felt a sense of hope. Whether things worked out with Griff or not, I was going to enjoy this trip and experience as much as I could.

CHAPTER 11

LUCA

Holy crap.

HOLY CRAP.

This couldn't be where Griffin worked, could it? He must be employed by someone famous. But who? Someone I knew?

Peeking out of the RV window as we parked on Via Cerritos, I turned to Doc. "This is insane."

"Is it possible that Griffin is well-to-do and lives here? Based on the company name, I'd assumed we were going to a business, not a residence."

"I don't think so, but honestly, I'm so confused. The truth is, I don't even know if the address on that eBay receipt has anything to do with Griffin at all. It was just an assumption based on the word *music*." Now, I was starting to wonder if this entire trip had been a waste of time.

Doc peered out of the window with his binoculars. "It's probably only a matter of time before we get kicked off this street. We should perhaps inquire as to who that house belongs to before that happens."

A few minutes later, I spotted a woman exiting the gates of a mansion that was a few houses down from the one allegedly linked to Griffin.

"Should I approach that lady and ask her if she knows who lives there?"

"Can't hurt," he said.

I stepped down out of the RV when she got closer to us.

"Excuse me. Hi. Can you tell me who lives at that property over there . . . Twelve Via Cerritos?"

She tugged on her dog's leash to keep it from moving and narrowed her eyes at me. "What, are you on some kind of sightseeing tour? The residents don't appreciate your *curious* kind around here. My boss is one of them. I'll have you know she'll call her security if—"

"I'm not on a tour. I'm looking for a friend. Can you just tell me who lives there?"

"That's Cole Archer's house."

"Cole Archer? Is he someone famous?"

"Yes. The lead singer of the band Archer."

Archer?

"Not sure I've ever heard of them."

An incredulous look crossed her face. "Have you been living under a rock?"

I laughed at the irony of that. "Basically, yeah."

She looked behind me at Doc, who was now outside of the RV looking up at a tree. "Why does he have binoculars, then, if you two aren't spying on the rich and famous?"

"He's looking for birds, not Beyoncé."

"Well, I suggest you move that RV off this street before someone has you arrested."

"Thank you for your time," I said before walking back toward Doc. He put down the binoculars. "What did she say?"

"She said the person who lives there is named Cole Archer. He's apparently a famous musician. Maybe Griffin works for this man." As Doc and I reentered the RV, I said, "You brought your laptop, right? Can we connect to that hot spot?"

"Sure. Are you going to look up this musician?"

"Yes. I need to see who Cole Archer is."

After he handed me the computer, I pulled up YouTube and typed in *Cole Archer*. A plethora of results came up. On second thought, I was pretty sure I'd heard of the band Archer, but since my taste in music tended to be less current, I didn't know anything about them and couldn't name any of their songs.

The first video I played was titled *Archer Live at the Pavilion*. Someone had taken professional footage of one of their performances. It looked like a smaller concert venue. The lead singer, presumably Cole Archer, was sitting on a stool and playing guitar while making love to the microphone during a slow ballad. His voice was powerful, hypnotic, and a little bit gritty. He was extremely attractive, exactly how you would imagine the lead singer of a band: thick hair that looked like he'd just had sex, chiseled features, and a great body. A few silver rings adorned his large hands that were wrapped around the guitar handle.

Since this video really wasn't telling me anything, though, I went in search of another to watch.

The next one I clicked on was titled *Archer Interview, Liam Stanley Tonight*. The band members were sitting in a row answering questions from the interviewer.

"Tell me how you guys got together."

Cole answered. *"Well, not sure how much time you have. It's a bit of a long one."*

I immediately noticed that Cole had a *British* accent.

Wait.

A rush of adrenaline ran through me. It was the first time I considered the unthinkable. *No.* It couldn't be. Griffin couldn't BE Cole Archer. *Could he?* No way. No how. The accent had to be a coincidence. At least that was what I wanted to believe.

"Have you found anything?" Doc shouted from the corner of the RV.

"Not anything that would lead me to Griffin's connection to Cole Archer. I have to keep looking."

I was reluctant to admit to Doc that I suspected Cole could be Griffin. It still seemed too crazy, and I had no evidence to substantiate it.

Over the next hour, I scoured the internet for any bit of information I could find on Cole Archer. His Wikipedia page did indicate that he grew up in England, which wasn't news given the accent, but there was no information alluding to anything else that would lead me to believe this man was Griffin.

It wasn't until I came across the comments section of an article in a music magazine . . . that I got my answer. It was clear as day right in the middle of an insulting jab.

> I don't get the appeal. His voice sucks. It's like he can't decide whether he wants to sound British or American. Oh and his real name isn't even Cole Archer. It's apparently Griffin Marchese.

My eyes were glued to the word.
Griffin.
Griffin Marchese.
Griffin Marchese.
Marchese Music.
Oh. My. God.
My body completely froze as all the blood in it traveled to my head. My heart was racing. *Griffin IS Cole Archer? Cole Archer IS Griffin? Griffin is . . . a superstar? MY Griffin?* I kept pausing the video at different spots to see if I could catch a glimpse of the twelve-year-old boy I remembered from that one picture he'd sent. There was one frame that truly sealed the deal. It was the same exact expression from the photo.

"Luca, what's wrong? You look like you've seen a ghost."

After several seconds, I finally mustered the ability to answer him. "I don't even know what to say . . . I . . . Griffin is . . . he's . . . he *is* Cole

Archer. That's why he lives in a place like this." I put the laptop down and covered my mouth. "He's famous. This is . . . unbelievable."

Doc covered his mouth. "Oh my. Are you thinking this explains why he didn't want you to know his identity?"

I thought back to the words in his last letter: *Sometimes when you follow your dreams, you realize they aren't free, and the cost is far greater than you'd ever anticipated.*

It was a figurative cost he'd been referring to, not a literal one. He wasn't poor, but perhaps he had paid a price for fame.

"That's it, Doc. It's starting to make sense now. He must have thought my knowing would change the way I saw him."

The reality of this situation was hitting me in waves. Griffin is a rock star.

A fucking rock star.

I could only assume his lifestyle is one of fast cars, sex, and crowds of people. It was likely the polar opposite of my secluded existence. Truly understanding this also meant realizing that we very likely *couldn't* ever be anything more than friends. That epiphany was heartbreaking. *Could we BE more different? Why am I hearing Chandler Bing from* Friends *at a time like this?*

Panicking, I asked, "What now? This was the last thing I ever expected. What do I do, Doc? I seriously feel paralyzed."

"We came all the way out here, Luca. Now that you know what he's hiding from you . . . why not just go to him, tell him the truth, and nip this in the bud? It's going to come out eventually. I think it would be extremely hard for you to hold in what you know now and to pretend that nothing has changed."

Doc was right about one thing. This did change *everything*.

"How do I even access him? There is no way his security will let some crazy girl anywhere near him."

After I grabbed the laptop again, he asked, "What are you doing?"

"I just need to watch him a bit more."

I kept scrolling through the videos. I became transfixed whenever I looked into his eyes and realized this man was my Griffin. Come to think of it, the more I watched, the more I could again see glimpses of the face I remembered from that photo all those years ago.

There was one video that showed Griffin—Cole—signing a bunch of autographs in the midst of a swarm of sex-crazed women. He seemed frustrated and tired, yet he signed every single one until there were no more people waiting.

Not to mention, any one of those women would have been happy to stand by his side while he performed the duties of his job. Me? Just the thought of being in that crowd made me start to panic.

I swallowed hard. It felt like I had the heaviest weight on my chest. I was suddenly in mourning, having to say goodbye to the imagined future I had with Griffin. There was no way to make this work. I could totally see now why he felt the letters were all there could ever be between us. Honestly, it might have been better if I'd never uncovered this.

Just when I thought nothing else could surprise me today, my eyes landed on one of Archer's music videos. It was the title of the song that caught my eye: *"Luca."*

What?

Before I could click on it, a loud knock on the RV door startled me. Upon peeking out of the window, I felt my heart fall to my stomach. The most beautiful man I'd probably ever seen in the flesh was standing there with his arms crossed, wearing—a bathrobe?

Oh no.

Oh my God. Oh my God. Oh my God.

"Who is it, Luca?"

Feeling ready to collapse, I looked over at Doc and cried, "It's Griffin."

CHAPTER 12

GRIFFIN

One Hour Earlier

I hadn't heard from Julian in two days. When I hired him, I'd figured he'd snap a few pics, maybe tail Luca for a bit to see what her daily life was like—nothing too crazy. Yet my little snoop job had turned into a cross-country expedition at this point.

Luca hadn't mentioned in her last letter that she'd been planning a road trip. So when Julian called to say she'd gotten into an RV carrying a suitcase with the old guy, I told him to follow her and see where they were heading. Twelve hours later, he called and said he'd just crossed over the Ohio state border. I figured I was in this far, might as well see where the two of them were going. Plus, I was curious. So far, they'd gone to three different national parks, spent two days in Nebraska at some crazy-looking lady's house, and then hit the Grand Canyon. Not that Luca owed me any explanation for her whereabouts, but I thought it was screwed up that she'd tell me her fantasies but not mention an upcoming fifteen-state road trip.

If I didn't have to be at the studio every day this week, I would have hopped in the damn car and driven to Nevada myself, just to get an in-person glimpse of Luca. The thought of her being so close to me had me distracted all day. But when my phone rang at 6:00 a.m., I had no idea just how close she really was.

"What?" I hadn't even looked at the caller ID when I answered. Whoever was on the other end of the line better have a damn good reason for calling. I'd been in the studio until after two in the morning last night, or rather today.

"Wakey, wakey, Mr. Rock Star. I have some very interesting news."

Hearing Julian's voice, I sat up in bed. "What happened?"

"Your little chickadee has arrived at her next destination."

"Where is she now? Mexico?"

"Close. A little farther north. You'll never guess."

"I'm paying you by the hour, so how about we save the guessing games and you just cut to the chase."

"She's in Palos Verdes Estates."

What? She's here? In my little town? That couldn't be a damn coincidence. What the fuck?

I hopped out of bed, grabbed a pair of sweatpants, and started to pull them on. "Where is she?"

"Via Cerritos, my friend. She's parked that heap of metal about half a block down from your house and turned off the lights. Hasn't come out yet."

My heart started to race out of control, and my mind reeled even faster. A million questions hit me all at once.

What the hell is she doing here?

She knows who I am?

How long has she known?

What the fuck?

WHAT THE FUCK!

"You still there?" Julian asked. I'd forgotten he was on the phone, even though I still had it held up to my ear.

"Yeah, I'm here."

"What do you want me to do?"

91

I raked my hand through my hair. "I don't know. Stay on her. I need a few minutes to think. Call me if she gets out of the RV."

"You got it, boss."

I hung up and stared at my phone for a solid five minutes. I seriously couldn't believe what was happening. Luca was here . . . after eighteen years, the girl who I'd never met yet knew me better than anyone without knowing my real name . . . and she was right outside my house.

What the hell was her plan? Was she going to knock on my door?

How did she think she'd get past the guard at my gate?

How the hell did she find me?

Better yet, what was I going to do now that she had?

I was pissed off, but did I really have any right to be pissed if she'd hired someone to find me? After all, I'd done the same damn thing. Of course, I hadn't hopped into an RV and driven across the country to knock on her door.

Which brought up another series of questions—why the fuck hadn't I?

I have no balls.

No goddamn balls.

Luca has bigger balls than I do.

Shit. Balls. FUUUUCK.

I needed some coffee if there was any shot in hell that I'd make sense of things. So I headed to the kitchen to make a pot. While it was brewing, I looked out the windows. The tall hedges that bordered my property line blocked the view of the street, so I couldn't see down the block. That had been one of the things that first attracted me to the house—privacy.

When my coffee was done, I dialed Julian for an update. He answered on the first ring. "All quiet on the crazy bus still."

That shit might've been funny if I wasn't so anxious. "So they're just parked there. What are they going to do, camp out on my block?"

"No idea. But the way the police patrol this ritzy neighborhood, I'm sure they'll be escorted off the block pretty quickly. Sun isn't even awake yet. Cops are getting their doughnuts and coffee, so they'll be around soon."

He was joking, but he also wasn't wrong. My area had its share of celebrities. The police really did enforce the *no loitering* rules around town. Which meant, whatever she was doing here—she might not be doing it for long.

"Let me know if anything changes in the meantime. But I'll be out in a few minutes."

"You're coming out? Want me to handle this for you?"

"I don't think so. This is something I need to handle on my own."

"Alright. I'm here if you need me. I'll keep an eye from where I'm parked down the block."

"Thanks, Julian."

I hung up, tossed my phone on the table, and drained the rest of the coffee from my mug. When I opened the front door, the chilly morning air hit me. I only had on a pair of sweats, so I grabbed a bathrobe hanging on a hook and slid on some slippers. I looked like James Gandolfini from *The Sopranos* about to go grab the morning paper and wave to the FBI. I really hoped that a car full of teenyboppers didn't pass by as I headed down the block.

At the bottom of the driveway, a security guard sat in a little booth next to my tall gates. I waved. "Hey, Joe."

"Morning, Mr. Archer. You heading somewhere?"

"Just down the block."

"Not sure that's a good idea. I'm keeping my eye on a strange vehicle that pulled up a little while ago. Figured I'd give it fifteen more minutes and then call the local guys to escort it out if it's still here. Could be an eccentric fan or paparazzi."

Oh, you got the eccentric *part right.*

"It's fine. Don't call quite yet. I'm going to handle this one myself."

"You sure?"

"Positive."

Joe pressed the button to open the gates, and I slipped outside onto the street. Sure enough, there was the RV parked a few houses away. I was used to excitement—getting onstage with a stadium full of cheering fans pumped up the adrenaline. But that feeling had nothing on the anticipation I felt as I walked down the street.

Eighteen years.

And it all came down to this.

As I approached, I saw there was no one in the driver or passenger seats. A curtain was drawn so that I couldn't see into the interior of the RV. Guess my visit was going to be a surprise attack.

Arriving at the door, I took a deep breath. It did nothing to slow my racing pulse.

Luca. Luca. Luca. What are you up to?

I guess I'm about to find out, my eccentric, beautiful girl.

My chest felt like it had a runaway train locked inside, and a thin sheen of sweat formed on my forehead. Lifting my hand to knock, I was barely able to stop it from shaking long enough to pound on the door. God, I was a wreck. I couldn't remember the last time my nerves had gotten to me like this. But that was nothing compared to what I felt when the door swung open.

My heart nearly stopped at the sight of her. Her beautiful, gigantic eyes seemed to be staring through to my soul, causing me to completely blank on what to even say. I had to think quickly and opted not to out her just yet. I wanted to see where this would go if I didn't immediately come clean—namely whether she knew "Cole" was *me*.

"You realize it's illegal to park here, don't you?" I finally said.

She swallowed and forced out words. "Who are you?"

While I couldn't be 100 percent certain she knew it was *me*, I suspected based on her apparent nerves that she did.

"I'm Cole Archer." I pointed behind me. "My property is right over there."

Her eyes seemed to be examining every inch of my face. "Oh."

Beautiful, beautiful Luca.

Wow.

It's really you.

I wanted to pull her into my arms and devour her plump lips, swallowing up all of those nerves. Instead I said, "You should move the vehicle before someone calls the police."

She shook her head. "Oh yeah . . . sure. We can do that."

"Going right now," the old man said as he jumped up from his spot in the back. I hadn't even noticed him until he spoke.

He moved into the driver's seat.

I'd only told them to move as my excuse for coming out here. I didn't want them to *actually* move, because then what? I could lose her.

Before he was about to turn the ignition, I held out my hand to stop him. "Wait."

He looked over at me, expecting more.

Think.

"I . . . suppose there's no harm in what you're doing, just parking here. I can't guarantee that no one else will call the police, but you're good with me. Stay here as long as you like."

Luca blew out a relieved breath. "Thank you. We really appreciate it."

"No problem." Our eyes were stuck like glue to one another as I nodded. "Very well, then."

I turned around and headed back toward my house, shaking my head at this predicament.

Although I'd wanted so badly to take her into my arms and tell her I knew who she was, it was easier said than done. I was also hoping she'd fess up to me, but she never did. While I was now fairly certain she knew who I was based on the way she looked at me, I also couldn't be 100 percent sure.

I had a lot of questions. Did she maybe recognize me as Cole Archer and not know that it's really *me*? Could that also explain the reaction? Was she still looking for Griffin? Or worse, did she realize that I was Cole and then decide that she wanted a piece of me just like everyone else? That didn't sound like Luca, but honestly neither did this entire road trip she'd embarked on. I was so goddamn confused. I felt like the only way I could really learn if she wanted me for *me* was to continue this charade a little longer. If I told her the truth too soon, I might never really know her true intentions.

◆ ◆ ◆

I spent the rest of that afternoon looking out the window at the RV parked in the distance. I'd made a few calls to ensure the cops didn't have them removed. I couldn't understand why she'd come all the way to California if she didn't plan on telling me who she was. Then again, I'd completely blown my own opportunity to bare all.

If I knew Luca, she was second-guessing everything, stuck as to how to handle this just as much as I was. I needed to draw her out, make it easier for her to open up to me. There was no way I was letting her leave California before getting to explain myself properly. *Jesus.* She'd come all the way out here, despite her agoraphobia. That really spoke volumes about how much she needed to find out the truth.

I had to go out there before she made a rash decision and left. It would be nice if I took off my damn bathrobe this time.

After replacing the robe with a halfway decent shirt, I once again passed my very confused security guard and headed down the road to where the RV was parked. She'd never agree to go anywhere in public with me, and given her issues, I wouldn't put her through the hell of having to deal with paparazzi. But I needed to get her alone, maybe even have a little fun before I pulled the lid off everything tonight.

There was only one way to handle this clusterfuck and that was to wing it.

I knocked on the RV and waited.

Luca opened the door, once again looking flustered.

I waved. "Hey. Me again."

She blew out a breath. "You again . . ."

"I just wanted to apologize if my knocking on your door earlier was intrusive."

"Oh . . . uh . . . not at all."

"What brings you to the neighborhood?"

She looked back at her friend, then said, "He and I are on a road trip. This looked like a nice, safe place to stop."

"I'm sorry, I was so rude earlier that I didn't even get your name?"

"My name? I'm . . ." She hesitated, then looked to her left. "Mirada. And this is my friend Chester."

"Mirada . . . ," I repeated.

"Yes."

"Well, it's very nice to meet you. Welcome to California. I'm Cole."

I held out my hand, and she took it. Touching her for the first time felt electric.

"Nice to meet you, Cole."

"What are your plans while you're here?" I asked.

"Can't say I have any. Just going wherever the wind takes us."

Or the hot air . . .

I needed to move this nonsense forward.

"Might you have some time to join me for dinner tonight?"

While Luca didn't say anything, the old man answered for her. "She'd love to."

She turned to him. "I would?"

"Yes, you would."

She looked at me again. "I guess I would."

"Brilliant, then. Say about six? I'll give my guard your name . . . *Mirada*. He'll let you in."

She feigned happiness. "That's great. Thanks. Looking forward to it."

I knew she was probably dying inside. I hated that, but this had to be done.

As I walked back to my house, all I could think was how ridiculous this situation was; I didn't have very long to figure out how the hell I was going to handle it.

CHAPTER 13

LUCA

"Mirada? Mirada! I couldn't come up with anything better than the brand name of the RV we're driving?"

"That *was* an interesting choice." Doc chuckled.

"I freaked out and glanced over at the dash, and that was all that came out."

"I have to say I was very curious as to how you were going to handle that whole situation."

"I didn't handle it. I completely made a mess of things for myself. Thanks for accepting his date offer, by the way. It would have been nice if I'd had a choice."

"You don't have a choice, Luca. You must face the music."

"I never thought the *music* would end up being literal." I sighed. "Seriously, how am I going to handle this, Doc? He's going to think I'm a nutjob for following him here and lying about my identity."

"You're not the only one who lied. His was a lie of omission."

"Am I really doing this? Having dinner with him?"

"Yes."

"What do I say?"

"He's giving you the chance to say anything you need to. The fact that he came back here and invited you into his home saves you the trouble of having to figure out how to get him alone. He's handed the opportunity to you on a silver platter. Now it's up to you to decide what to do with it."

◆ ◆ ◆

An hour later, I was dressed in the only nice outfit I'd packed—a simple red sheath dress. I hadn't exactly planned on going to dinner with a celebrity in his fancy mansion while out here stalking Griffin. I most definitely hadn't expected *Griffin* to be that celebrity.

With wobbly legs, I made my way over to his massive house.

I spoke to the guard. "Hi . . ." *Jesus, I nearly forgot my supposed name.* "Mirada here to see Cole Archer."

"Yes. He's expecting you." He directed me to head to the front entrance.

As I continued toward the door, I wondered what "Cole" wanted with me anyway. Griffin didn't know my identity. He thought he was inviting a random woman for dinner. Did he do this all the time? Was he attracted to me? Or was he just being hospitable? I couldn't figure out why he'd invited me here. Before I was able to ponder it much, the gigantic wooden door to the Spanish-style house opened. A short woman dressed in housekeeper's garb nodded at me as she let me in.

Griffin was nowhere to be found. My heels echoed against the marble floors as I looked around the impressive foyer. Some framed vinyl records adorned the walls. This was definitely what I'd imagined a rock star's house to look like.

All I could think right now was *I'm so proud of you, Griffin.*

His voice startled me. "The record label sends those to me. Might as well hang them up. I'm really not an egomaniac. I swear."

"I wasn't thinking that at all. You should be proud. You've really done well."

When I turned to look at him, I noticed he'd changed into sleek black pants and a fitted gray T-shirt. His hair was wet. He was seriously hot as fuck. I couldn't believe this was my Griffin.

"Depends on how you define *done well*. I've definitely accumulated wealth and managed to impress a certain percentage of people with my music. But it can be hard sometimes. It can be a very lonely life."

That tugged at my heartstrings. "Yeah. I can imagine."

"Can I get you something to drink, Mirada?"

"Sure. Anything is fine."

"I have a bar bigger than *Cheers*. What suits your fancy?"

"A glass of wine would be nice."

Griffin led me into the massive living room. All the furniture was white. I just knew I was going to dirty it somehow before I left. He ventured over to the large bar in the corner of the room and prepared my drink himself.

He returned and handed me a large glass of red wine. "Sorry . . . dinner is a little late. My chef is off tonight, and, well, I didn't want to poison you with my cooking, so I've ordered out. Hope that's okay."

"That sounds delicious."

"You don't even know what it is yet."

"That's true. But I'm sure it will be good."

"You sure have a lot of blind faith in me."

What did he just say?

Blind faith?

He must just use that term freely. I wouldn't read into it.

I cleared my throat. "Apparently."

He clapped his hands together. "So . . . dinner. Hope you like scallops wrapped in bacon? I've chosen that for an appetizer. Then garlic pork roast with thyme for the main course."

Pork? Is he kidding?

I swallowed. "Sounds delicious."

He squinted at me. "You look so familiar. Are you sure we haven't met?"

Nervously twirling my hair, I laughed. "What do you take me for, a groupie?"

"Ha! No, no, no. I just felt this familiarity from the moment I met you." His eyes were searing into mine.

I was seriously starting to burn up from the intensity of his stare. *Can he possibly know it's me? How?*

My plan was to tell him the truth, but the longer this charade went on, the harder it was to blurt it out for some reason. I kept waiting for the perfect window to confess, but it never seemed to come. Not to mention, his penetrating stare sort of left me speechless.

"Who is that man you're traveling with?" he asked.

"He's a good friend."

"So no funny business going on there?"

"Gosh, no. He's only my traveling companion. I don't travel alone."

"Ah. Gotcha. Yeah, traveling alone is for the birds."

Birds.

"Right."

He smiled. "So did you recognize me? You didn't seem like you did."

My heart was beating out of my chest. "You mean . . . did I know you were . . . Cole Archer?"

Griffin tilted his head. "What else would I mean?"

I blew out a relieved breath. "I did actually know who you are, yes."

"That sucks. I was kind of hoping you didn't."

I looked deeply into his eyes. "It must be crazy, huh? Being you?"

"Yes, but what in particular do you mean?"

"Everything?"

He just looked at me for a while before he answered. "Sometimes I just wish I could hide in my house and never come out."

Sounds familiar.

My heart beat faster.

He continued. "I envy people who aren't recognized everywhere they go."

"I can imagine."

"What is it that you do, Mirada?"

What do I do?

"I . . . A little bit of everything. Sort of at a crossroads right now."

"Why are you hiding it? If I can be forthright, certainly you can as well. What, do you . . . write porn or something?"

"No, nothing like that."

"Too bad." He winked.

Suddenly, the housekeeper led a bunch of people through the living room into the adjacent dining room.

"Ah. Dinner's here," Griffin said.

I put my wine down on an end table and followed him into the dining area. A full staff of people were setting up a grand table. One gentleman carried a gigantic covered silver platter.

"This looks like a meal fit for a king," I said.

When the man took the top off the platter, my stomach sank. It wasn't just pork but an entire pig with the head still on it. I looked away. I couldn't stomach it. It was like watching Hortencia burned at the stake and laid out at her funeral.

Griffin's eyes were practically bugging out of his head. His cool stance was no longer. He turned to the man. "What the fuck! I ordered the pork, not an entire animal. What the hell are you bringing into my house? It's disturbing. Please cover it up and take it back."

The man hurriedly did as he said but asked, "What did you think pork was, sir?"

"I get what you're saying, but there's no need to *see* my dinner staring back at me." He looked over at me. "Clearly you can see my guest is extremely upset."

I was shaking. Honestly, I didn't even know what to say anymore.

After the room emptied out, Griffin rushed over to me. "Are you okay?"

"That was . . . that was unexpected."

"Fuck. I was just having a little fun in ordering the pork. I knew you wouldn't eat it. I would never have done that to you on purpose. I know how much she means to you."

Wait.

What?

What's happening?

He placed his hands around my face. "You look like you're about to cry. I've fucked this all up. I would never want to hurt you like that. You mean so fucking much to me." He backed me up against the wall, pressing his rock-hard body against mine. "Luca . . . my beautiful Luca."

My voice was shaky. "Griffin?"

"How did you find me, my impulsive girl?" He shook his head. "Never mind. Don't answer that yet."

He leaned in and smashed his lips against mine, kissing me so hard, I was practically seeing stars. My entire body felt weightless as I melted into him, our tongues colliding in a wet and delicious frenzy as we made up for years of lost kisses.

"Goddamn, Luca, you taste so good," he muttered over my lips. "I feel like I've been waiting my whole life for this."

Raking my fingers in his lustrous hair, I couldn't help the sounds that were coming out of my mouth. No one had ever kissed me the way Griffin Marchese was doing right now. Breathing him in like this was everything I'd ever dreamed of.

Our kiss was interrupted when the housekeeper entered carrying three large pizza boxes.

Feeling like an animal in heat, I panted and asked, "What's that?"

"Our real dinner. Pineapple pizza—your favorite."

A feeling of nostalgia warmed over me. "You remembered."

"How could I forget? I remember everything, Luca."

◆ ◆ ◆

"Tell me what you're thinking right now."

I blinked a few times and my vision came back into focus. I'd been staring down at a slice of pineapple pizza and when I looked up, I found Griffin watching me. I'd heard him speak, but the words seemed to have swooped in one ear and bolted out the other. "I'm sorry. What did you say?"

He stood. We'd been sitting across from each other at the dining room table. Today had been surreal—from finding out Griffin was Cole Archer, to seeing him for the first time after all these years, to that kiss. *That kiss.* Griffin extended his hand. "Come on. You have too much on your mind to eat right now. Why don't we go sit in the living room and talk?"

I nodded and put my hand in his. He led me over to the massive sectional, and when I sat, he knelt down in front of me and slipped off my heels one at a time. "I'm taking these off so that you're comfortable, but I also have an ulterior motive. I'm going to get us some more wine from the kitchen, and I'm going to keep one of these with me so you can't bolt out the door while I'm gone for two minutes."

I thought he was joking, but he actually took one of my shoes with him. He returned a few minutes later carrying two fresh glasses of wine and my high heel.

"Nottingham Cellars cab." Griff extended a glass of my favorite wine. The thing was full to the brim. "I wasn't sure what year you liked so I got a few different ones. This is the 2014. Which do you usually buy?"

"Um. Whichever one is the cheapest."

"Shit. I went in the other direction."

I smiled. "It's fine. I'm not really a wine aficionado, so I doubt I'd be able to tell one year from the next."

Griffin sat down on the couch next to me and pulled one knee up, turning to face me. He looked completely at ease, whereas I was concentrating hard to keep my hand from shaking. I really didn't want to slosh red wine all over his white furniture. He noticed and put a hand on my knee. "Relax. I'm not going to bite." An adorable boyish grin tugged at the corners of his mouth. "Unless you want me to."

I gulped down half the glass of wine.

Griffin arched a brow. "Feel better?"

I shook my head. "Not really."

He slipped the glass from my hands and set it down on the coffee table, along with his untouched one. Then he took both my hands into his and looked back and forth between my eyes. "You're even more beautiful in person."

Heat crept up my cheeks. "Thank you. I can't believe you even recognized me. How old was I in the one photo you've seen of me? Twelve?"

Griffin looked down at our joined hands and squeezed. "I think we both have a lot to come clean about. So I'm going to start right now. I didn't recognize you from the picture that you'd sent me in middle school. I hired a private investigator to follow you and take some photos of you."

My eyes bulged from my head. "You what? When?"

"A few weeks ago. He took some pictures of you coming out of the post office. And then . . . he followed you across the country over the last week."

Not knowing someone had been watching me made me suddenly feel very violated. I pulled my hands from his. "Why would you do that?"

Griffin raked his hands through his hair. "I wanted to see what you looked like."

"I *asked* you to exchange photos. You were the one who said you didn't want to."

"I wanted to see *you*. I just didn't want you to see *me*. But I guess you knew who I was all along, so the joke was on me anyway."

My brows drew down. "What are you talking about? I only found out this morning who you are."

He looked genuinely confused. "Then how did you happen to arrive on my block?"

"You left an eBay receipt in the bottom of the box of Furbys you sent me. It had a shipping address of Marchese Music. I figured that was where you worked."

Griffin shook his head. "But if you didn't know who I was, why did you drive all the way across the country?"

The fact that he'd even had to ask that question told me so much. This beautiful man with this big, beautiful house thought people were attracted to him for his fortune and fame. This time, it was me who did the assuring. I reached out and took his hand in mine, looking into his eyes as I spoke. "Because I had a crush on the boy who wrote me letters all those years ago, but I started to fall for the sweet man who seemed to like me for who I am—broken or not—and I needed to see if maybe we could have a chance if we met in person finally."

Griffin leaned in a little closer. His eyes jumped back and forth between mine, searching for something. "You really had no idea who I was until this morning?"

I half smiled. "I hate to bruise your ego, Mr. Rock Star, but not only did I have no idea who you are, I'd never even listened to your music."

Even though I'd just insulted him, Griffin smiled like my answer was the best thing he'd ever heard. His eyes lit up. "What if you came all the way out here, and I was homeless, bald, and had a few missing teeth?"

I covered my mouth and laughed. "That's pretty much what I was expecting. You said your career choices had cost you more than you anticipated. So I thought maybe you were poor and ashamed about it."

Griffin looked bewildered. He squinted. "And yet you drove three thousand miles anyway?"

I shrugged. "I liked you for you. I was willing to accept whatever your situation was. But don't get me wrong. The fact that you look"—I waved my hand at his face—"like this . . . is a very nice surprise."

Griffin wrapped his hands around the backs of my knees and tugged me closer to him. "Oh yeah? Are you saying you like the way I look, babe?"

Babe. I definitely liked that. I tried not to smile but failed miserably. "I guess you're not so hard on the eyes."

He cupped my cheek. "Is that so? Well, you're not so bad yourself." His eyes fell to my lips and he rubbed his thumb over my bottom one. "This pouty mouth. I spent hours staring at it as a teenager. You don't even want to know all the things I used to fantasize about doing to it."

I swallowed. "Yes, I do."

Griffin's eyes darkened, and he pushed his thumb into my mouth. Without giving it any thought, I swirled my tongue around it and then closed my eyes before sucking hard.

"*Fuck*, Luca." The hoarse rumble of his groan sent shivers across my skin. Suddenly, I was lifted from my seat and was being hauled across Griffin's lap. He wound his hands into my hair, his lips sealed over mine, and his tongue replaced his finger inside my mouth. I'd thought our first kiss was electric, but this one, it made my body feel like a live wire. His lips were so soft, but his touch was so firm. This was a man who knew how to kiss. I was pretty sure I'd spend hours analyzing that fact later, but in the moment I didn't care how he'd gotten good at it, only that his expert tongue was inside my mouth, and it felt like damn heaven. He kissed me long and hard, with just the right amount of aggressiveness to make me let him take the lead and follow him anywhere.

I distantly registered a sound, but the roar of the blood rushing through my ears made everything else seem so far away and faded. Which was why, at first, I didn't realize the noise I heard was a doorbell ringing. Until it rang a second time. "That's the . . ." I tried to speak between our joined lips, but Griffin pressed his harder to mine.

"Ignore it . . . ," he mumbled.

Since I wasn't anxious to stop, I pretended I hadn't heard it. But when the bell rang a third time, it was Griffin who pulled back.

He stumbled to his feet, panting. Dazed at the sudden change in what was happening, I lifted my hand to cover my bruised lips. "I thought . . ."

That was when I heard what had made Griffin stop. Unfortunately, it was the voice of the one person I couldn't ignore.

Doc.

CHAPTER 14

GRIFFIN

"Where's Luca?" The old man marched past me as if I didn't exist.

I shut the door and cleared my throat. "She's in the living—"

Luca staggered into the kitchen looking frazzled. Her lips were swollen and her hair was a disheveled mess. Yet I wasn't sure if her being freaked out was from our kiss or her being worried about the old guy. She looked pretty panicked. "Doc? What's the matter? Is everything okay?"

He made a beeline for her and placed both his hands on her shoulders. "Are you okay? You didn't text like you were supposed to."

Luca let out a relieved breath. "Shoot. I'm sorry, Doc. Griffin and I, we started to . . . We just got caught up, and it slipped my mind that I was supposed to let you know I was okay."

Doc gave her a thorough once-over, then looked suspiciously at me and back to her. "You're sure everything is okay?"

"Yes. I'm fine. Griffin . . . he knows who I am now."

Doc's forehead smoothed out. "Oh. Okay. Well, I'm glad to hear that. I was worried about you. I didn't mean to intrude."

I knew he was important to her, so I extended my hand. "Griffin Marchese. Sometimes known as Cole Archer, Dr. Maxwell. I've heard a lot about you."

The good doctor warmed up. "Call me Chester, please."

It dawned on me that security hadn't called to let me know they were letting anyone come up to the house. "Did you come through the front gate, Chester?"

He shook his head. "I climbed the fence at the far end of the property."

My eyes widened. My fence had to be eight feet tall. "You climbed . . . the fence?"

"Luca wasn't answering her phone, and I was worried."

I started to crack up at the visual of this seventy-year-old man scaling a giant fence to save his patient. These two were one hell of a team.

Luca smiled at him warmly. "I'm so sorry for making you worry, Doc."

He held up a hand. "No need to apologize. I just wanted to make sure you were okay. I'll leave you two alone, then."

There was absolutely nothing I wanted more than to be left alone with Luca, to pick up exactly where we'd just left off. But when I looked over at her and saw the sweet smile she wore melt to a frown, the stupidest thing came out of my mouth. "No. Stay. Why don't you join us for dinner?"

◆ ◆ ◆

"So how long are you two planning on staying in California?"

Luca sighed, and I knew before she spoke that I didn't want to hear the answer. "We have to get back on the road the day after tomorrow."

Heaviness settled in my chest. "Why so soon?"

"It's a three-thousand-mile drive. We took a little longer than we'd planned to get out here, and we need to leave six days for getting back. If I'm behind the wheel too many hours in a day, I start to daydream and forget I'm driving. I missed half of Colorado plotting my next book in my head. It's not exactly safe."

"What about if I get someone to trailer the RV back and you guys take a plane? I'll book you a private flight."

Luca smiled sadly. "That's very sweet. But I . . . I don't go on planes." She looked down. "Or trains or buses. I don't even go to the grocery store like a normal person, Griffin."

Doc piped in. "She did great at the pet store last week, though."

Luca shook her head. "My life is . . . complicated."

Doc caught my eye. "Yes, Luca's life is complicated. But I'd venture to guess that Griffin's isn't uncomplicated. Where there's a will, there's a way."

It was easy to forget about Luca's issues while looking at her. Hell, it was easy to forget everything while admiring her beautiful face. But Doc was right; my life was as complicated as hers, maybe even more so—just in a very different way. I stared at Luca—we only had a day and a half, and I didn't want to waste a minute of our time together.

"Doc, I have a small pool house in the back of my property. It's got a bedroom and a kitchenette. Why don't you camp out there for the next two nights? I'm sure the beds in that RV can't be too comfortable. We can pull the camper into the driveway so that it's secure, and you can have some privacy."

Doc seemed hesitant to accept my offer. So I told a little white lie that I knew would sway things in my favor. "There're some great birds out there. I just installed a new feeder, so I bet it's like an aviary first thing in the morning."

Doc's eyes lit up. "Have you seen the spotted towhee? I hear she's quite the stunner."

The spotted what? "Sure, sure. Definitely have some of those out there."

Doc looked to Luca. His face reminded me of a little boy with his nose pressed up to the glass ice-cream display at the store while he waited for his mom to say he could get a scoop.

Luca smiled at Doc. "That sounds like a great idea, Doc."

He beamed. "Alright. Thank you for the offer, Griffin. But only if we can really pull the rig into the driveway behind the gates. I don't want Luca sleeping in the RV all by herself out on the street."

Oh, don't worry about that. I have no intention of letting Luca stay in that RV, either. "Of course. Why don't we go take care of that now, and I'll show you to the pool house."

The three of us headed out, Doc walking through the front door first. I extended my hand to tell Luca to go ahead of me, but she stopped, turned to face me, and pushed up on her tippy-toes to whisper in my ear. "You better find a way to make birds appear back there by morning, *liar.*"

Cole: Need you to do me a favor.

Aiden: Whatever you need, boss.

Cole: Find a 24-hour Home Depot and pick up a dozen bird feeders and seed. Hang them all around my pool house by the time the sun rises. I need birds out there bright and early. Buy a dozen parrots from the damn pet store if you have to.

Aiden: Okay . . .

Cole: And don't wake up the old man sleeping inside the pool house.

My assistant had received way stranger requests than this. One of the things that made him good at his job was that he never asked questions. So I powered my phone off, confident that Doc would be happy in the morning, and turned my attention to the woman standing in my kitchen.

Her beautiful mouth stayed in an unreadable line.

I walked toward her, focused on those lips. I wondered if she'd mind if I bit them. But Luca put her hand up and pressed against my chest, stopping me from finding out.

"I'm not sleeping with you."

I raised one brow. "Not ever?"

"Not tonight."

I nodded, amused. "Okay. So tomorrow night it is, then."

"That's not what I meant."

She still had her palm to my chest, so I tested the waters by giving a little nudge forward. She didn't stop me, so I leaned down and buried my face in her neck, kissing my way along her pulse line up to her ear to whisper, "Are you saying you're not attracted to me, Luca? That's a shame, because I'm *very* attracted to you."

She shook her head. "I . . . I am. Very. But . . ." Her words fell away. I had no doubt I could convince her to change her decision if I set my mind to it. Though Luca meant more than just a quick fuck to me.

I pulled back to look at her and cupped both her cheeks. "I respect that, Luca. I'd be lying if I said that the thought of burying myself inside you wouldn't be a dream come true. But I'd never ask you to do anything you didn't want to do."

She looked genuinely relieved. "I'm just afraid. Meeting you was such a huge step, and I don't want to get even more attached than I already am."

Hearing her say that was more of a disappointment than her *no sex* declaration. She'd only been in my home for a few hours, but I was pretty sure I was already more attached to her than some of my appendages. "Why don't we go relax a bit? I have more than one guest room when you're ready to get some sleep. I don't know about you, but I'm nowhere near ready to stop talking to you."

She smiled. "Yeah. That would be perfect."

In the living room, I lit the fireplace and filled our abandoned wineglasses from earlier. Luca pulled her feet up and tucked them under her. "Can I ask you something?"

"Anything." I sipped my wine.

"Why didn't you want to tell me?"

I shook my head. "I don't know. I guess I liked us being just us. I was afraid things would change if you found out the truth."

"Did someone you trusted do that to you? Change because of your fame?"

I wasn't surprised she'd hit it on the head. Luca could read me better than anyone, without us ever having met. Now that she sat in front of me, I didn't even need to say the answer aloud. She saw my face and spoke again before I did.

"I'm sorry they did that to you. That sucks."

Since we had limited time together, I didn't want to focus on all the negative shit that had gone down in my life, so I gave the abbreviated version. "Friends who I thought were friends turned out not to be. And women . . . well, they want to be with me because I'm Cole Archer, not for who I really am. If that makes sense."

She nodded. "It does. You know, the funny thing is—your being famous is probably the worst attribute in a man for me. I don't do crowds and busy places, and from the limited stuff I saw on the internet today, your life is one giant crowd and busy place."

"I guess . . . sometimes anyway. But the last few weeks, I've mostly been recording in the studio, so it's been pretty low-key. Honestly, I love the music but the crowds and the fame got old pretty quickly. I never appreciated anonymity until I didn't have it anymore. Things can get insane in this business."

"Like what? Tell me the craziest thing that's ever happened to you."

I thought about it. I had enough stories to write a dozen books, but one in particular stuck out. "I once came home to a woman cooking me dinner in the buff in my kitchen."

Luca's brows knitted together. "I would think a man would be happy to find his date cooking in the nude, not think it's crazy."

"She wasn't my date. I'd never met the woman before in my life. She broke in and acted like she knew me, calling me *honey* and stuff. It was like something out of *The Twilight Zone*. She had my name tattooed over her heart and had legally changed her last name to Archer. In her mind, we were married."

Luca's eyes bulged. "Oh my God. That's terrifying. Did she go to jail?"

I shook my head. "No. I agreed to drop the charges as long as she went for psychiatric counseling. She obviously wasn't right. But after that, I hired the security guard team that sits at the front gate twenty-four seven. I needed it anyway. A week after Miss Archer was arrested, one of those celebrity tour buses added me as a stop on their map, and now there are always people trying to get on the property."

"How can they do that? What about your privacy?"

I shrugged. "I traded my privacy for fame, Luca."

"That's crap. I can understand people wanting autographs and trying to take your picture when you're out and about. But your home—that should be your sanctuary."

"Yeah. People sort of forget I'm a real person."

Her shoulders slumped. "And here I just did the same thing to you, didn't I? I showed up in an RV without being invited. In fact, you specifically told me you didn't even want to exchange photos."

"That's different. I'm glad you took this leap for us, Luca. I really am. It needed to be done. Though I hope you can understand why I was hesitant at first. People don't show up to see Griffin. They show up to see Cole."

"But I didn't even know you were Cole when I made this trip."

"I know that now. And I'm sorry I ever doubted you."

"I'm sorry I pushed you outside your comfort zone. God knows I hate being outside of mine."

My eyes roamed her face. "Thank you for coming all this way. I know it couldn't have been easy."

She nodded.

Luca went quiet for a long time after that. She stared down at her wine, seemingly lost in thought. After a minute, I slipped my finger under her chin and lifted. "If we only have a day and a half, you're going to have to tell me what's on your mind. While I'd love to get inside that head of yours and try to make sense of how it works, I'm afraid we don't have that luxury."

She nodded. "I was just thinking that . . . you must have a lot of women throwing themselves at you all the time."

There was no point in lying. All she had to do was Google and she'd find women flashing me their tits from the front row of almost any of my shows. And I'd indulged my fair share when everything first hit. The paparazzi had captured more walks of shame leaving my dressing room than I wanted to remember. I wasn't proud of the man I'd been in the beginning, but I'd learned my lesson. "I'm not going to sit here and tell you that I'm a virgin, but those women, they aren't throwing themselves at Griffin Marchese. They're throwing themselves at Cole Archer—a man who doesn't even really exist."

"Have you had any serious girlfriends?"

My jaw clenched. "I thought I did, but it turned out I didn't. Haley lived with me for about three months. She was an aspiring singer. On my last tour, I decided to surprise her and come home between shows when I hadn't been scheduled to. I found her in bed with my forty-five-year-old agent."

"Wow. I'm sorry. That's awful."

"Yeah. That was just the beginning of finding out a bunch of dark shit about the people I thought cared about me."

Luca stroked my forearm. "I guess I can understand why you wanted to keep your current life a secret from me."

This conversation had taken a turn toward depressing. I reminded myself that we only had a little time together; the clock was ticking. I scratched at the stubble on my chin. "I have an idea. Do you remember that little game we used to play as teenagers? The one where we would tell each other a couple of true things and a lie and we'd have to figure out which was which."

Luca grinned. "Two truths and a lie. How could I forget? Like when you got your driver's license and thought you were so cool going to the drive-through line at McDonald's the first time, and you placed your entire order yelling into the trash receptacle?"

I laughed. I had forgotten all about that. Figures Luca hadn't. "That's the game. The winner used to have to send the other stickers, if I remember correctly."

"I stickered an entire closet door because I beat you so often."

"I used to let you win, cocky girl," I lied.

"Sure you did."

"I'm thinking it's time for a rematch. We only have a day and a half to get to know each other again. What better way than to play our old game?"

"I'm down for that. But I don't have any stickers with me, on the off chance you actually get something right."

"That's okay. We're not going to be playing for stickers this time."

"We're not? What exactly are we playing for, Mr. Quinn?"

"Kisses. Winner gets to pick where they want to give them."

CHAPTER 15

LUCA

The way I saw it, no matter who won this little game, I was going to come out a winner if it ended in a kiss from Griffin.

We got comfy on the couch.

"I'll go first," he said. "Two truths and a lie." He rubbed his hands together. "Okay. I once won a pair of Elton John's old knickers on eBay. Also, during one of my earlier concerts, I blanked out and forgot the words to one of the songs in front of thousands of people. Lastly, for your consideration . . . I haven't spoken to my father in two years."

I let the choices sink in as I massaged my temples. "I feel like this is sort of a trick. The knickers thing sounds so bizarre that it almost *has* to be meant to seem like a lie, but really it's the truth. While I don't want to believe you haven't spoken to your dad in that long, based on your past relationship with him, I'm afraid that's possibly true as well. So I'm going to go with you forgetting the words to the song as being the lie."

Griffin stared at me for a few seconds before making a sound that mimicked a buzzer.

"I'm wrong?"

"Yep." He laughed.

"Damn. I'm losing my touch."

"What would I want with an old pair of Elton John's knickers? That was the lie."

"I don't know! You seemed to enjoy perusing eBay before your account got shut down, and I remember you used to like him a lot when we were younger. So . . . it made a little sense?"

"I like him. But not *that* much!"

I wiped my eyes from the tears of laughter before turning serious when I said, "Okay, so . . . oh my gosh. Two years since you've spoken to your dad, Griffin?"

A frown washed over his face. "Yeah."

"Why?"

He blew out a breath. "Well . . . you remember he never supported my musical aspirations growing up. That never really changed. It wasn't until I made it big out here that he ever started to acknowledge that I might have made the right decision. Anyway, our relationship had always been strained because of how he treated my mum before she died, but even so, I still tried to keep the peace. That ended when he gave an interview to a British tabloid for a large sum of money. The article was titled something like, 'Cole Archer's Father Spills All His Secrets' or some garbage. Anyway, I stopped talking to him after that."

That hurt my heart. Griffin's dad was the only immediate family he had left after his mother died. I could relate to how awful it felt to be an only child and have almost no one. It must be a different kind of pain, though, to have your parent betray you.

"I'm really sorry, Griff."

He shrugged. I could tell from the way he sucked in his jaw that talking about it had upset him. "His loss. Maybe someday I'll get over it and call him, but that day hasn't come yet."

I reached for his hand and squeezed it. Touching him even in this innocent way felt absolutely electrifying.

"Anyway . . . ," he said. "The night I forgot the words to the song was recorded and is now on YouTube. You can find it if you want the proof. Early on, when the fame had gone to my head, I'd gotten caught up pretty heavily in the drinking and partying. That concert was the last straw. The label threatened to boot me. Got my act together real fast after that embarrassment. Never drank before a show again."

"Wow. If you can bounce back after blanking out in front of thousands of people like that, you can survive anything. Just standing there in front of them would be my biggest nightmare, let alone having to sing and remember words." I shivered at the thought.

"Your turn, love. Two truths and a lie."

I took a deep breath in and thought about what I was going to say.

"Okay. Two truths and a lie." I paused. "I've developed an intense fear of spiders . . . I've never had sex with the lights on, or . . . my readers think I'm a man."

His eyes widened. Then a look of amusement flashed across Griffin's face. "Why do your readers think you're a man?"

"How do you know that's even the truth?"

"It's so obvious the spiders thing is a lie. Anyone who lives with a pig must have a high tolerance for creatures of all kinds. Plus, there is no possible way you have arachnophobia *and* agoraphobia."

I chuckled. "Okay. You're good."

"Yes. I am . . . in *many* ways." He winked.

Feeling my body heat up, I said, "So my readers think I'm a man because my name is . . ." I braced myself. "Ryan Griffin."

He took a moment to let that sink in. "Griffin? Ryan . . . Griffin."

I nodded. "I never mentioned my pen name, and you never asked, but it's our two names combined. Well, my fake last name and your real first name. My actual last name is Vinetti."

"Vinetti. Italian like your dad. I love it."

"Thanks."

"So Ryan Griffin. That's wild—and amazing that you held on to me in that way. I'm honored. Now that you know about my fake persona, I can't wait to properly explore yours. Will you let me read your books?"

"It's not like I could stop you if you really wanted to, now that you know my pen name."

"You're wrong about that. If you didn't want me to read them, I absolutely wouldn't violate your trust."

I sighed. "You can read them. You might think I'm even more screwed up than you already do . . . but you can read them."

"Nah. Not possible," he teased. "Seriously, though, I wanna binge them all, find out what my Luca's intricate mind can conjure up. I can't fucking wait, really."

I rolled my eyes and laughed. "Great." As much as his reading my novels made me nervous, I was also kind of curious as to what he'd think about them. I wanted to make him as proud as he made me.

"So you've never fucked with the lights on. That's easy enough to change. Any particular reason why, though?"

"Well, my first time was in a dark car, and the other times, I made them shut off the lights. Just never felt like letting those guys see me. Not even really sure why that came to mind. I guess I couldn't think of anything else on the fly."

"You thought about it because being around me makes you think of sex." He wriggled his brows. "You imagined us both naked in broad daylight fucking against that wall over there. Am I right?"

I gulped.

Well, I wasn't before. But now I certainly am imagining that!

"Jesus, Luca. You're turning red. Did that turn you on, babe?"

"A little."

"Just a little?"

"Maybe more than a little."

"You're so fucking adorable." He leaned in and whispered in my ear. The heat of his breath gave me goosebumps when he said, "That reminds me. I need to collect my prize, don't I?"

I got chills. "Where are you going to kiss me?"

"Well, there really is no wrong choice here. I'd love to kiss any part of you that you'd let me. But given that you've made it clear we won't be taking things too far tonight, I should probably ask you what my options are first."

I wanted him to kiss me everywhere, but I knew opening up the "options" could lead to things I wasn't ready for. "Can I think about it?"

"Of course. And if you don't want me to kiss you again tonight, you can just tell me. I can take a rain check for my prize—because I do really hope to see you again. I wish to God you could stay longer than just one day."

I thought about that. Honestly, if I *could* have stayed longer . . . how much would I even be able to blend in to his life here? Pretty sure the answer was: not at all.

He must have noticed the look of worry on my face. "What's wrong, Luca? Talk to me. I'm still the guy you can tell anything to, despite all this ostentatious crap you see around you right now. Ignore all that, and tell me what's on your mind."

After a few seconds of silence, I looked into his eyes. "How could this ever possibly work, Griffin?"

He took my hand in his. "Crazier things have happened. For one, I've been in a relationship with pieces of fucking paper and words for the past several weeks. They were my only window into your soul. And you know what? They made me happier than I have been in a very long time, even with just the letters and nothing more."

"But now, we can't ever go back to that, can't ever go back to what we had. You deserve more than some woman who can hardly leave her house except to go food shopping in the middle of the night. It's only a matter of time before you figure out that there is no way for this to realistically work. You don't realize how limited I am."

He stared off in thought. When he looked into my eyes again, he asked, "Will you do me a favor?"

"Yes."

"Can you put all of the reasons we're wrong for each other on hold for one night and just *be* with me? Because while you're worrying about the future, I can't stop thinking about how damn lucky I am that my dream girl drove all the way across the country to see me—the real me. I'm on a high right now that you can't even imagine, Luca. And while you're sitting here trying to convince me that it could never work between us, all I can think about is whether you taste as good as you fucking make me feel." He squeezed my hand. "Can you do that? Can you just be with me and fuck the rest for a little while?"

How can I say no to that?

My eyes were watering. "Yeah. I can do that."

"Good." He stood up. "How about I show you around a little bit?"

"I'd love that."

Griffin gave me the grand tour of his massive house. One of the stops was the downstairs home theater that featured several rows of plush seats along with a popcorn machine.

We plopped ourselves down into two of the seats.

He rubbed his hand along the arm of the velour chair. "I have this great theater that I don't even use. When I do watch movies, it's usually alone at night in my room after a long day at the studio. I can't remember the last time I watched something down here."

"That seems like such a waste."

"Yeah . . . well, this room is made for more than one person, and when you can't even count on one hand the number of people you trust, well, it's kind of hard to fill a theater." He shook his head, seeming to catch himself getting into serious territory. "I'll tell you one thing, though, *Ryan* . . . when they make a fucking movie out of one of your books, you'd better damn well bet I'll be screening it down here."

That made me smile.

Next, he took me upstairs and showed me the bedrooms. There were five in total. The one at the end of the hallway was his—the master.

Stepping into Griffin's bedroom felt a little intrusive for some reason. I looked around for a bit. There was a lit electric fireplace. His bed had a massive fabric headboard. The heavy drapes were made of gray satin.

"This is gorgeous." I walked around, then turned to him. "I can imagine this room has seen more action than your theater?"

Even though I was sort of teasing with that statement, a part of me knew I was really digging for information about exactly how promiscuous he'd actually been.

He didn't look the least bit amused. "You'd be surprised. I haven't really taken many women into my bedroom. To me, that's a very intimate thing. Like I said, I had only one serious relationship since all of this happened."

I continued to look around, dumbfounded, as if I'd just entered a sex dungeon. But it wasn't; it was just a regular bedroom, but somehow I was freaking out being inside it. Then Griffin placed his hands on my shoulders.

"Why don't we talk about what's really concerning you right now? I didn't want to talk about serious stuff when I only have you for a short time, but I do feel like this needs to be said." He blew a breath out. "I know what you were thinking when you walked into this room. It scared you a little. *I* scare you a little—maybe a lot. You have this idea that I'm a manwhore. As I told you before, it was like that for a while. There weren't hundreds—but maybe dozens in the beginning. It gets old real fucking fast, Luca. You know what happens when you can have literally anything? Ironically, you don't want any of it anymore. I miss the chase. I miss being a normal human being. Instead of walking into this room and wanting to lie with me, wanting me to hold you, you were worried about all of the supposed women who had been here before you. That makes me a little sad, really. Especially because at this moment, I can barely remember much of anything that happened before Luca Vinetti showed up at my house."

My heart fluttered.

"I'm sorry for making you feel like you had to explain yourself."

"Don't apologize. I get it. One of the people you trusted most isn't who you thought he was. But I'm trying to tell you that I *am*, Luca. I *am* still him. You just have to look past all of the bullshit to see me. I'm here."

I looked deeply into his eyes before pulling him in for a hug. We held each other for the longest time. With each second that passed, my fears seemed to melt away little by little. Or at least they faded into the background—for now.

"Where am I sleeping tonight?" I finally asked.

"Wherever you want. You can take your pick of the guest rooms. The only thing I ask is that you *not* insist on sleeping in the RV. I want you under my roof tonight. Because in a little over a day, I lose you again."

I felt the need to better defend my behavior tonight. "The reality of the situation is just hitting me in waves, Griffin. But I am going to try to spend the rest of this time focusing on the now and not on anything else beyond that."

"Your concerns are normal. Just promise to always be honest with me. I promise to do the same moving forward. You need to tell me what you're afraid of, especially when the object of your fear is me. There shouldn't be any elephants in the room . . . or pigs for that matter." He smiled. "But please, I'm begging you. Don't be afraid of me. Trust what's in your heart, trust in what made you get into that RV and come here in the first place. I promise, if you can do that, I'll try like hell not to let you down."

"Blind faith," I whispered.

"Yes. Except the blind part isn't so literal anymore—now that we can look at each other, and perhaps do some other things when the time is right." He flashed a crooked smile.

Griffin and I hung out by the electric fireplace and talked until the wee hours of the morning. He told me more about the road to becoming a star. It turned out he'd actually been discovered by an American talent agent while singing in a bar in London. The agent then paid to have Griffin travel to the United States, but that arrangement never went anywhere. Ultimately, while here, Griffin met his current bandmates when each was auditioning at the same time for a music competition show. The group of "rejects" formed a bond and eventually became Archer.

Later, I showed him all my books online and bit my nails as he purchased and downloaded each one to his e-reader.

When it was nearing 2:00 a.m., I could no longer keep my eyes open. I was still so exhausted from the trip out here. Griffin set me up in one of his guest bedrooms. I chose the one closest to him.

As tired as my body was, I just couldn't fall asleep. I was completely wired. Not to mention, I had to pee. This particular room didn't have its own bathroom, so I would have to use the one that was down the hallway.

After I ventured over there, just as I was exiting, I smacked right into Griffin's hard chest.

"Whoa. Shit. Are you alright? I didn't see you in the dark," he said.

"Yeah, I'm fine."

He rubbed my forehead. "You sure?"

"Yeah."

"I was just headed to the kitchen for a glass of water," he said. "Can I get you anything?"

"No. Thank you."

I suppose one of us should have moved. Instead, we stayed close. I could feel the heat of his breath. His mouth lingered over mine, but he didn't kiss me right away. Our mouths were inches apart as he wrapped his hand around my back. I closed my eyes for a moment, and that was when I felt him devouring my lips.

For the next five minutes, we just stayed there in the dark hallway, making out like teenagers. I knew he would respect my wishes not to try to have sex with me tonight. Yet I wasn't exactly sure I cared anymore at this point.

I felt the heat of his cock through his pants pressing against my abdomen. He was so hard. Wetness began to pool between my legs.

He whispered over my lips, "I know you don't want to take things too far. I respect that. But let me make you come with my hand."

So desperate for it, I nodded, unable to form words.

Griffin licked his fingers before lowering his hand down into my panties. My back was against the wall as he kissed me so hard while his fingers moved in and out of me. He used his thumb to massage my clit.

It amazed me that despite our years apart, despite my earlier anxiety, his touching me this way felt so natural.

He kissed me harder as he moved his hand faster, pushing his fingers deeper into me with every thrust of his hand. At one point, he stopped, and it was almost painful. He took his hand to his mouth and sucked the fingers that had been inside me. His eyes were closed as he savored the taste. It was so sensual and erotic, like nothing anyone had ever done to me before. My clit was throbbing.

He stuck his fingers back inside me, but this time there were three. So turned on, I was ready to come. I bucked my hips. He must have felt my muscles contract when he said, "Come, baby. Come all over my hand. Pretend it's me inside you. I'm so incredibly hard right now."

I bent my head back against the wall and just let myself go, my muscles pulsating as I came against his hand.

"I love the sounds you make when you come, Luca. So insanely beautiful. I've fantasized about that for so long, but nothing came close to the real thing. Nothing."

What could I even say? What he'd just done was selfless, really.

Panting, I said, "Thank you for that."

"The pleasure was all mine. Believe me." He kissed my forehead. "Go get some rest. We have a big day tomorrow. And I need to head straight to the shower."

I didn't have to wonder why he'd be showering now.

"Okay," I said. "What's happening tomorrow, though?"

"Don't worry. We won't go anywhere. It'll be a big day simply because we're together."

CHAPTER 16

GRIFFIN

Despite only getting a few hours of sleep, Luca and I were up before 9:00 a.m. As she stood across from me sipping her coffee, I thought about how surreal it was to have her here with me in my kitchen. The sun shined through the window, bringing out the subtle red highlights in her dark hair. This was a moment I'd never forget. I still wasn't entirely sure how I was going to let her go tomorrow.

When she caught me staring at her, I asked, "Have you heard from your friend?"

"No, actually."

"You think he's up?"

"Oh, Doc gets up at the crack of dawn. He probably thinks we're still sleeping. I'm certain he's been up for a while looking for the birds you promised." She lifted her brow. "How did you handle that exactly?"

I nudged my head. "Let's go take a look."

Reaching for her hand, I led her to a sliding door that opened to the part of my property that overlooked the pool house.

In the distance, we could see the good doctor lying out on a lounge chair, surrounded by a variety of birds perched atop the surrounding bird feeders. I was glad to see Aiden had come through for me.

Luca's jaw dropped. "This is a problem."

"Why?"

"He may never want to go home, and then I'll have to find another way to get back."

"Well, we can leave him here in California, and I'll take you back." I winked.

She probably didn't think I was half serious, but I would have loved to take a trip with her, to escape this craziness for a while and just enjoy the open road with Luca. Basically, leave Cole in LA and live as Griffin for a bit.

"Are you here in California for a while recording, or do you have any travel coming up?" she asked.

I cringed. "Actually, I have to fly to Vancouver in less than two weeks. We're part of the lineup at a music festival out there. Until then, I'll mostly be back in the studio, recording."

Luca pushed out a smile, but I could see it was bullshit. "That's great. I'm sure you'll have a good time."

I chose to not call her out on her comment. Time was ticking, and I didn't want to waste another minute of it talking about how different our lives were. What I needed to do was show her that I was still Griffin—even when I was playing the part of Cole. "How about if I make us some breakfast and then we take a little trip in the RV?"

Luca immediately looked panicked. "I'm not good in traffic, Griffin."

I figured she might say that, so I'd already mapped out a route that avoided the busiest roads. The twenty-minute trip might take us an hour, but I didn't give a fuck because that hour would be spent with her by my side. "I know. We'll avoid the 405 and leave about eleven, after rush-hour traffic passes."

"Where would we go?"

I brushed a lock of hair from her face and looked into her eyes. "Can you just trust me that I won't do anything to hurt you, love?"

Her fear was palpable, yet she took a deep breath in and nodded. *That's my girl.*

Now, if only I don't fuck this up . . .

It was a miracle to not hit traffic on the way to the studio. Seriously, a fucking miracle. The gods were definitely watching over me today, because in the years since I'd moved to LA, I'd never seen fewer cars than I did on the drive this morning. I'd talked Luca into letting me drive the RV—well, actually, she'd originally refused, but after pressing her up against the driver's side door and kissing the shit out of her, she reluctantly agreed. For the first half of the drive, she sat white-knuckled in the passenger seat, holding on for dear life. But after a while, she eased into it and now it was me who was more nervous than she was. Not about the trip itself but about the piece of shit I was currently driving. I couldn't believe she had driven this hunk of junk clear across the country. It pulled to the right and swayed with the slightest gust of wind.

"How old is this thing?"

"I'm not sure. It's Doc's sister's. He said she's had it for a long time. I know it's older-looking, but it has barely any miles on it."

I stopped at a stop sign, and the engine trembled and revved for a minute like it was stuck in gear before sputtering back to normal. "When was the last time the tires were checked? I think you have an alignment issue."

Luca shrugged. "It pulls a little to the right. But you barely notice it when you're going seventy on the interstate."

Great. That makes me feel a lot better. We drove a few more blocks in silence, mostly because I was making a mental checklist of shit to set into motion once I got to where we were going.

Find an RV mechanic to go through this hunk of metal with a fine-tooth comb tonight.

Pick up a portable electronic navigation system to set up on the dash.
The amount of folded maps and printed directions on the floor was truly mind-boggling. I couldn't imagine Luca driving this big thing through Colorado, up and down the mountainous roads as it swayed in the wind, no less while looking at maps at the same time. It seriously freaked me the hell out. I'd be calling her all day, every day, until she got back to Vermont. Which reminded me . . .

Get Aiden to go to Best Buy and pick up a phone cradle, mount, and headset. When I called to check on her, it would be nice if she could answer without taking her eyes off the road.

We turned down the street of our intended destination, and I smiled. Aiden was standing curbside waiting for us and had done exactly what I'd asked. Seeing us approach in the RV, he waved and walked into the street to collect some of the orange cones he'd put out to reserve our spot. He'd also blocked off two car lengths in front and behind where the RV would be parked.

Luca looked at the man standing in the street and then at me. "Are we here? Who is that guy?"

"We're here. And that's my assistant, Aiden. I had him come early this morning to block a spot for us to park and make sure no one was parked too close to us."

She looked around outside. "But where is here?" The blocks surrounding this particular recording studio were heavily industrial. It was mostly just old warehouses that had been turned into artist lofts, storage facilities, and various unmarked filming sets and music studios.

"This is where I'm recording today. But relax, I don't expect you to come in. Give me a minute to park this thing, and I'll explain."

Of course, the piece of shit didn't have a rear camera system, so I was glad that Aiden had blocked off all that extra space, and I could just pull in once he'd cleared the cones. I turned off the ignition and reached over and took Luca's hand. "You're doing great. Just keep trusting me, babe."

She nodded, though she looked nervous again. I got out and spoke to Aiden privately for a moment before opening the back door to get into the living area of the RV. "Do you mind if I let Aiden in for a minute? He's just going to set up some equipment, and he'll be out of your way in no time."

"Sure, of course."

I waved Aiden into the RV and did the introductions. "Aiden, this is my girl, Luca. Luca, this is the man who saves my ass on a daily basis—Aiden."

Aiden leaned forward and shook Luca's hand. "Nice to meet you, Luca."

It took him less than five minutes to set up portable Wi-Fi, a Mac monitor, receiver, and speakers. He handed me a set of Bose wireless headphones. "All done. Here you go, boss."

I nodded. "Thanks. Can you let them know I'll be in and ready to go in five minutes?"

"You got it."

Aiden said goodbye to Luca and climbed out of the RV. She was still sitting in the front passenger seat, so I extended a hand for her to climb from the front into the back.

"What in the world are you up to?" she asked.

I closed the privacy curtain once she was in the back. "Take a seat, and let me show you."

She settled into the couch, and I positioned the monitor on the table across from her and handed her the headset. "I have to record for a few hours today. I want you to watch, but I know you don't like crowds and public buildings. Between the sound guys, the mixers, the recording team, and the label execs, there're at least ten guys in the studio while I work. So I had them set up a video camera in the booth so you can watch while I record, and this headset will let you listen. It'll be like you're watching but without the crowd."

When I saw her face fall, I thought maybe she was disappointed. It had been pretty egotistical to assume she'd want to sit alone in a camper and watch me record, hadn't it? "Sorry. You don't have to watch if you don't want. I can tell them I need an hour and take you back home."

"No, *God no*. I can't wait to watch. I just feel bad about all the trouble you had to go through for me."

I knelt in front of her. "Wasn't any trouble at all. And even if it were, you're worth it."

Her face softened. "Thank you, Griffin."

I kissed her. "You can thank me later. I'll have Aiden make a sign for after I'm done. *Don't come a knockin' when the RV's a-rockin'.*"

I went to get up, but Luca tugged my hand back down. "You called me your girl."

My brows drew down. "I did?"

She nodded. "When you introduced me to your assistant, you said, 'This is *my girl*, Luca.'"

I hadn't even noticed. But the truth of the matter was, she *was* my girl. I shrugged. "You are my girl, Luca. You'll figure it out, too, soon."

CHAPTER 17

LUCA

"Check. One, two, three. One, two, three." Griffin had on a set of headphones and leaned into the microphone to speak. I heard some other people talking in the background, but the camera had been set up inside the little recording booth, so the only thing I saw on the big monitor was Griffin's face. Which was fine by me. Honestly, I'd wanted to spend some time staring at him since he knocked on the camper door. This was the perfect opportunity to gawk without him catching me.

For the next fifteen minutes, Griffin went through a bunch of sound system checks and testing. He stood in the booth repeating words and talking to people. My eyes were glued to the monitor, combing over every inch of his handsome face. He was seriously even more gorgeous than I could have imagined. He had big, beautiful brown eyes with thick, dark lashes lining his lids that almost made it look like he had eyeliner on. His skin was tanned to a light shade of golden brown and his masculine jaw had day-old stubble on it. I *really, really* liked the stubble. Just as I was staring, Griffin looked directly at the camera, and his voice dropped low. "Guys, this message is for my girl, so close your ears." He flashed a sexy, crooked smile and then whispered into the microphone. "Babe—I forgot to tell you, I left you a little something in the center console in case the mood strikes while you're watching today."

My belly fluttered. The man was as sweet as he was sexy. Although it was a dangerous combination that seemed to turn my brain into mush. I had to tear myself away from watching the monitor to go to the center console. When I opened it, I started to crack up.

Okay, so he was sweet and sexy *and a pervert*. The crazy man had left me a vibrating Furby key chain. Lord knows how many of these things he actually bought.

Smiling like a goofball, I climbed back into the rear of the RV carrying my makeshift vibrator. But I froze hearing Griffin start to sing.

Oh my God. His voice is amazing.

I knelt on the floor right in front of the monitor, completely entranced at his gritty, soulful voice. Griffin was singing a ballad of some sort, and I felt every word of the song inside my chest in the most overwhelming way. When the song ended, he opened his eyes, and I realized I'd been holding my breath the entire time.

I inhaled a few lungfuls of air and let out controlled exhales in an effort to slow down my racing heart.

God, I was totally screwed.

Totally screwed when it came to this man.

I shook my head and looked down at the furry stuffed animal still clutched in my hand. "What are we going to do, Mee-Mee? This man is going to break our hearts."

Mee-Mee had no answers, so I folded the key chain back into the palm of my hand and shut my eyes. "I'm *definitely* going to be needing you later."

◆ ◆ ◆

"So . . . what did you think?" Griffin opened the door and climbed into the back of the RV, where I was still sitting on the couch. He'd spent about three hours singing, and I'd spent the same amount of time glued to the monitor. It had been an amazing and surprisingly intimate experience—he'd talk to me between takes, and at the end of each song he'd flash his boyish smile at the camera or give me a wink.

"I think I'm a groupie."

He closed the distance between us, taking a seat on the couch next to me. "Oh yeah? You want to play groupie and rock star?" He tugged me up from my seat and guided me to straddle his lap.

I nodded, wrapping my arms around his neck. "Do I get to take off my panties and throw them at your feet?"

Griffin's eyes darkened. "You take off your panties, and I'll kiss your feet."

I giggled and pressed my forehead to his. "Seriously, Griff. That was absolutely incredible. Your voice is just beautiful. I don't even know what to say. It's like you sing from your heart. I could feel so many emotions in your words. I loved every minute of today, but that song you sang at the end—the one about heaven needing her more than you—that song just made me melt. I actually cried a little listening."

"I wrote that for my mother."

I nodded. "I figured you did. I know I never knew her personally, but I'm certain she's listening and as proud of you as I am."

Griffin leaned in and kissed my lips tenderly. "That means a lot to me. Thank you."

A knock came from behind me. Someone was at the camper door. I went to climb off Griffin's lap, but he held me in place. "Stay. It's probably Aiden."

"Boss?" a voice called through the closed door.

Griffin yelled around me. "Are we all set?"

"The car will be there at six."

"Sweet. Thanks for taking care of everything."

"Text me if you need anything else."

"See you tomorrow, Aiden."

I looked at Griffin. "That was rude. You just had an entire conversation behind a closed door."

Griffin smirked. "Babe. Scooch your ass toward me a little."

My brows drew together, so Griffin nudged me a bit, pulling me farther down his lap until I felt warmth between my legs. *And something hard.* He saw the knit of my brows lift to understanding.

"More polite to talk behind a closed door than with my hard-on trying to escape from my pants, don't you think, sweetheart?"

Sweetheart.

I really liked that name, too.

I also really liked the way our bodies were aligned. So I leaned in and kissed him, grinding down on his erection as I threaded my hands into his hair. God, I wanted to feel him inside me so badly it hurt. Griff's fingers dug into my ass and he started to guide me to rock back and forth on him. We both had on jeans, but the friction between us made the heat rise to an incendiary level. I seriously thought I might be able to come from just our dry humping.

But . . . it wasn't my turn. As much as I was terrified to connect with Griffin and get hurt, I didn't want to be selfish, either. I broke our kiss and nuzzled his ear. "Did you lock the door behind you?"

He blew out his frustrated answer. "I didn't."

I debated getting up and latching the door shut, but I really didn't want to cool the moment. So I threw caution to the wind and whispered back, "Well then, if anyone comes in, I guess they'll be getting a good show."

I started to kiss down his neck. When I slipped my hands between us and began to unbuckle Griffin's belt, he groaned. *"Fuck."* His head fell back against the couch, and the desire in his voice fueled me. I wanted to make him feel desperate, as desperate as he'd made me.

Grabbing the hem of his shirt, I dipped my head and licked my way from his chest down to his taut abs. I could have spent all day tracing the sculpted lines of his muscles, but I had more pressing things to get to. Sitting up again, I leaned back and unbuttoned his jeans. The sound of each tooth separating as I dragged the zipper down filled the air around us.

Griffin watched me as I lifted from his lap and knelt on the floor in front of him. Yanking at the waist of his pants, I slid them down his thighs. The thick bulge that greeted me from his tight boxer briefs heightened my arousal, and I unconsciously licked my lips.

"Fuck, Luca," he groaned. *"*That mouth. *That fucking mouth."*

It was seriously a toss-up who wanted this more. I couldn't wait to make him feel good. The two of us grabbed for his boxers at the same time, both pushing them down in haste. Griffin's erection sprang loose and my mouth salivated. *Oh my.*

Of course he had to be that big. As if his gorgeous face, flawless body, and sexy voice weren't enough—God seriously pulled out all His tricks when He made this man.

Leaning up on my knees, I wrapped my hands around the thick girth of him and looked up before lowering my head.

Griffin's voice was strained when he spoke. *"You're so beautiful right now."*

I smiled and, without a word, wrapped my hand around the base and took him into my mouth—our eyes staying locked the entire time.

"Jesus Christ."

I bobbed up and down a few times, finding my rhythm, and fluttered my tongue along the underside of his crown. Griffin groaned and fisted handfuls of my hair. I loved how his lust made him grow rougher. His bound hands guided my head down farther and then tugged to make me rise again. I'd started this, but he was definitely taking over control. *"Fuck. Just like that. That feels so good."*

Griffin lifted his hips and began to pump into my mouth. I was so turned on that I was certain if I reached down and touched myself for even two seconds, I'd set myself off.

"Luca . . ." Griff gave my hair a slight tug—a warning. But I fought against it and kept going.

He spoke louder, likely thinking I hadn't heard him the first time. "Babe. I'm gonna come."

I lifted my eyes to meet his, letting him know that I'd definitely heard him, and then sucked him as deep as I possibly could.

"Fuck . . ."

Griffin gripped my hair even harder and pumped twice more before stilling my head. His entire body shook as the heat of his orgasm spurted into my throat.

After, his chest heaved up and down. I was the one performing neck aerobics with a full mouth, yet he was panting like he'd just run a marathon. Griffin released my hair and struggled to catch his breath. "Jesus, Luca. You're *really* fucking good at that."

I felt gratified at his praise. "I told you, the For Dummies series of porn."

He laughed. "What else do they have? I'm ordering every movie they ever produced as soon as I get the strength to lift my arms and take out my phone."

I got up from the floor and snuggled up against Griffin's side. "Pretty sure they had *Anal for Dummies*, *Sixty-Nine for Dummies*, and *Ménage à Trois for Dummies*, too. But I only watched the one."

"I'll be buying the first two but not the *Ménage* one. Not sharing you, babe."

Warmth spread through me, but then a thought hit me and a chill pushed back whatever comfort I'd started to enjoy. *Groupie and rock star.* This was the life that Griffin led. I was certain he had a line of women who would do what I'd just done for him after every performance. They probably believed he was singing to them, too.

I'd gone quiet and Griffin noticed. He stroked my hair. "What's going on in that head of yours, babe?"

"Nothing."

He pulled up his jeans and boxers and turned to look at me. "Talk to me, Luca. What just happened? We were good, and then we weren't."

I shook my head and looked down. "Sorry. It's stupid."

Griffin tilted my chin to look up at him. "Spill it, Vinetti."

I sighed. "I guess . . . well . . . you said you weren't sharing me, and I was just thinking you must have dozens of women ready to drop to their knees after a concert. Or at the snap of your fingers, even."

Griffin held my eyes. "I wish I could make you feel better by telling you that I don't. But I'm not going to lie to you. There definitely is opportunity. But that doesn't mean I want to take it. I know you just got here, and our situation is a little unique, but I wasn't kidding when I said you were my girl. You *are* my girl, Luca. And you know what? That's probably not the most convenient thing for either one of us, considering our circumstances. But that doesn't change how I feel. I haven't been with another woman in almost two months—since you answered my first letter again. Just because I might have women willing doesn't mean *I'm* willing. You're my girl, Luca. We're going to figure this shit out."

My eyes started to water. I wanted to have his optimism and courage, but I was terrified. Griffin had been honest with me, so I did the same. "I'm scared to be your girl."

He smiled sadly and cupped my cheek. "It's okay. I know you, Luca. Being scared only lasts for a little while, then you do something brave. We're not in a rush. We've waited so many years already. What's a little longer?"

I turned my head into his hand and kissed his palm. "Thank you, Griffin."

He kissed my forehead and kept his lips pressed against me. I felt his smile grow against my skin. "Pretty sure I should be thanking you after what just went down."

CHAPTER 18

GRIFFIN

I really wanted Luca to enjoy her last hours in California. I knew that meant doing everything in my power to make sure we continued to avoid crowds tonight. While I hoped that someday she could overcome her phobia, it wasn't going to happen overnight and certainly not during this trip. I had to roll with it and try not to push her in any way.

Aiden had arranged for a car to pick us up at my house. The driver was instructed to take back roads. I'd rented a private room at my favorite restaurant, which had a back entrance frequently offered up to celebrities. It allowed access right into a dining room, which was kept separate from where the other patrons ate. I knew the manager pretty well and trusted his discretion. Marcus was also good at making sure his employees kept mum about my presence. So I felt confident taking Luca there.

She and I sat across from each other at our candlelit table, enjoying an intimate dinner. We dug into our salads while waiting for the main course.

Luca picked at her greens. "Is it weird that I'm actually going to miss the letters?"

"Not a bit. But who says they have to stop?"

"I guess we never discussed it. But I can't imagine we'll continue writing handwritten letters now that we've met?"

Putting my fork down and reaching across the table for her hand, I said, "I want to stay in touch, Luca. I want to hear from you every day whether it's an e-mail, a phone call, or a fucking singing telegram from someone dressed as a wiener. I just want to hear from you."

I could relate to that feeling of impending loss over the letters, though. Our invisible connection was a huge part of us. We would never experience that intimacy quite the same way ever again. I hoped things would be even better now, but Luca's concerns about my life weren't exactly unfounded. I just didn't quite know if I would be able to prove her wrong about whether this could work. I had the will . . . but did I really have the way? My situation was complicated. Actually, it was more like a complete circus.

Our food finally arrived. I'd ordered the filet mignon and Luca got trout in a garlic-lemon sauce.

As I cut into my steak, I asked, "Have you heard from Doc?"

"He called me right before the car came to pick us up. The connection was staticky, so I couldn't really make out what he was saying, but he sounded so happy. Where did you have the driver take him?"

"I called the zoo and asked if I could rent out the aviary after it closed. That's where he is right now. He has it all to himself."

Luca smiled wide. "Wow. He must be overjoyed. Thank you for arranging that. For someone who adopted a minimalist life back home, Doc sure seems to be getting acclimated to your pool house, housekeeper, and all of the special treatment."

"Well, he's welcome back anytime. Any friend of yours is a friend of mine. I hope you know that."

"Thank you. Truly. Thank you for your hospitality."

"It's my pleasure. I owe Doc a lot for helping to get you here. It was a gift. Lord knows how long it would have taken me before I figured out how to tell you about Cole. I'll always be grateful for him . . . and my little stalker."

She wiped her mouth. "It was reciprocal stalking if my memory serves me correctly."

"That it was."

Our eyes locked. My mind wandered to that amazing blowjob she'd given me earlier. My dick stiffened. I wanted nothing more than to return the favor tonight.

"So when do you leave for Vancouver again?" she asked, interrupting my fantasizing.

The thought of my upcoming trip filled me with dread.

"In about a week."

"It's a music festival, you said?"

"Yeah. It's called Beaverstock."

"Beaver?"

"It's a vagina festival."

Her eyes widened. "What?"

"I'm joking. The name apparently comes from the urban beavers that dwell in the city."

"Wow. Okay."

"This is our second year doing it."

"When do you go on tour next?"

"The US leg is in about a month. A dozen cities. Then we have a small European tour a few months after that."

"Twelve cities in a row?"

"Yes."

"That must be so hectic. Is it nonstop?"

"Pretty much. Sometimes you get a day or two in between, but I much prefer it that way. I would rather get it over with and have a chunk of time to myself again."

I could practically see the fears swirling around in her head, visions of girls in tour buses, bras being flung everywhere. Booze spilling. Music blaring. Cocaine snorting. Her fear was palpable.

"As crazy as my life can be at times," I said, "there are lulls . . . weeks at a time where I can go away, do what I please. Things are busy now with recording the new album, but once that's done and the tour is over, things will calm down a bit."

That statement was an attempt to try to convince her that my life did contain some small periods of "normalcy."

"What will you do when you get home, Luca?"

She sighed as if the answer was daunting. "I plan to get started on the book I daydreamed about on the ride here."

"Do you have to turn it in by a certain time?"

"No. Because I'm way ahead of my deadline, I have lots of wiggle room. I stick to a schedule, but it's not the end of the world if it changes a bit."

"That's brilliant. Tell me about your newest character. What's his or her deal?"

"Well . . . he's British."

"Oh yeah?" I winked. "Inspired by anyone in particular?"

"Well, I'd be lying if I said my interactions with you didn't influence that decision. But you're not a serial killer. And he is. So there's that. That's the main difference."

I shrugged. "Details . . ."

We got a good laugh at that, and apparently it faded into my staring at her as I often did, which prompted her to ask, "What?"

"Nothing. Sometimes I just still can't believe I get to look into your eyes. There's not one time I've looked into them that I haven't thought about how lucky I am to be able to do that."

Luca blushed, and it was beautiful, really. I hoped that someday I could see her do that very thing while our bodies were connected as much as our souls always seemed to be.

The evening so far had gone off without a hitch. And I should've known that was too good to be true. Because after dinner, when we exited the *supposed* private door to head to our waiting car, a rush of flashes greeted us. A few paparazzi had been camped out waiting for us to exit. Apparently somewhere beneath the smiles of the people who had served us tonight, there was a mole.

Luca's big, beautiful eyes were filled with confusion.

Never in my entire career had I ever lost it with the paparazzi—until now.

"Back the fuck off," I shouted. "It's okay when I'm alone, but this is not cool! She didn't ask for this."

Their questions all seemed to blend together.

"Is she your girlfriend, Cole?"

Flash.

Flash.

Flash.

"What's her name?"

Flash.

Flash.

"How's the new album coming?"

Flash.

Flash.

Flash.

I wrapped both my arms around Luca protectively. Thankfully, the car was right there, and we didn't have to wait for it.

After we got inside and I closed the door, it became eerily quiet.

I misdirected my anger toward the driver. "Why didn't you warn me they were out here?"

"I tried to call your phone, sir. There was no answer."

I checked my phone. There were no missed calls.

What the fuck?

I didn't know what had happened, whether he had dialed the wrong number or what. That didn't matter.

"Take us home, please," I told him.

I had one job. *One job.* That was to give Luca a normal night out without interference. I should've known better.

I pulled her close. "Are you alright?"

"It happened so fast, yeah. I didn't have much of a chance to react."

"Yeah. That's how it is sometimes."

"How did they know we were in there?"

"Someone at the restaurant probably ratted us out. Employees are told not to say anything, but all it takes is one person—one waitress texting her friend or whatever. Then word spreads like wildfire. Normally it doesn't matter. I deal with it. But I wanted so badly to escape it for one night with you." My voice was strained. "I'm sorry, Luca."

She caressed the stubble on my jaw. "I know it's not your fault."

"Yes, it is. I should've known that I couldn't take you anywhere in public and have it be a hundred percent paparazzi-free."

Things were quiet until the driver let us off in front of my place. The silence continued to follow us into the house and up the winding staircase.

She looked tired.

I led Luca to her room. "Wait for me here, okay, love? Lie down and relax. I'll be back in about five minutes."

I ventured down the hall to my main bathroom and ran the water in the large tub, testing it with my hand to make sure it was just the right temperature. I was still fuming. All I wanted was to help Luca relax so that she could sleep well tonight. She needed a good night's rest before having to hit the road.

After the tub was filled, I returned to her room and held out my hand.

"Come."

She took it and followed me down the hall.

When she spotted the tub filled with suds, she asked, "Am I supposed to get in there?"

"*We're* gonna get in there."

She swallowed. I realized she might have been thinking I had *other* ideas. Understandably so.

"I'll keep my knickers on. I just want to hold you."

I turned around as a cue for her to undress and get in the water. "Just say when."

After a couple of minutes, she said, "When."

Only her head was visible. She gazed at me as I removed my shirt and pants, taking off everything but my boxer briefs. She seemed to notice the tattoo on my chest for the first time and squinted. It was my mother's name intertwined with roses and barbed wire.

"Libby. Your mother." She smiled.

"Yeah. Got this about a year after Mum died."

"It's beautiful."

"Thank you," I said as I slipped into the water behind her. Wrapping my arms around her waist, I pulled her into me, resting my chin on her head before I kissed the top of it. Many thoughts went round and round in my mind. Was I crazy for thinking that this could somehow work? I knew how badly I wanted it to, but was that enough?

"A part of me wishes I could just stay here in this water with you forever and not have to worry about anything else," I said.

"If I was the type of person who fit into your lifestyle, you wouldn't be feeling that way. This would be easy."

"Just because something is easy doesn't make it better. We have our issues. But being with you still feels better than anything in the world. Sometimes the best things are also the most challenging. And that's just the way it is."

When my hand shifted for the first time and brushed against the underside of her breast, I realized she'd taken her bra off, too. Since I hadn't seen her undress, I wasn't sure if she'd opted to keep it on. My cock stiffened at the thought, and I readjusted my position so that she didn't feel it poking into her. As intimate as this bath was, it didn't seem like the appropriate time to get a stiffy.

"This feels so good," she said. "And I do feel safe when I'm with you, Griffin. I need you to know that. It's everyone else who scares me."

"I know that, baby. Right now, it's just us. Let's enjoy it."

Luca didn't say anything for the longest time. Then I heard her breathing change. When I leaned my head around to look at her expression, I realized she'd fallen asleep on me. This trip had exhausted her.

Later, Luca woke up just long enough to dry off and slip into one of my long T-shirts. I carried her back to her room and placed a chaste kiss on her lips before watching her drift to sleep again. I never went back to my room. Instead, I slipped in beside her and stayed up all night watching her sleep. I knew I would pay for it in the morning, but I couldn't justify willingly falling unconscious at a time like this.

The morning sun streamed through the window. Her eyes blinked open as she took notice of me lying next to her.

"I didn't know you were here."

"I couldn't bring myself to go back to my room."

"You were here . . . next to me . . . all night?"

"Yeah. Does that creep you out?"

"I write about serial killers, have a pig for a child, and drove cross-country to stalk you . . . safe to say, nothing should creep *me* out." She smiled, then it faded into a frown. She looked pensive.

"What's wrong?" I asked.

"I was just thinking about what one of the photographers shouted at me last night before we got in the car . . ."

My stomach sank. I'd been too busy swearing at them, I hadn't heard every single thing that was thrown in our direction.

"What did he say?"

"He said, 'Eve . . . is that you? You look great. Keep up the good work.'"

My head fell.

I had to explain.

"Eve . . . is Eve Varikova."

"Who is that?"

"She's this . . . model I dated briefly several months ago. It was nothing serious. But she's very well known, so the press had a field day when we were spotted out together."

"Do I look like her or something?"

"You have dark hair. That's about it. I think that person must have been smoking crack, because she's about a foot taller than you."

"Why did he say 'keep up the good work'?"

"Because Eve had a drug problem that I didn't know about when I started seeing her. Soon after, she went into rehab. I haven't spoken to her since, but I hear she's doing well."

I took a deep breath in, because I could tell by the look on Luca's face that she was overthinking everything again. She was probably going to start Googling Eve the second she got into the RV, and that would lead to more searches resulting in false information about me. It truly made me sick.

"Will you promise me something?" I asked.

She nodded. "Okay . . ."

"Will you try not to Google me? Most of what you find will be garbage. Or even better . . . Google me, but do it *with* me while I'm on the phone or beside you. Just let me be there to explain what's truth and what's not. I'll never lie to you. I just hate the idea of you reading all of this shit and not knowing what to believe."

She looked like she was struggling with that. I knew it would be extremely hard for her to really follow through on that promise. If I put myself in her shoes, I wasn't entirely sure I could stop myself.

She blinked for a while, seeming to seriously consider my request. "Okay," she finally said. "I had to think about it to make sure I could make that type of a promise and mean it. I promise not to Google you . . . without you knowing."

I breathed out a sigh of relief. "Thank you. I know it won't be easy, but I promise, you're not missing anything of value. I can tell you everything you need to know that's important. And if you ever have any questions, you just have to *ask* me."

She reached her hand out and brought my face into hers. The desire bubbling inside me transformed quickly into urgent need as I kissed her passionately.

"Are you sure there's nothing I can do to convince you to stay longer?" I whispered over her lips.

She didn't have to answer. I already knew.

While the price of fame was high, I'd never downright wished I could make it all disappear. That was before Luca. At this very moment, if given a choice, I would have forgone the fan-crazed twelve-city tour I had coming up soon enough for a road trip across the country in a broken-down RV.

CHAPTER 19

LUCA

I'd never heard Hortencia oink so much in my life. After picking her up from the farm she'd been staying at, I unlocked my front door to find that somehow the place that had always been my safe haven felt a whole lot emptier.

It was still early, too early to call Griffin on West Coast time. So I sent him a text, hoping he'd receive it when he woke up.

Luca: Made it home safely.

To my surprise, he immediately responded.

Griffin: Thank God. I was so worried about you in that damn clunker.

Luca: What are you doing up?

Griffin: I haven't really been sleeping.

Luca: Well, I'm safe and sound.

Griffin: I miss you like crazy. I have a million things to do, but I have no energy. I'm fucking depressed.

Luca: That was how I felt when I walked in here. Home is usually my happy place. It feels different now.

Griffin: You left your Furby here. The housekeeper brought it to me with a confused look on her face.

Luca: If she only knew the half of it!

Griffin: Siiiiiiiigh. Luca, Luca, Luca. I need to see you again.

I wanted to ask him when and if he thought that would be possible, but at the same time, I wasn't sure he could know the answer. He was just finishing an album and now had to leave for Canada soon.

Luca: Are you all packed for Vancouver?

Griffin: That would be a negative. Like I said, no motivation.

I'd had a lot of time to think during the ride. One of the things nagging at me was the need to listen to the song Griffin had written. The one that I had assumed was about me based on the title. Technically, that would have meant Googling him, which I'd promised not to do.

Luca: I have a confession.

Griffin: Okay . . .

Luca: I had to stop myself from Googling you several times on the ride home. I want you to know I didn't give in once. But there is one thing I really want to know more about.

Griffin: Alright. What is it?

I could sense his agitation.

Luca: Your song . . . the one called "Luca."

My phone suddenly rang. It was him.

I picked up. "Hey . . ."

"I was going to tell you about that. I wasn't sure if you knew. You never mentioned it, so I figured maybe you hadn't discovered it yet."

"Well, I saw it online and never had a chance to actually hear the lyrics."

"Luca . . . listen. When I wrote that song . . . I didn't know."

"I know that. It's okay. I won't take it personally."

"It's basically the musical version of the letter I sent you when I was drunk. A glorified angry rant . . . that happened to sell millions of copies."

"Can I hear it?"

He let out a long breath into the phone. "Of course."

"Is it okay if I pull it up on YouTube now?"

He sounded a little defeated. "Yeah. Sure. I'll be right here."

With Griffin on the line, I opened my laptop, logged in, and punched in *Luca Cole Archer* into the search bar.

A version of the video that had the words to the song listed as subtitles popped up.

I pressed "Play."

(Opening Music)

There was Griffin's gorgeous face as he sang the first words.

The letters were the window to your soul.
Before you left me with a giant hole.
When you disappeared into thin air
And proved you didn't really care.

Now I see your soul was black.
Because you're never coming back.
You're nothing but ink and lies.
A devil in disguise.

Luca, Luca, Luca
Were you just a dream?
Luca, Luca, Luca
You make me want to scream.

Luca, Luca, Luca
Are you happy now?
Luca, Luca, Luca
If so, baby, take a bow.

(Music)

Looks like the joke was on me.
So blinded by love, I couldn't see.
In the end,
You were never my friend.

The really messed-up part . . .
You're still living in my heart.
And if I had to do it all again,
I'd still have lifted that damn pen.

Luca, Luca, Luca
Were you just a dream?
Luca, Luca, Luca
You make me want to scream.

Luca, Luca, Luca
Are you happy now?
Luca, Luca, Luca
If so, baby, take a bow.

(Music)

Take a bow.
Take a bow.
Take a bow.

Luca, Luca, Luca.

Yeah, yeah, yeah.

(Music Fades)

◆ ◆ ◆

I must've listened to it a hundred times over the next twenty-four hours. While beautiful, the song had a heavy, sad vibe, which totally went with my melancholy mood. One particular part kept replaying in my mind over and over.

Luca, Luca, Luca
Were you just a dream?

Because last week was beginning to feel like just that—like it had been one big fantasy in my dreams. One that was incredible but would forever be just out of my reach. I dragged my ass around like someone had died for most of the day today. I'd managed to write, but I was pretty sure that my characters had caught my blues, and my thriller was turning into a women's fiction ugly cry.

Since I'd cleaned out my refrigerator before my trip to California, I had no food in the house, and a middle-of-the-night trip to the supermarket was inevitable. The parking lot was almost empty, and I breezed down the aisles without seeing a single person until I got up to the checkout line.

Doris was ringing up a young guy's groceries and smiled at me. I hadn't mentioned my road trip to California to her, or anything about Griffin for that matter, which I was glad about now, because the last thing I felt like doing was talking about it. My emotions were all over the place, and I probably would've burst into tears telling her how great it had been finally meeting the man I'd crushed on for more than a decade.

The guy in front of me in line sure did have a shitload of tattoos. When I finally stopped wallowing in my own self-pity long enough to take a good look at him, I noticed he also had safety pins outlining his jaw—actual safety pins just pierced through his skin and clipped right into his face. The two-in-the-morning crowd was always interesting. He caught me staring, and I diverted my eyes, failing at pretending I hadn't been scrutinizing him and wondering what the hell made him think it was a good idea to do such a thing.

My eyes landed on the candy rack next to me. Trying to look legit, I grabbed a Hershey bar from the shelf and tossed it into the cart. The shelf to the right of the candy held tabloids, so I picked one up and started to mindlessly thumb through. Until I hit *page three.*

My eyes bugged out of my head.

A picture of Griffin and me walking out of the restaurant.

I couldn't believe it.

Griffin had one hand held out, making sure the photographers kept at arm's length, and the other wrapped around my shoulders. My face was turned into his chest, away from the photographer, so it would be difficult for most people to even tell it was me from my partial profile. But of course, I knew.

I'm in the Enquirer.

Oh my God.

I read the caption below it.

Cole Archer and mystery woman get cozy at Mariano's in downtown LA. Is the crooner missing his old flame Eve Varikova by replacing her with look-alikes?

My stomach sank.

I wasn't sure what bothered me more—seeing my picture in a tab-loid or the mention that Griffin could be trying to replace an old girl-friend. I knew the latter was ridiculous because Griff had told me about her—yet it upset me for some reason anyway.

"Earth to Luca." I caught Doris waving in my peripheral vision. Looking up, I blinked a few times and realized Pinface was gone, and Doris had been waiting on me while I had an internal freak-out over some dumb magazine.

"Hi. Sorry. I . . . I . . ." I held up the *National Enquirer* in my hand. "I got caught up in one of the articles."

Doris leaned over to look at what had captured my attention. "Cole Archer. I don't usually go for men under forty, but I wouldn't kick him out of bed for eating crackers." She wiggled her eyebrows and whis-pered, "I'd like to lick the crumbs off that one."

My eyes widened to saucers, which Doris thought was the funniest thing. Of course, she thought it was because she'd shocked me by talk-ing dirty about a young guy, since she had no clue I'd actually *been* in Griffin's bed last week. My cheeks began to flush and I became flustered.

I put the tabloid on the checkout conveyor. "I like to read the articles."

Doris chuckled, thinking I was being coy. "You and me both, sister."

For the next ten minutes, I was in a total haze while emptying my cart and chatting with Doris. I couldn't get over the fact that my face was plastered all over a supermarket tabloid. It gave me a funny feeling in the pit of my stomach, yet I wasn't sure why. Being inside the grocery store always made me anxious, but this heightened that feeling. It felt like someone had violated my personal space, even though it was only a photo and no one would likely recognize me from it. At the last second, right as I was about to swipe my card to pay, I turned and grabbed all of the copies of the *National Enquirer* from the shelf.

Doris's face scrunched up. "You want to buy *all* of those?"

"Yes."

"They all say the same thing, you know."

"I . . . I got a new bird and need something to line the cage."

"Oh. I can probably get the manager to set aside some of the newspapers that don't sell for you, if you want. We just rip off the front page and give it to the delivery guy for a refund credit. The rest goes into the recycle bin."

"Um. Yeah. Sure. That would be great, Doris. Thank you."

"No problem." Doris scanned the tabloids, and I swiped my card to pay. "What's his name?"

"Huh?"

Her brows drew down. "Your bird. What's its name?"

God, I was digging myself deep. I said the first name that popped into my head. "Chester. My bird's name is Chester."

"That's a good strong name."

"Yeah. Chester the bird. He's something else." I tossed the last of my bags into my cart, anxious to get out of there. I'd been in such a rush, I almost forgot to leave Doris the items I'd picked up for her. I took a few steps back after saying goodbye and lifted the bag of treats onto the counter. "Have a good night, Doris."

"You too, honey. I'll see you soon."

Once I was safely inside my car, I took out the tabloid again and stared at it. A thought hit me as I sat there with the engine idling—there had been a few photographers, so might I be in other papers, too? Maybe with my head at a different angle so that my face was identifiable? Even though being in the confines of my car usually brought me relief after my supermarket trip, I suddenly felt the same type of panic that I experienced right before going inside.

It was 2:30 in the morning in Vermont but only 11:30 in California. Griffin was a night owl, so I dug out my phone and called him. He answered on the first ring.

"Hey, baby. You're up late."

My shoulders relaxed a little just hearing his voice. I sighed. "Hey."

"Everything okay?"

"I just went to the supermarket."

"Oh. How'd that go? What crazy shit did you see tonight?"

I'd forgotten that I'd shared with him some of the bizarre things I'd seen during my middle-of-the-night trips. Though the thing I'd seen tonight topped them all. "I saw a picture of me—a picture of us—in the *National Enquirer*."

Griffin hissed. "Shit. Damn that Marty Foster."

"Who?"

"One of the photographers from the restaurant. I had my assistant reach out to the others and buy the photos they'd taken. But Marty wouldn't return our phone calls. I was hoping it was because he didn't get a good shot and had nothing to sell. Guess I was wrong." From the tone of his voice, I pictured Griffin raking his hand through his hair. "I'm sorry, Luca. I tried."

"Oh my God. Don't be ridiculous. It's not your fault. I can't believe you bought the other photos. I didn't even realize you could do that."

"Money buys pretty much anything in this town. Paparazzi don't care who buys their work, only that they get paid. Plus, I offered them more than they'd fetch with the tabloids, so the other three were happy to sell them to me."

"It's so sweet that you did that. But really, it's not necessary. I don't want you wasting your money on stuff like that."

"Anything I spend that might make you happy or less stressed is a good use of my greenbacks, Luca."

That anxious feeling in my chest settled a little bit more. "Thank you, Griffin."

"No need for thanks. Just trying to look out for my girl."

I took a deep breath in of *my girl* and exhaled out the *National Enquirer*. "So did I wake you? What were you doing?"

"Nah. I have some company tonight. The guys in my band came over. We're celebrating wrapping the album this afternoon. We were slated to finish tomorrow, but we were able to knock it out a day early."

"Oh wow. Congratulations. That's amazing. You must be so happy."

"Yeah. I'm pretty stoked about the way it came out."

"That's great. But I'll let you go. I didn't realize you had company. It's so quiet in the background."

"I stepped out into the backyard when I saw your number come up. I'm sure I'll get a good ribbing when I go back inside."

"What would they tease you about?"

"They're calling me whipped."

"Whipped?"

"As in pussy whipped. Apparently that's a popular expression in America. It means your woman has you on a tight leash."

I laughed. "I know what it means. I was just asking why they would call you that?"

"Oh. Normally, when we end a tour or wrap a recording, we have a wild party to celebrate. But I wasn't up for wild tonight. So I told the guys they could come over, but no women allowed. And now I'm on the phone with you."

"You didn't want their girlfriends to come?"

"They don't have girlfriends, Luca. Their idea of a party is booze, a bunch of groupies, and a few strippers."

"Oh."

"Anyway. It's just us blokes tonight."

"I should let you get back, then."

"Nah . . . rather talk to you than listen to their stories. I've heard every one of them ten times by now. Shit tends to get repeated when you spend months traveling on a bus with the same people."

I smiled. "I bet."

"So tell me . . . how did you handle seeing your face in the tabloids for the first time?"

For the first time. "I might have hyperventilated a little."

"It gets easier."

I'd been so caught up in how I felt seeing my face plastered in print that I never stopped to think about what it must be like for Griffin. The tabloids only took my picture because I'd been with him. This was just a small taste of what he must go through every day. "How do you handle it?"

"You learn to ignore it. The worst part isn't even the pictures. It's the shit they make up about you to sell a story. I once touched the belly of a very pregnant fan while signing an autograph. She'd told me that her baby was a superfan and jumped around during my concert. She swore every time she put on one of my songs, the little bugger would start to dance in her belly. Her husband was standing next to her and said he thought it was true, too. So I leaned down and started to talk to her belly as a joke—see if the baby would start to move around. And when it actually did, they told me to hold her belly and feel it. It was pretty cool. But the next day, photos were plastered on the cover of every tabloid with stories of how the woman was carrying my love child, and her husband had come to the concert to beg me to allow him to adopt my soon-to-be son."

"That's crazy. They need a verifiable source to print that stuff."

"Some celebrities have sued and won to make a point. But the payout on the occasional lawsuit is less than they earn selling papers, so it doesn't stop them. The only people who win in that mess are the lawyers."

I sighed. "I guess."

"Anyway . . . I was doing some thinking tonight. We have the festival up in Canada the day after tomorrow, and some appearances lined up after that to start to promote the new album. But if it's alright with you, I'd like to see if I can move things around and come down to Vermont for a few days."

My heart started to race. "I'd love that. When?"

"I'm not sure yet. My schedule is pretty packed, but I figured I should be able to work it out with my publicist and assistant to rearrange things and clear a bit of time. Maybe next week or the week after?"

"That would be great."

"Are there any particular days that are better for you?"

"No. Anytime, really. One of the few perks of being a reclusive, agoraphobic writer who works from home is that my social calendar is pretty empty."

Griffin laughed. "You think you're making your life sound bad, but every time you talk about it, I get a little more jealous of how much freedom you have."

"That's funny. I feel like freedom is the opposite of what I have. Most days I feel like a bird locked in a cage because of all my fears."

Loud voices started to shout in the background. *There you are. Who you on the phone with, Mr. Pussy Whipped?* Griffin chuckled. "I better get going. The natives are getting restless with me not inside."

"Okay."

"Are you okay now?"

I thought about it. Talking to Griffin had really relaxed me a lot. "Yeah. I think I am. You calmed the savage beast."

"See. We can totally do this together, babe. You'll see. We got this. But be careful driving home."

"I will. Have fun with the guys."

I swiped my cell off and sat in my car for a few more minutes. God, I hoped Griffin was right—that we could do this. Because at this point, it was going to hurt like hell if we couldn't.

CHAPTER 20
GRIFFIN

"You need to be seen. Stop being such a shut-in." My publicist, Renee, marched into my house without waiting for an invitation.

"Come on in," I grumbled and shut the door behind her. I'd planned on calling her today. But apparently she got tired of waiting for me to return her calls and thought a seven-in-the-morning unannounced drop-in was a good idea. The guys had only left at five, so I wasn't happy.

"It's early, Renee." I followed her into the kitchen. She went straight to the coffeepot and started to open cabinets and pull shit out to make a pot of coffee. I leaned against the doorway, watching her spring into action. "Do you think we can do this a little later? I only got to bed two hours ago."

"We could have done this on the phone if you'd answered even one of my calls over the last week."

I had been avoiding her calls. But every time I talked to her, ten things got added to my schedule. And the only thing I wanted on my calendar was some alone time in Vermont with Luca. It had been more than a week since she'd left, and I'd come to realize that it was more than a week too long to be away from her.

Though I needed Renee's help to move some shit around and get out of this town for a while. So I walked to the cabinet where I kept the coffee, pulled out a canister, and handed it to her. She took it and looked me up and down. "You don't appear so bad for the morning after a wrap party."

"It wasn't the usual mayhem."

She raised a brow. "Oh yeah? Why is that?"

I was going to need to tell her about Luca anyway, since I needed her help. So I told her the truth. "Have a girlfriend now. Didn't feel up to the guys bringing over two dozen strippers and groupies."

Renee pushed a bunch of buttons and handed me the coffee canister to put back. "Girlfriend, huh? Is that the woman in yesterday's *National Enquirer*? And I assume also the reason you're overpaying every paparazzi in town to buy the copyright of pictures of the two of you?"

I lifted a brow. "How do you know I paid off the photogs?"

She shook her head. "It's my job to know what you're doing—*who* you're doing, for that matter, too."

I only *wished* I were doing Luca. Taking a seat at the kitchen table, I laid what I needed on the line before Renee had a chance to rattle off what she wanted from me. "I need some time off to go to Vermont and visit my girl. Think you can clear some of my scheduled appearances for a few days?"

Renee folded her arms across her chest. "I need to *add* more to your calendar. You've been avoiding anything PR-related for a while. We need you to start getting some publicity. You have an album coming out and then the tour. Tell me about this girlfriend. Is she a celebrity—someone I can turn into media hype?"

"Definitely not. She's very private, and I'd like to keep it that way. She's not big on crowds or attention."

Renee shook her head. "So of course, the logical choice for her is to date a musician who plays to sold-out stadiums and draws a crowd by stepping outside."

I sighed. "Can you clear me a few days? I really need to get out of here for a while to spend time with her."

Renee's eyes roamed my face. "You really like this girl, don't you?"

I nodded. "She's special."

The coffeepot beeped, and Renee turned and reached up to the cabinet where I kept the mugs. Filling two, she sat at the table across from me and slid one steaming mug to my side. "Let's negotiate. When do you need to leave? Can we get a few public appearances in before then and schedule a few late-night TV appearances for when you get back?"

"I'm in Vancouver tomorrow for the music festival. But I can do whatever you need the day after that. Can we do your PR stuff in one day?"

She frowned. "You're a pain in my ass, you know that?"

I smiled from ear to ear, knowing that was her way of saying yes. "You're the best, Renee."

She wagged a finger at me. "You're giving me a full day. I want one or two good-doer deeds that I can leak to the paps, and then you're going to have lunch someplace outdoors and sign stuff for fans. Kiss some babies and let the teenagers take selfies with you and follow you into a few stores."

"I can do that."

"You're going to have double the work when you get back. You can't complain about it, either."

"Yes, ma'am. No complaining. I got it." A thought popped into my head. I scratched at the stubble on my chin. "Can I pick the good deeds and where I go shopping?"

"What do you have in mind?"

I grinned. "Something to make Luca enjoy the tabloids a little more next time."

"You could've picked a place that smelled better." Renee held her nose while she sidestepped to avoid a giant pile of shit.

"I told you it was a farm. What the heck did you wear those heels for?"

"You said it was a sanctuary. I figured you'd be doing a photo op with some cute little animals roaming rolling green hills, not doing hard labor and shoveling crap on a dilapidated pig farm."

I'd driven past Charlotte & Wilbur's Farm once and remembered the sign outside asking for volunteers. When I'd called and explained who I was and that I'd like to donate some time, bring a few photogs to help raise awareness of the cause, and make a sizable donation, the owners were thrilled. Working at a pig sanctuary wasn't exactly a fashionable celebrity cause. I wiped my brow and looked around. This place was really run-down. The rickety old fence that lined the property needed replacing, and the barn looked like a good gust of wind could lift the caving roof right off. But the struggling farm housed eighty rescued miniature and potbellied pigs. The little porkers were pretty damn cute—and smart, too. Charlotte, the older woman who ran the place, said that in the late eighties, pigs had become popular pets, and at one time they had over two hundred abandoned animals. Apparently people brought them home not realizing how big and messy the pigs could get, and there was nowhere safe for people to bring them. This farm was the only no-kill shelter in the area.

I'd gotten here bright and early this morning and helped out the entire day before the paparazzi showed up. Then I posed for a boatload of pictures with various pigs. Wearing a red bandanna and some dirty, torn jeans, I looked more like one of the farmhands than a guest donor. But Renee had made me hold one of the little miniature pigs in one arm and use the other to lift my shirt and wipe sweat off my forehead, which of course exposed my abs. The paparazzi ate that shit up.

"You ready to go?" Renee said. "I hope you're planning on showering before your little shopping excursion."

I opened my arms wide and grinned, walking toward her. "Have I thanked you for rearranging my schedule for me? Come here, give me a big hug."

She held her hand out. "Touch me smelling like that, and you'll be booked on two dozen teenybopper shows by sundown. You won't have time to see your little girlfriend for months."

I laughed. "Thanks again, Renee. You can leak to the paparazzi that I'll be at my next stop by seven, and I'll stick around to sign autographs for at least an hour because you're the best."

She shook her head. "You won't be saying that when you get back and you're double-booked for everything. But you and your girlfriend have fun off the grid."

"We will. Thanks."

I plan to have a damn good time—and so will Luca, as soon as she opens the door and finds out I'm coming earlier than she's expecting.

CHAPTER 21

LUCA

"Oh my God!" I shrieked and covered my mouth. "He's so out of his mind."

For the second day in a row, I received a delivery of three dozen multicolored roses and a box of supermarket tabloids wrapped with a big red bow. Yesterday's magazines had been filled with pictures of Griffin working at a pig sanctuary. I melted at the sight of the mega rock star all dirty and bonding with pigs. It was the most bizarre yet sweetest thing he could have done after I'd freaked out seeing my own photo in the papers last week. But today's papers nearly made my eyes bulge from my head—photo after photo of Griffin in a bookstore. In some he was signing autographs, some he was perusing the shelves, but in every single photo, he had a copy of my hardcover book in his hand!

I couldn't believe what he'd done. If I'd had any doubt that he was out in LA with all the beautiful, flashy women and already forgetting me, he certainly knew how to put those thoughts to rest. I tried to call him, but his phone went right to voice mail. He'd said he would be traveling to some important meeting this afternoon and would call me after, but I couldn't wait.

Lately we'd been video chatting every evening, so I thought it might be fun to repay the thoughtfulness he'd shown me by getting myself all done up and wearing something sexy for our call later. I ransacked my underwear drawer to find just the right thing and then started to fill the tub for a bath. My skin had been really dry the last few days, so I pinned my messy hair on top of my head and painted on a moisture-intense mud mask to wear while I soaked. Just as I was about to step into the tub, my cell rang. Griff's name flashed on the screen. I laughed to myself, glad that he'd called and not FaceTimed, because there was no way in hell I'd want him to see the mess I looked like at the moment. I answered on speakerphone from the bathroom.

"Hey."

"Hey, babe. Sorry I missed your call. I was driving to my meeting."

"Oh. It's okay. I just wanted to say that I got your delivery. I can't believe you did that. It was seriously sweet." I took off my bathrobe and let it fall to the floor. "I'm planning on something sweet in return, but it isn't quite ready yet."

"Oh yeah? When will it be ready?"

I dipped a toe into the bath to feel the water. It was nice and warm. "In like an hour or so."

"I can't wait. I need to get to my meeting. But I wanted to ask you something first."

"What?"

"When you said I could come see you in Vermont anytime, did you really mean it?"

"Of course. I can't wait for you to come visit. I hope it's next week and not the week after." I climbed into the tub and was just about to sit down when my doorbell rang. "Shoot. Someone's at my door, and I just got into the tub and have a mud mask all over my face. It's probably UPS with a delivery I've been waiting for. I hope he leaves the box, because I can't answer the door looking like this."

"Well, I also sent you another delivery. You need to sign for mine, so you might want to get it."

"Oh. Shoot. Okay. Hang on a second. Let me get the door, and I'll be right back." I got out of the tub and wrapped myself in my big fuzzy robe. Catching my reflection in the bathroom mirror, I shook my head. *The delivery person is going to think I'm scary. But oh well. He'll be right.*

I rushed to the front door, more anxious about what else Griffin might've had delivered than caring what I looked like.

Opening the door, I was greeted by an enormous bouquet of flowers. The thing was so big that it covered the delivery person's face. I smiled. "Oh wow. Shoot. Let me grab a tip. Give me one second."

I turned to grab my wallet but froze when a voice stopped me in my tracks. "Do I get to pick the type of tip you give me?"

My eyes widened and my head whipped back around. "Griffin?"

He moved the flowers to reveal his beautiful, smiling face. "You said *anytime*. Hope now is okay."

My heart felt like it was going to leap from my chest. "I can't believe this."

"Believe it. I'm here and all yours for the next few days."

I wanted to cry tears of happiness. Griffin looked so sexy, dressed in a leather jacket and ripped jeans. His hair was tousled from all the travel, but honestly, he was even hotter messy. I, on the other hand, was just a *hot mess* right now.

He handed me the flowers.

Gesturing to my face, I said, "Look at me. I'm a disaster."

"Rolling around in the mud with Hortencia again, eh?"

"It's a beauty mask, which is pretty ironic, because it's far from attractive."

"Even with mud on your face, you're still the most beautiful girl in the world." He opened his arms. "C'mere."

"I'm a mess. I—"

He didn't listen to me when he pulled me into him and planted a huge kiss on my lips despite the goop on my face. Now some of it was on his face, too.

After a few seconds of breathing him in and tasting his tongue, though, I stopped caring about how I looked. All that mattered was that my Griffin had come all this way to see me and that I had him all to myself for a little while.

Hortencia ran into the room and started to oink. It was only then that Griffin broke away from me.

He rubbed his swollen lips as he said, "Ah. The famous Hortencia." He bent down and spoke to her. "Pleasure to meet you, lovely lady. You know, I saw some of your mates the other day. They say hi."

Groink.

I laughed and said, "Let me go wash my face real quick and get you a towel to wipe yours."

I put the flowers down on a table and Griffin followed me to the bathroom.

When he noticed my filled tub, he said, "So sorry I interrupted your bath time." He smiled. "Actually . . . I'm not."

"I had this whole thing planned. I took out lingerie and was going to change into it for our call. But I was going to take a bath first. Obviously you came to the door and thwarted that."

"Well, by all means, don't let me interrupt your plans."

I rubbed his cheek. "You must be exhausted from the flight."

He took both my hands into his. "Doesn't matter. All worth it. I've been dying to get to you."

"From the photos I've seen, you've been so busy. You've hardly had a moment to breathe over the past week. It means so much to me that you came."

"Everything I've done has been all about getting here. Believe me. I want to make the best of these three days."

I really needed to get this mud off my face. "Let me just take a quick bath, get dressed, and then I'll meet you out there. Why don't you relax for a bit? Make yourself at home. There's some iced tea in the fridge, or I have some red wine on the counter you could open."

He sighed. "Alright. Don't take too long."

Not wanting to waste a single minute of this time with him, I washed off the remaining mud from my face and scrubbed my body quickly in the tub. I put on the lingerie that I'd laid out and walked back into the living room. Griffin was lying down on the couch with his eyes closed. Poor guy must have been so tired.

"I'm back."

His eyes blinked open as he sat up. He was speechless as he got a look at my scantily clad body, dressed in a purple Chantilly lace teddy. I'd taken my hair down and let it cover my breasts, which otherwise would have been pretty exposed through the lace. I felt a little vulnerable standing there in almost nothing, but it was the least I could do, considering I'd greeted him looking like the Bride of Frankenstein.

"Luca . . . you . . . God." He rubbed his eyes. "Am I dreaming?"

"You don't mind if I hang out in this tonight, do you?"

"As long as you don't mind me sporting a perpetual hard-on or having to escape to the bathroom from time to time to wank off . . . no."

I laughed. "I can live with that."

"Alrighty then. We have a deal."

He stood up and walked toward me. God, he smelled so damn good, like sugar and spice. My nipples hardened.

I took his hand. His thumb brushed against mine.

"Can I show you around the rest of the place?"

His eyes were on my breasts. "Huh?"

Feeling my cheeks heat up, I laughed. "Do you want a tour?"

"A tour?"

"Of the house . . ."

"Oh . . . yes. Yes. Show me around." As we walked together, he placed his hand on my back, which sent shivers down my spine. "Sorry . . . ," he said. "I'm still a little distracted by you right now."

Griffin kept his body close as he followed me through the living room to the other side of the house. I showed him Hortencia's play area and finally, the room where I got much of my work done.

"This is my study. It's where I do most of my writing." I pointed to the wall. "These bookshelves came with the house. They actually open up to a hidden storage area behind them. So it's very practical."

"Brilliant," he said, except he wasn't looking at the shelves. He was looking at me . . . *through me*, his eyes dark and wanting.

Griffin was *starving*. He was trying to be patient and respectful, but I could tell holding back right now was killing him. Heck, I was starving, too.

Jesus, Luca. What are you doing?

The man came all this way. He'd been celibate for weeks. *And you think he gives a shit about practical bookshelves?* He was looking at me like he wanted to eat me, and quite frankly there was nothing I wanted more than to be devoured by him.

This house tour could wait. All of it could wait.

I suddenly leaped into his arms, wrapping my arms around his neck.

His hot breath on my skin gave me goosebumps. "Fuck, Luca. I missed you." He brought my mouth to his, kissing me so passionately that I practically melted into him.

I slid my hand down to rub the erection straining against his jeans. His cock was hot and throbbing and now so was I.

He hissed as he placed his hand over mine, pressing my palm further into him. "It's impossible to hide what I'm feeling right now," he said gruffly. "I want you."

Griffin kissed me harder as my fingers threaded through his hair. He lowered his head down to my breasts, sucking on my flesh through the fabric. My nipples were on fire. My entire *body* was on fire.

He pulled back to look at me. "Do you have any idea how beautiful you look tonight?" Lifting me up, he carried me over to the large wooden desk and placed me on top of it. "This desk is where you work your magic?"

"Yes."

Spreading my legs apart, he asked, "Will you let me work mine . . . right here?"

Swallowing hard and unable to speak, I nodded.

"Say it, Luca. I need to hear you say it, to make sure I'm understanding *exactly* what you want right now, exactly what I'm allowed to do here . . ."

Panting, I said, "I want you to fuck me . . . right on this desk."

"Thank God," he muttered. "Because I need you tonight."

"I know," I said softly.

He took my hand and placed it over his chest so that I could feel how fast his heart was beating. "Never doubt what this means to me."

I needed that. I needed to feel his heart, to know that this was so much more to him than another notch on his belt.

Reaching into the pocket of his leather jacket, he took out a condom and tossed it next to us.

He slipped his fingers under the straps of my lingerie top. "I want you skin to skin." He made quick work of removing my skimpy outfit before tossing it and taking a few moments to gaze at my naked body. I'd shaved a thin landing strip on my vagina and thanked my lucky stars that I'd had the good sense to groom myself, considering the surprise nature of his visit.

He took off his jacket and threw it down before slipping his shirt over his head, showcasing his chest, which was so perfectly sculpted and sun-kissed.

His pupils dilated as he stared down at me. I'd certainly never experienced this side of Griffin before—the sexual beast ready to be unleashed.

Our tongues danced in a frenzy of hunger, a competition of who could taste the fastest. The metal from his silver rings was cold against my breast as he squeezed it.

His warm skin against my bare chest felt amazing. My needy fingers scratched along his muscular back.

Lowering my hands to his belt, I undid it as fast as I could. After I pushed down his boxer briefs, his massive cock sprang forward, exhibiting more girth than I'd remembered. He began to rub the head of it across my clit, teasing me with his precum and circling the hot tip over my flesh.

When it seemed he couldn't take it anymore, Griffin grabbed the condom, ripping it open with his teeth before sliding it over his shaft. He squeezed the tip before looking into my eyes one final time. Then he slammed into me in one hard thrust, rocking my entire body—my world.

My legs were wrapped around him as he fucked me so hard that I was practically seeing stars. It hurt a little at first, but I didn't care. Soon enough, the pain was gone, replaced by sheer ecstasy. His balls slapped against the skin of my ass. Never in my life had I been fucked like this, so urgently, so deep within me. As my nails dug into his back, I just couldn't get enough.

"Harder. Fuck me harder, Griffin."

I wanted him to ravage me. I'd been on the verge of orgasm since he'd entered me, a tingling bliss radiating throughout my body but ready to explode at any given moment. The sensation finally reached its peak when he grabbed my waist and went even deeper, thrusting with more force. My skin tightened, and a rush of heat ran through me as my orgasm rose to the surface, causing my entire body to shake.

When Griffin looked into my eyes and came inside me, it was the most intense feeling I'd ever experienced, certainly unlike anything I'd ever felt before. We both screamed out in unison, our groans of pleasure echoing throughout the room.

Breathless, I lay under him on the desk, a pile of sated mush as he covered my face in kisses.

"Hey," he said through heavy breaths.

"Yeah?"

"The lights are on."

I looked around. "They are, aren't they?"

"I'm your first." He smiled.

"You are."

It hadn't even fazed me that the lights were on, that he could clearly see every inch of my naked body. I knew that was because I fully trusted Griffin. Not to mention, I was too busy losing myself in him. He'd taken me with every ounce of energy he had left in him, playing my body like an instrument—fucking me like the rock star he was.

CHAPTER 22

GRIFFIN

I was starting to think I could seriously live this recluse life forever.

First off, who else could say they got woken up in the morning being kissed by a pig? Not sure if that was what Hortencia was doing, but her snout was on my mouth, so I had to assume it was something along those lines.

Our first day together consisted of morning sex, followed by a walk with Hortencia, followed by more sex, then a two-hour lunch of tapas made from whatever the hell she had in the fridge. We topped off the afternoon with Luca reading me some of her latest book while I rubbed her feet and then talked her into more sex before a nap. Then we woke up, had dinner, and stayed up talking until it was time to go food shopping.

Ironically, heading to the supermarket in the middle of the night actually worked quite well for a celebrity trying to hide from prying eyes. It was as if some of Luca's strange habits were made for me, really.

In Los Angeles, I had to wear a hat and sunglasses anywhere I went day or night if I didn't want to be recognized. Here, I wore nothing, deciding to risk it as we ventured to the market during Luca's usual time.

It was nearly empty. And it was bliss.

As Luca tapped with her index finger on a watermelon, I couldn't help but notice how cute she was. She held it close to her ear. With her focused expression, you would have thought she was listening to the ocean inside. Her life may have been sheltered, but she certainly appreciated the little things. I was starting to see that the little things—these moments with her—were the *big* things. I wished I had more time here in Vermont to experience them.

"What are you doing?" I finally asked, referring to her examination of the fruit.

"I'm trying to see if it's any good. There is a process with picking watermelons."

"And here I was thinking *I* was the expert in fondling melons . . ."

"Oh, believe me. You definitely are." She winked.

I laughed. "So what's the trick to knowing whether it's a winner?"

"Simple. If it's hollow inside, it's probably good."

"Sort of the opposite of humans, eh? That's how I felt before I found you. Hollow inside. Makes for a great melon but a rotten human."

She put the watermelon down and placed her hand on my cheek. "That makes me sad."

I grabbed on to both of her wrists. "I don't feel that way anymore. Not here with you. I feel like a human for the first time in years. This—just being at the grocery store with you—it feels so freeing. You'd think that having all the money in the world gives someone freedom. But it's different when you're a celebrity. The real you is essentially imprisoned by your persona. You can't ever really get the life you had before—the anonymity—back. So anytime you can feel halfway normal again, even if it's fleeting, is like a gift."

"Do you regret it at all?"

Pondering her question, I really had mixed feelings. "I'm proud of what I've accomplished. Music has always been an important part of my life, and to be able to do this for a living shouldn't be taken for granted. But there's no doubt I didn't quite know what I was getting myself into.

Even if I regret it now, I can't change anything. So I try to just look forward not back. What I need . . . is to figure out a way to have some kind of happy medium." I looked around. "And this conversation is far too deep for the produce aisle."

Luca pulled me into a hug. "Well, I'm really proud of you, of everything you've accomplished, if I haven't already made that clear."

"I'm proud of you, too. You're successful in your own right. I create music and perform, but you create entire imaginary worlds. That's no small feat, love."

As we resumed wheeling the cart through the desolate aisles, I found myself grabbing everything I wanted on impulse, mostly packaged foods that I wouldn't be caught dead eating back in LA.

"Are we having a Super Bowl party I don't know about?" she joked.

"No. But I'm happy, so I feel like celebrating—being bad, eating things I can't typically eat."

Including you.

I hadn't realized how much I was starving for normalcy until I finally got a taste of it during this trip. Granted, food shopping in the middle of the night wasn't exactly "normal." But I could really get used to this, hiding out with Luca, having sex all day, then venturing out only at night for sustenance.

As we approached the register, Luca said, "I'm just warning you that Doris is a fan, and she'll probably recognize you. I haven't mentioned anything, so I'm not sure how she'll react. She might blow your cover."

Luca had previously told me about this cashier, a warm and friendly face who always worked the graveyard shift.

"I think I'll live if she outs me, given there are only two other people in this entire place besides us. Hardly a potential stampede."

We approached the register with our cart.

"Hey, Doris."

"Hey, Luca."

Doris started to scan the items before she finally noticed me. Her eyes went wide as she mindlessly proceeded to scan the same item numerous times. She was in shock.

Luca cleared her throat. "Doris . . . this is—"

"You're . . ." She pointed. "You're . . . Cole Archer."

"Yes, I am."

"You're . . . in my supermarket."

Looking around, I nodded. "I seem to be, yes."

She looked at Luca and then back to me. "You're . . . here with Luca?"

Luca seemed to struggle to find the words. "Doris . . . Cole is my . . ." She hesitated.

I realized at that moment that Luca didn't know how to categorize me. Understandably so, because we'd never discussed a formal title. I'd referred to her as *my* woman but never referred to myself as *her* man.

I finished Luca's sentence. "Boyfriend."

Luca turned to me. "Boyfriend?" I couldn't tell if she was taken aback.

My heart sank, wondering if I'd fucked up in being presumptuous. "Is that not okay?"

When her mouth curved into a smile, my pulse slowed down a bit. "It's perfect," she said.

"Good," I whispered. "Very good."

Our eyes locked until Doris's voice interrupted.

"How did this happen?"

"How much time do you have, Doris?" I asked.

With stars in her eyes, she sighed. "All night . . . all night for you."

"Alright, then."

She gazed at me, eager for my explanation.

"Well, first off, my real name is Griffin. And our story started long before I ever became famous. When we were kids, Luca was my pen pal. We wrote letters to one another, didn't even know what the other looked like. I fell in love with her through her words, but I never told her that. Due to a terrible misunderstanding, we were estranged for a long time. I was heartbroken. Then one night this past year, I got drunk and wrote to her again, never thinking she'd write back." I looked over at Luca and kept my eyes on her. "We realized our mistake and picked up right where we left off. Except this time, we took some big chances. We found each other for the first time, and I realized that I'm even more in love with her than I thought." I studied Luca's shocked expression for a moment, then turned to the cashier. "I'm in trouble, Doris. I'm worried, because everywhere I go, people know who I am—or they think they do. It's not a normal way to live. And my girl . . . she gets scared around crowds. It's the worst possible combination of factors. It feels like everything is against us sometimes. But my greatest hope is that she'll continue to believe in me, to believe that what we have is stronger than anything else working against us. I'm just so happy to be here, Doris—with her and with you."

A carton of eggs that Doris had been holding slipped out of her hands and smashed onto the ground.

She seemed unfazed by the broken eggs as she fixated on us. "That was the most beautiful thing I've ever heard. I'll . . . I'll get you a new carton of eggs. I'm sorry."

She ran away before I could say anything else.

I took the opportunity to turn to Luca and say, "I hope that was okay to admit, that I've . . . fallen in love with you, Luca. I love you. I'm crazy about you."

Luca was in tears. "I love you, too, Griffin. I really do. I always have."

We embraced, and I whispered in her ear, "I wasn't exactly expecting that to come out the way it did, but now that it has . . . I want you to know that I mean every word."

Doris returned, panting. "New carton of eggs for ya."

She busily returned to scanning the rest of the items, seeming to rush nervously to make up for the previous delay.

After paying for everything, I wanted to give her a little something extra. I handed her a hundred-dollar bill. "Thank you for looking after my Luca when I can't."

"My pleasure." She grinned. "Thank you so much, Mr. Archer."

"I'll see you soon, Doris," Luca said.

"You'd better," she said as we walked away.

Luca and I took the groceries to her car. After packing the trunk, I stopped to look at the sky. It was a beautiful starry night and, even more beautiful, there was absolutely no one in sight.

Freedom.

I grabbed Luca impulsively and started to slow dance with her in the middle of the parking lot. With her hand in mine, we rocked back and forth in silence. When else in my life could I do this without someone snapping my photo? I wanted to dance with my girl under the stars with no one watching but us.

I didn't know why, but the first song that came to mind was "Maybe I'm Amazed" by Paul McCartney. It just seemed fitting. Luca continued to rest her head on my shoulder as I started singing the song softly.

It was a beautiful few minutes of peaceful rocking with the lady I adored. It felt like a dream indeed. If only my real life wouldn't be coming to wake me up in a couple of days.

As our dance came to an end and we entered the car, I asked, "Would you ever consider a threesome?"

She was adorable as shock overtook her face.

"No. Never."

"I wasn't referring to *that* kind of threesome. But I was thinking . . . maybe you'd let me interfere in your Furby action tonight?"

I didn't want to leave. And I didn't mean the day after tomorrow—I meant *ever*. Luca's head rested on my chest, and a cute little snore made her lips vibrate with each exhale she let out. Jesus, I even loved her snore.

I was screwed.

Totally screwed.

How the hell was I going to go on the road for weeks, sometimes months at a time, without seeing her? I didn't want to go one single day. Plus, I really loved her lifestyle. Even the two-in-the-morning supermarket run felt more normal to me than anything had felt in years. I could see myself raking the leaves out front in the fall, shoveling the snow in the winter, and taking long walks in the spring with Luca by my side. Even though I had all the money I'd ever dreamed of, it always felt like something was missing. I just didn't know what it was. Until now.

I fucking love this girl.

And now that I knew what made me happy, there was no way I was letting it slip through my fingers. So I slunk out of bed, careful not to wake Luca, and went to her office. I remembered she had a big calendar in there, one of those old-school desk blotters, and I needed it to lay out my plan.

◆ ◆ ◆

"What smells so good?" Luca came up behind me at the stove and wrapped her arms around my bare chest. I set down the spatula and turned to bury my face in her neck.

"You. *You* smell good. It's about time your lazy butt got up. I'm starving."

"You could have eaten breakfast without me."

I slipped my hands beneath the hem of the T-shirt she wore, *my* T-shirt—which I loved her in—and grabbed a handful of ass. "I ate breakfast three hours ago. I was talking about lunch. I'm eating you, sweetheart." I pointed my chin to the kitchen counter next to us. "Right up there. I'm going to spread your legs wide and lick you until you say yes."

She pulled her head back. "What are you asking that you want me to say yes to?"

I shook my head. "In good time. In good time. We'll get to that. But first, I made you all your favorites." I lifted a paper towel. "Bacon—*turkey* bacon. So you can enjoy the taste and still look your little buddy in the eye afterward." I took the top off a pot on the stovetop. "Mashed potatoes. The real kind, not the powder shit you said you buy when you're cooking for one. I have four Band-Aids on my fingers to prove I peeled the spuds myself." I opened the oven door, where I had the main course keeping warm. "And crispy fried chicken battered with cornflakes."

Luca licked her lips. "Oh my God. I can't believe you did all this. I didn't even have most of the ingredients for any of that in the house. You must've gone to the stores, too."

That reminded me. I'd also stopped at a bakery during my outing—no hat and no sunglasses all morning, and not one person tried to take my picture or seemed to recognize me. In fact, the old man at the bakery grumbled at me. *God, I love Vermont.* I walked over to the refrigerator, opened the door, and took out the white cake box. "Cheesecake with strawberry preserves on top. Though I admit that one is more for me than you. I can't wait to smear it all over your gorgeous tits and lick it off."

Luca's eyes went soft. "I can't believe you remembered all my favorite foods and made them. No one has ever done something like this for me."

I kissed her lips. "Sit. Let's feed you. Because you'll be much more content with a full belly. Then we can talk."

Luca made little humming sounds when she ate something she really liked. I couldn't help but wonder if I could get her to make those while she was on her knees.

"What?" She put down her chicken leg, wiped her mouth with a napkin, and squinted at me. "You look like you're thinking something dirty."

I smiled. "How could I not be? You're sitting at the table with no knickers or bra on. And *fuck*, I'm getting a hard-on watching you sink your teeth into that chicken leg. *Sitophilia*—I looked it up while you were feasting on my potatoes. I never knew I had a food fetish."

Luca bit her bottom lip. "Speaking of fetishes, I bet you must have . . . done a lot of things . . . you know, experimented with women. I'm sure there's been lots of opportunity."

This was most definitely a conversation that I shouldn't have. So I redirected where it had been heading. "I want to do a lot of things with *you*."

Luca tilted her head. "Like what?"

"Off the top of my head? Well, I'd like to take off your shirt and titty fuck you. Slip and slide my cock through those big, beautiful baps and come all over your delicate neck."

Her cheeks pinked up and her hand rose to touch her neck. "What else?"

"Well, since you're asking . . . I'd like to bend you over my knee and smack that sexy ass a few times—hard enough so you feel it, and I leave a handprint on your fair skin. Then I want to hold you down with your cheek pressed against your desk and take you from behind while looking at my handiwork."

She swallowed. "Oh. Wow. Okay. What else?"

There were a million things I wanted to do to her. So many ways I wanted to have her—in every orifice, in every position. But there was one particular thing I'd wanted to do with her ever since I first set eyes on her outside of my house in California. It wasn't erotic in the least, yet it was what I wanted. "You know what I'd really like to do? Maybe we can give it a go tonight?"

"What?"

"Drink a bottle of wine, fuck, then order pizza and eat it in bed naked."

The two of us started to crack up. Luca stood and walked over to sit on my lap. "I honestly couldn't ask for a better way to spend our last night together, Griff. That sounds perfect."

She was right; it was perfect. Only I needed to correct one little detail. And she'd given me a seamless segue to have the conversation I'd been itching to have since before the sun rose today. I locked my hands around her. "It is a perfect way to spend tonight. There's just one thing we need to fix about that plan."

She smiled. "Okay. What's that?"

"Let's not make it our last night together. I need to spend more time with you, because soon enough I'll be on tour again and life will be crazy. I want you to come away with me now while we have the chance, Luca."

She was more freaked out than I thought she'd be.

I'd written my schedule for the next month on Luca's calendar and laid it in front of her to explain what my plans were. I pointed to Friday.

"I have to be in New York the day after tomorrow for the taping of a late-night talk show. Saturday I head to Connecticut for an interview at some college radio station, then back to New York for three different morning radio station appearances on Monday. Tuesday is a down day, but I have to be in Detroit on Wednesday night for a private showcase my label put together with some industry people. We're going to play a few songs from our upcoming album for magazine reviewers and the big music bloggers. Thursday we go on to Chicago for three days to shoot the video for the first single. Then I'm off for a week before the tour starts. This is what I was thinking." I took one of her hands in mine and brought it to my lips for a kiss. "Hear me out. Keep an open mind."

Luca closed her eyes for a minute in an attempt to keep calm. When she opened them, I smiled.

"That's my girl. Okay . . . here we go. First, we drive to New York. We do that late tomorrow night so the roads are empty. I reserved an Airbnb on the Lower East Side—it's a two-story brownstone, and I took both floors so there wouldn't be anyone else in the building but us. The place has a nice big desk that looks out a window where you can work while we're there. We'll stay there Thursday through Tuesday. I'll do a day trip to Connecticut on Saturday and come back at night. You can write while I'm gone. Sunday we can spend the day in bed, maybe trying out some of those things I can't wait to do to you and watching old movies. Monday you'll work while I go do the last of the radio shows, and then we'll drive to Detroit at night before going on to Chicago. After that, we drive back to Vermont and stay here for a week. My assistant will pack up my guitars and send them here, and he found a studio that I can use to practice during the day so I'm not loud during your writing time. The tour comes after that, but we use the next two weeks to ease into things, and we won't worry about that schedule for a while."

Luca's eyes started to well up. I pushed a lock of hair behind her ear. "Talk to me," I said. "Tell me what you're thinking?"

One big, fat tear rolled down her cheek. It caused an ache in my chest as I wiped it from her beautiful face.

"I want to. I *really, really* want to. But I'm afraid, Griff. What if I have a meltdown in the middle of the trip?"

"What if you don't have a meltdown and you have a great time?"

She frowned and closed her eyes. "You're the sweetest. But I'm serious. I don't think you fully understand how debilitating a real panic attack can be. Simply making plans causes an irrational amount of stress for me. I don't just have anxiety the minutes before walking into a building, Griffin. I obsess over the possibility of even having a panic attack. It's all I can think about when I know I have to do things that I'm uncomfortable doing. Every day my fear builds and builds until I get to a place where I start to crack."

"How about if we take it one day at a time, then? Just go with me for one night. Don't plan to stay two. After day one is done, you can decide how you feel about the next day. I can drive you back at any point."

"I don't know, Griff. You have a schedule. You don't have time to run your agoraphobic girlfriend home if she becomes a basket case."

I felt like I was starting to lose the battle. "Don't worry about my time. A relationship is about give and take. You'll be going outside of your comfort zone for me because I want you with me, and if I need to take a day and run you home, then that's what we'll do. My mum used to have a saying about relationships. To be honest, I never quite understood it, but I think that it's because I never had a real relationship before."

"What was the saying?"

"She used to say, *What comes easy won't last long, and what lasts long won't come easy.*"

Luca smiled sadly. "Your mom was a smart woman."

"She was." I cupped my girl's cheeks. "So what do you say? Will you give it a try? We'll start with one day and see how we do."

She looked back and forth between my eyes. I could see the sheer terror in her face. But I knew we could make it work together. She wrapped her hand around my wrist while I held her face. "Can I think about it?"

Just then the doorbell rang. The timing couldn't have been more perfect.

"Oh God. I'm not dressed, and I wasn't expecting any company."

"I'm expecting company." I cradled Luca in my arms and stood, taking her with me. "Go put some clothes on. I borrowed your phone to call Doc. I invited him over."

Her brows furrowed. "Doc? Why?"

I kissed her nose before setting her down on the floor. "Because I knew you would need someone to talk to about what I just asked you."

Luca graced me with a real smile this time. She pushed up on her toes. "I really do love you, Griffin."

"I love you, too. Now go get dressed so you can talk through stuff with Birdman, and we can get back to our plans for tonight."

"Plans?"

"You've forgotten so soon? Drinking, fucking, and naked pizza in bed."

CHAPTER 23

LUCA

"I think this is a very good opportunity for you to continue your desensitization therapy, Luca."

Doc and I walked side by side through the woods. It was a little chilly today, so I had a light jacket on. My trusty therapist, on the other hand, had a crew neck Christmas sweater on with a cartoon picture of Jesus holding up two fingers in a peace sign. It read LET's PARTY BECAUSE IT's THE BIG GUY's BIRTHDAY. Doc kept his off-season clothes in the trunk of his car, since his tiny house didn't have much storage room. Apparently that was the first thing he could grab for our walk.

"I know, but I don't think our relationship is ready for this. It's so new . . . we've only just met in person for the first time less than a month ago. What if I can't hack it and have a bad panic attack and it . . . it scares him away?"

Doc stopped and looked at me. "Let me ask you something. Does the fact that you've only met in person a short time ago make your feelings for Griffin any less real?"

"Well, no . . ."

"Okay. So how you got to the place you are now in your relationship is irrelevant. I'll admit your circumstances are a little unique—but you've gotten to know this man over more than a decade. It's not like you're jumping into something with a stranger. I'm assuming you're in love with him?"

I sighed. "I am. Very much so."

"Well, then you need to find out if you can make this life together work. It sounds to me like he's willing to bend as much as he can to figure it out. Wouldn't it be worse if you got even closer than you already are and then discovered that you couldn't fit into each other's lives?"

"I guess . . ."

"Let me tell you about the agapornis."

"The what?"

"The African parrot—we call them lovebirds."

"Oh. Okay. What about them?"

Doc extended his hand for me to start walking through the wooded path again. He liked to tell his stories as we strolled. "Most people think of lovebirds as the bird that your sweetheart gives you for Valentine's Day as a romantic gesture—because they mate for life. But they actually don't need to pair up and mate in order to survive. The lovebird requires companionship, and that bonding can come from a human if there isn't another bird available. We're a lot like the lovebirds. You don't need to pair up in order to live. In fact, I'm sure you'd survive just fine spending the rest of your days with only Hortencia by your side. But when the lovebirds pair up into a monogamous relationship, they become calmer and more stable."

"Are you saying that *I'd* be calmer in a relationship?"

"I am, Luca. It's not uncommon for people with panic disorders to alienate themselves like you have. They try to hide the condition to avoid shame or fear of having a panic attack in front of others. This is why a support network is so important. Once you see that people you love and trust accept you for who you are and don't judge you, you'll be more likely to take some risks that could result in others outside of your network seeing your panicked state. Allowing a loved one in is the next logical step for you. You've made wonderful progress with me over the last few years, but together we can only go so far. *You* need to now decide to take a chance."

Griffin didn't ask what Doc and I had discussed. Nor did he pressure me to talk any more about what he'd proposed earlier that day. Instead, he gave me space, and we had a great night of sex and eating pizza in bed. After, we both dozed off, or so I thought.

It was about 2:00 a.m. when I stirred awake. My eyes fluttered open to find Griffin's big brown ones watching me. He smiled.

"Is it creepy that I really like watching you sleep?"

My voice was raspy. "Sort of."

He chuckled. "Did I wake you by creeping on you?"

I pushed back hair from my face. "I don't think so. I think I just woke up because I have a lot on my mind. I tend to be a restless sleeper when something is bothering me."

Griffin nodded. He didn't need to ask what was weighing on me. Instead, he just leaned and brushed his lips against mine. "Anything I can do to help you sleep? Make you some warm milk or rub your back?"

"No, I'm good. Thank you."

He wiggled his brows. "I hear strenuous exercise is a good method of inducing sleep."

I smiled. "If that's so, I should have slept for a week after the last few days."

Griffin ran his thumb across my bottom lip. His touch was so tender that it made my insides melt. "Well, as long as you're up," he whispered, "can I tell you something that's on my mind?"

"Sure. Of course."

Griffin looked deep into my eyes. "I'm scared, Luca."

I sat up on one elbow. "What are you scared of?"

"I'm scared that you don't want anything from me. That you don't *need* anything from me."

My heart sank. "Oh God, Griff. You couldn't be more wrong. I *do* want something from you." I reached out and put my hand on his chest. "I want this. I want your heart."

"But you don't *want* to want it."

God, I'd fucked this whole thing up. I had been so busy worrying about how afraid I was to take a chance that I never once stopped to think that maybe Griffin was nervous about falling in love, too. He'd been burned by women and friends and had his own doubts. Yet this beautiful man had still taken a leap of faith with me—telling me he loved me, rearranging his life to make his fit with mine. I had tons of doubts and fears, but I didn't doubt his intentions or that he wanted to be with me. And that was because Griffin didn't just *tell* me he loved me—he'd shown me in so many ways.

I needed to do the same—*show* him that I loved him. Taking a deep breath, I decided I wanted to be a lovebird.

"Let's do it. I'll go with you on the trip."

Griffin's face lit up. "You mean it?"

I nodded. "I'm terrified of what might happen—the panic that might hit me. But I'm more terrified of letting you walk out the door tomorrow without at least trying to make it work. You already have my heart, Griff. If you leave without me, you'll just be taking it with you, and I'll be empty inside."

Griffin grabbed me and pulled me into a bear hug. He spoke with his head buried in my neck. "I love you, baby. Thank you. I promise I'll do everything in my power to make sure you don't regret making this decision."

I knew the words he spoke were true. I just didn't know if him doing everything in his power was enough to make it work between us.

◆ ◆ ◆

We'd dropped Hortencia off at the farm that she normally stayed at whenever I was away.

Griffin was packing the SUV he'd rented when I ventured to my room and snuck a phone call in to Doc. I only had a few minutes before we would be taking to the road. Since we planned to drive in the middle of the night, it was late, but I'd told Doc to expect my call.

He picked up on the first ring. "Have you left yet?"

"We're just about ready to leave. I wanted to touch base before I got into the car."

"Of course. How are you feeling?"

I breathed into the phone. "Anxious."

"To be expected . . ."

"After our conversation yesterday, I felt like I owed it to myself to take the chance on this trip, but I'm still wondering if I'm making a huge mistake. It's a long time to be away from home, several locations . . . a lot of opportunities for disaster . . . I—"

"Luca . . . ," he interrupted. "What is the number one rule that we always talk about?"

I had to think about it for a moment, then answered, "Staying in the present."

"Yes. If you stay in the present moment and not go where your mind is trying to lead you, then you will always be safe. There is safety in the now. Right now, you are in your bedroom talking to me. And that is all there really is. Your worries stem from past experiences and fear of the future. Neither the past nor the future is real. Only the present exists. If you stick to this mantra, you will be okay in anything you do.

If you can only remember one thing on your trip, remember to stay present. Listen to the sound of the car moving, focus on the raindrops, taste the delicious food that I'm sure Griffin will feed you. Practice those mindfulness tools."

"Okay. I'll try. But please be on standby for some calls in case I need you."

"Always, my dear. And for the record, I'm incredibly proud of you for taking this step."

Griffin entered the room and smacked his hands together. "Ready, Freddie?"

I nodded. "Okay, Doc. I have to go."

"Good luck, Luca. If you see any sandhill cranes in Michigan, please take some pictures for me."

One-track mind.

I chuckled. "Okay. You got it."

After hanging up, I looked over at Griffin, who seemed to be observing me.

He tilted his head. "You alright, babe?"

My heart was racing, and I felt very cold, which often happened to me when I was really nervous. "Yeah. Just some last-minute panic trying to creep in."

He wrapped his hands around my waist and spoke close to my mouth. "Ah. Well, I just so happen to have the cure for last-minute panic."

"Yeah? What is it?"

"I've heard that sitting on your lover's face takes care of it."

My mouth hung open. "Oh really . . ."

"Yes. It's called CBFS, actually."

"CBFS?"

"Cognitive behavioral face-sitting."

I burst out in laughter. "So how does this work exactly?"

"Well . . . we start to attack your way of thinking by challenging the questions in your mind that cause you fear. Simultaneously, you're sitting on my face while I work to bring you to orgasm. The eventual realization is that none of the other shit matters—aside from coming on my mouth."

I laughed. "Ah. Seems like a very specialized therapy. Does one need a degree to administer it?"

"It's self-taught. In fact, I need some practice, actually. And you look like you could use some CBFS right now. So . . . win-win."

My brow lifted. "You want me to . . . sit on your face?"

"Car's all packed. We're ahead of schedule. I'm thinking that might be a good use of time, yeah."

I couldn't argue with that. Maybe an orgasm would do me some good to calm my nerves. But sitting on his face? Wasn't sure if I was comfortable with that.

He could sense my apprehension. "It'll calm you down. I promise."

Griffin lay back on the bed and pulled his shirt over his head. The ripples of muscle on his chest never ceased to amaze me. The tattoo over his tanned skin accentuated the whole package. It never took long to get into the mood with Griffin. All I really had to do was look at him.

His voice was gruff. "Stay right there where you are. Undress yourself slowly while I watch. Start with your bra. I want to see your tits pop out one by one."

I did as he said, taking my clothing off piece by piece. My nipples puckered as Griffin unbuckled his pants and took out his engorged cock. From where I was standing, I could see the tip was already wet. I licked my lips from the urge to suck on it. He began to pump into his hands as he watched me undress until I was fully naked. I loved how turned on he was; it made me crazy.

"Play with your clit while you watch me jerk myself off."

I pressed two fingers against my clit and began to rub it in circles. As he ran his tongue along his mouth, I kept thinking about how it was going to feel when it touched me. Getting wetter by the second, I actually had to stop myself from coming. Watching him masturbate, watching his big hand moving up and down his thickness, turned me on so much. This was a first for us. It was an unexpected but welcome monkey wrench thrown into my otherwise stressful evening.

He gestured with his index finger. "Come here."

I walked, then crawled onto the bed and over to him. He continued to stroke himself as he positioned me over his face. The heat of his mouth between my legs in this position felt foreign—but amazing. His scruff felt prickly against my tender skin. I had never actually sat on a man's face before. Any potential apprehension was quickly squelched once I became lost in how incredible it felt. There was something very dominating about it, and that made the sensations running through me all that much more intense.

He spoke under me. "Tell me what's worrying you now, Luca . . ."

Unable to form words, I simply moaned. "Uhhhh . . ."

His mission was accomplished, because my previously overactive brain had turned to mush. Not only could I not remember what I'd been worrying about, but I could barely remember my own name.

My tender clit was throbbing as he continued to lick and suck me while I grabbed onto his head and pushed him harder between my legs.

"Ride me, baby. I love devouring you like this. I can feel everything, taste everything. I'm gonna come so hard."

His tongue was hitting all my erogenous zones. I couldn't take it anymore. One of the most powerful orgasms I'd ever had rocketed through my core. With one hand on his cock and one wrapped around my ass, Griffin's breathing from under me became erratic. I knew he was coming. The muffled sound of his own pleasure vibrated against my sensitive skin.

He licked me gently, his tongue moving in slow circles, as we both recovered.

"That was . . . amazing. I've never done that before," I said, out of breath.

He flipped me over, pinning me under him, his mouth glistening from my arousal. "Another first I get to claim. Just the way I like it."

CHAPTER 24

GRIFFIN

We'd made it through the beginning part of our trip with no complications. The Airbnb I'd rented for us on the Lower East Side of Manhattan was as private as expected. So I'd had no qualms whatsoever about leaving Luca alone while I traveled to Connecticut on Saturday. I'd checked in on her a couple of times, and she'd reported that she was getting some good writing time in.

On the drive back that night, I couldn't wait to get to her. I'd had the entire evening planned. We'd order some of the best pizza in New York—with pineapple on top of course—open a bottle of wine, and then just "Netflix and chill" all night. Tomorrow, I had no obligations. We'd have the entire day to just lounge around. That was my idea of heaven—a lazy Sunday.

"Honey, I'm home," I announced upon entering the brownstone.

The place was quiet. *Hmm.* Perhaps Luca was sleeping?

I yelled out, "Luca? I'm back!"

Still nothing.

After thoroughly searching the first level, I could see she was nowhere to be found.

"Luca?"

I headed upstairs to find that she wasn't in bed. My heart started to speed up a bit. She wouldn't have gone out on her own, would she?

"Luca?" I repeated.

It was then that I heard a sound coming from the bathroom that was located off our room.

Her voice sounded weak from behind the door. "Griffin? Griffin . . . help me."

I ran to open it only to realize it was locked. *She's locked inside.*

"Open the door, Luca."

She was sobbing. "I can't. It won't open."

Fuck!

"What do you mean it won't open? You didn't lock it yourself?"

"No. It's broken. It locked behind me. I can't get out. I've tried everything. It won't open."

"What the fuck? How did this happen?"

I shook the doorknob with all my might. It wasn't budging. I was going to have to break the door down. But I knew the bathroom was small and I didn't want to hurt her.

Think. Think. Think.

Taking a deep breath in, I said, "Okay. Here's what we're going to do. I'm going to need you to stand at the far edge of the tub. I'm going to kick the door in."

She wasn't responding, but I could hear her whimpering.

Leaning my head against the door, I asked, "Are you with me, baby?"

"Yes . . . yes," she said through tears.

"Okay . . . tell me when you're ready."

After a few seconds, she said, "Okay. I'm standing on the edge of the tub."

"On the count of three, I'm going to kick the door in as hard as I can. Stay back and cover your head, just in case it goes flying toward you."

She didn't answer.

"Luca . . . answer me."

"I hear you," she finally said, her voice trembling.

"Alright. Here we go. On the count of three. One . . . two . . . three." *Boom!* I kicked the door with all my might. It opened but fell off the hinges. It was now leaning against the tub. Luca came out from behind it, thankfully safe and sound.

We'd gotten lucky. The bathroom was so small that I could have seriously injured her in the process of breaking the door down. The only light was coming from the bedroom. I now knew why she was so panicked. There was no light in the bathroom. It had been pitch-black while she was locked inside.

Luca was shaking as she fell into my arms. She then burst into tears.

How the fuck did this happen?

"How long were you in there, baby?"

She shook her head over and over before speaking. "I don't know. Maybe a half hour. I lost any concept of time. All I'd tried to do was go pee. I shut the door behind me thinking the light switch was inside the bathroom, not remembering it was outside the door. There was no light. I tried to kick the door down but wasn't strong enough. I didn't have my phone with me. Thank God you came home when you did."

I wrapped my arms around her. "You're okay. It's okay. You're safe." Leading her to the bed, I cradled her as we lay against the headboard. "God, I thought there was nothing that could possibly go wrong in this place, that I could leave you with no problems. I never imagined something like this would happen. I would have never left you had I known."

"It's not your fault. Anyone else probably could have handled it. I can't handle *anything*, Griffin, least of all being trapped in any way."

"Don't blame yourself. Anyone would be freaked out to be stuck in a tiny, dark bathroom with no windows, even if they didn't have a panic disorder. You had no idea when I'd be back. Your reaction is completely understandable."

She wiped a tear. "I just kept praying the whole time, praying that you'd come home. Eventually you did."

After Luca calmed down a bit, I ended up calling the owner of the property to give him a piece of my mind for having a door that could trap someone in the first place. That was a major hazard. After taking out my anger on him, I drew a bath for Luca and myself in the other bathroom and ordered takeout.

Holding her in my arms as we watched a movie that night, I vowed to do whatever it took to make the rest of the trip a positive experience for her. After all, how much worse than tonight could it get?

◆ ◆ ◆

After a stop in Detroit, the rest of the trip had been uneventful until we got to the last destination—Chicago. The original plan was to stay at a bed-and-breakfast just outside of the city. Then the owner called to say a pipe burst and that we wouldn't be able to stay there. It had been late when we got that news, and no one was returning my calls for last-minute Airbnb vacancies. Somehow I'd convinced Luca to stay with me in the penthouse suite of a high-rise hotel. I'd stayed there several times in the past and knew it offered a private elevator for penthouse guests. I figured it was the best option for us in the city and offered the least opportunity to be noticed.

This particular penthouse was one of the nicest I'd ever stayed in. Overlooking downtown Chicago, the four-thousand-square-foot space featured panoramic views and ornate furnishings. It was lavish, to the point where I'd worried that maybe she would think I was showing off. But thankfully, Luca seemed to be able to relax a little and really enjoy staying there.

I'd go to shoot the music video during the day, and Luca would stay in the suite and write by the window. She said the view of the city had given her lots of inspiration for the urban-based story she was plotting.

It would be set in Chicago. I was thrilled that we would be ending this trip on a positive note.

Unfortunately, that all changed on our third night. Luca and I were sound asleep when a loud noise caused us to jolt out of bed. It took me a few seconds to realize it was the fire alarm.

Fire?

No.

Please, no.

Anything but this.

This was bad. Very bad. Worse than anything that could have transpired.

Her eyes were half shut. "What's happening?"

"It's the fire alarm. We have to go. Get your clothes on."

Luca froze. I was an idiot if I thought she was going to be able to calmly get dressed at a time like this. I knew I needed to help her find her clothes and get her dressed myself. After grabbing her long T-shirt that was lying on the floor, I slipped it over her head. I threw on my jeans and a T-shirt and went in search of her flip-flops and my shoes. After we were both clothed, I grabbed her by the hand and led her to the door. I knew it wasn't safe to take the elevator in the event that this was a real fire. We would have to take the stairs. Unfortunately, the stairwell wasn't private.

Her hand trembled in mine as we made our way down the first set of stairs. Her body was limp as she let me lead her.

"I've got you, baby. I've got you."

As swarms of people started to clog the stairwell, I knew this was becoming a very bad situation. Luca wasn't saying anything. She didn't have to. I knew this was her biggest nightmare come to life. And goddammit, I'd put her in this position; I'd failed her again.

"Stay with me, baby. It's going to be okay. We just need to go downstairs, and then I'll get you away from all these people."

"Do you think it's a real fire?" she finally asked, seeming in a daze.

"I don't know. Probably not. I bet it was some kids pulling the alarm."

Her face was turning white, and her teeth chattered. "What if it's real?"

"Then we'll still be okay. Just keep holding on to me."

As we continued down the multiple sets of winding stairs that seemed endless, I just kept praying that we could make it out of here unscathed. Ironically, it wasn't even fire I was concerned about but rather the prospect of getting mobbed with no security present. No one had recognized me thus far in the stairwell, but it was probably only a matter of time.

We'd gotten down to about the twenty-fifth floor when someone shouted, *"Hey, I think that's Cole Archer."*

I squeezed Luca's hand harder. Luckily nothing more came out of that little shout-out.

It took a long time to finally make it down to the ground level. When we did, we were greeted by a mob of people. There was no sign of any actual fire. But the real shit show—getting through this packed lobby to the door—was about to begin.

We could hardly make our way through the crowd as it was, without anyone having recognized me yet. Then the inevitable happened. A gaggle of girls eventually spotted me in the crowd.

"Cole!"

"It's Cole Archer!"

"Oh my God. Oh my God. Oh my God."

The recognition spread like wildfire.

Suddenly I felt people touching me—touching us—hands, squealing, chaos. Everything meshed together and was closing in on Luca and me. But I couldn't focus on any of it, couldn't afford to look at anyone or respond. Nothing fazed me—not the people grabbing at my clothing or yelling my name, not the camera flashes in our faces. The only thing

I cared about was getting Luca the fuck out of here, my eyes focusing on the revolving doors in the distance.

My grip tightened on her hand. When I looked over at her, she had tears in her eyes. They were also filled with terror. It crossed my mind that my being in this hotel might have somehow gotten leaked, causing someone to pull the fire alarm. Crazier things had happened. The cause didn't matter now, though. All that mattered was getting to the safety of the sidewalk.

When we finally made it past the mob and the cold night air hit us, I pulled Luca in my direction and just fled. Still holding hands, we ran as fast as we could from the hotel. I just needed to get away from all of it so I could think straight.

About three blocks down the road, we finally got to a point where there was no one else in sight. Luca was still shaking as I pulled her into an alleyway and leaned her against the wall of a brick building. I cradled her face in my hands, bringing her forehead to my lips.

Whispering, I said, "It's okay, baby. We're fine. Everything is fine. You're gonna be just fine. My brave girl. I love you so much."

But everything wasn't really "fine." She wasn't saying anything, and I knew she was still in shock. She just kept crying, shivering.

All I could think was that she had trusted me, and I'd greatly fucked up. I had asked her to step out of her comfort zone. I should have known that taking her to a commercial hotel was a bad idea. I thought with the safety of the penthouse and the private elevator, we could risk it. But I hadn't taken into account the possibility of an urgent situation. In the event of an emergency, all bets were off. I'd put her in what was likely one of the scariest scenarios imaginable, one that mimicked the very event that had traumatized her. I only hoped I hadn't caused any irreversible damage to her recovery.

"I'm so sorry, Luca. So damn sorry."

In my heart, I knew this situation was very bad. This trip had been about proving to her that we could make this work. I'd proven just the opposite, that I could hardly take her anywhere without something bad happening. I didn't want to lose the woman I loved, but at what cost? Making her life miserable just so I could selfishly have her by my side? Cole Archer could never be erased. He could never have a normal life. He'd never be able to truly hide or keep Luca 100 percent safe. I'd been so blinded by my feelings for this woman that I'd tricked myself into believing that it would be easier than it is. I wanted to believe that. It isn't easy at all. It's damn hard. As she continued to shake in my arms, the harsh reality of the situation was really starting to hit me, the truth I didn't want to accept: that we might not be able to make it.

CHAPTER 25

GRIFFIN

"What can I do? I need to do *something*." I yanked at my hair while pacing back and forth and talking on the phone with Doc. Luca was out cold in the bedroom, thanks to a healthy dose of Xanax he'd prescribed when I'd first called him a few hours ago. But she'd been against even taking one pill; I wasn't going to get her to take any more—which meant I needed to figure out how to fix what I'd fucked up. *Fast.*

"I'm afraid you're doing everything you can, Griffin. You're providing her emotional support and a safe environment. She'll calm down. It's just going to take some time."

"How much time?"

Doc sighed. "I can't tell you that, either, Griffin. Luca's fear of being trapped stems from a situation that she couldn't control. Over the last few years, we've worked on her believing that she always has control—whether that is to walk out of a building or simply get out of a car—but at the moment she's feeling like she had no control over the situation that occurred, and it's going to take some time for her to be able to see she actually did. She allowed you to take the lead and exited the building—that's giving permission to another person to help when she needed it most. However, I know our Luca, and I'm sure she doesn't see it like that—at least not right now. She's feeling like she was helpless.

And in good time, we can work to get her to see that sometimes allowing someone to help is the best decision to make and that doesn't mean you've failed. Just the opposite, actually. Allowing someone to have control over you is a form of exercising control in itself."

I creaked open the door to the bedroom to check on Luca while talking to Doc. She was still out cold. I'd taken her to a friend's house. A buddy I shared a label with lived on the outskirts of Chicago. Luca and I had only been sleeping an hour when the fire alarm went off, so we both needed to crash for a while, and I knew taking her to another hotel was out of the question. Luckily, Travis had answered his phone when I called at 3:00 a.m., and he was kind enough to let me stay over at his place. He was on the road for a gig, so we had the place all to ourselves for the night after a quick stop to wake up his housekeeper and borrow her keys.

"I'm not sure what to do, Doc. She wants to go home. I hate to take her, but before we started this trip, I promised her we'd take it one day at a time and if she wasn't happy, I'd drive her back home."

"I think that's probably wise. Luca will feel better in her own environment. After an event like she's just gone through, feeling in control of her surroundings again is of the utmost importance. And her home is where she feels the safest. I'll come by as soon as she's settled in, and we'll get right back on the bicycle. This is a setback, not the end of the road for Luca's recovery, Griffin."

I don't know what I expected the good doctor to say—taking her home was obviously the right thing to do. But hearing him confirm that I shouldn't even try to talk her into staying made my heart sink.

"Okay. Yeah. Thanks, Doc."

He must've heard in my voice how deflated I felt. "She's strong, son. Luca will come back from this. You need to have faith."

What was most important was that Luca would be okay. Whatever would become of our relationship took a back seat to her mental and physical health, of course. Though the selfish part of me couldn't help but worry—Luca might come back from this, but would we?

We'd been on the road for thirteen hours already and had about two hours left until we got to Vermont. Luca had been quiet the entire trip. Despite her preference to drive only at night to avoid traffic, we also traveled during some daylight hours to get home faster. She was calmer now, almost too calm. While she'd answer me if I asked her a direct question, it was clear that she didn't really feel like talking. Most of the time, she'd just stare out the window, lost in thought. I hadn't attempted to discuss what would happen when we got to Vermont, mainly because I was afraid of what she might say. But with two hours left, I needed to at least let her know the plans I'd been able to make.

I reached over and took her hand in mine. Bringing it to my lips, I kissed her knuckles. "The production company gave me until Monday to get back and finish the video shoot. So I booked a flight back tomorrow evening."

"Oh. Okay." She frowned. "I'm sorry you had to postpone everything. I'm sure the band isn't happy about the delay."

"It's not a big deal. At all. We once had to postpone an album cover photo shoot because Styx, our drummer, got his tongue stuck to a stripper's muff."

She squinted at me and shook her head, seemingly coming out of her fog. "Did you just say he got his tongue stuck to a . . . ?"

I nodded. "Muff. Her pussy."

Luca looked rightfully confused.

"Dumbass has a tongue ring. He went down on a stripper who had a clitoris ring, and the two somehow got connected, and they couldn't disconnect them. He didn't show up for the shoot and wasn't answering his phone. So I went over to his place and pounded on the door. I figured he'd gotten loaded the night before and was passed out inside. When he still didn't answer, I got the building super to let me in and found his head between her legs—they'd been stuck that way for four hours. Every time they tried to move, it hurt one of them, so they just lay in bed with his face planted between her legs and waited for his roommate to come home."

"Did you . . . unhook them?"

"Fuck no. I did what any good buddy would do. First I FaceTimed the guys to show them the shit I'd just walked in on, and then I called 911 and snapped some pics while the two poor paramedics figured out how to remove the dumbass's tongue ring without castrating the woman. Anyway, we missed that photo shoot, and a whole bunch of other shit for my mates' ridiculous crap. No one is going to give a shit that I need a few personal days."

Luca sighed. My stupid story seemed to at least get her attention away from the window. "Thank you for not pushing me to try to stay."

I nodded. "I told you we'd take it one day at a time and I'd drive you home if you weren't comfortable at any point. When I tell you something, I want you to be able to count on it. But I hope you know I would have done anything to get you to stay."

"I know, Griffin. And I appreciate that. I really do." She turned away and looked out the window again. "I've been thinking. When I first started working with Doc, I had photos of Isabella and me in every room of my house. The one in my bedroom was the first thing I looked at each morning when I opened my eyes. Doc convinced me to put them all away for a few days. He thought that if I stopped forcing myself to look at what I'd lost, it might make moving on a little easier. I hadn't wanted to do that, because I loved Isabella so much—not past tense: I *love* Isabella so much—but eventually he got me to do it."

I wasn't sure where she was going, but I was happy she was talking, at least. "Okay."

"You know what happened when I put them away?"

"You stopped thinking about what you'd lost as much?"

She nodded and turned back to look at me. Her eyes were glassy, and she was on the verge of tears. "I did. And I feel a lot of guilt over never taking them out again. But Doc was right; I needed to do it in order to move on. It doesn't mean I don't love her anymore. There are just times in life when love isn't enough, and being strong means being able to see that and making a decision that hurts."

I definitely didn't fucking like where this story was heading now. "Luca—"

She put up her hand and stopped me from talking. "You're a beautiful human being, Griffin, and I'll always cherish this time we've spent together."

My heart started to race. This was not happening. And this conversation was not one I wanted to have while driving seventy miles an hour on the highway. I needed to pull over. I was about to pass an exit, and I abruptly cut over three lanes to get off at the last second. Luca grabbed on to her door and started to freak out.

"Hang on, love. We're not having an accident. Everything is fine. I just needed to get off the highway so we can talk." Luckily, the exit ramp had an entrance to some sort of town storage facility. I pulled into a parking lot with a dozen parked yellow utility trucks equipped with plows and a giant salt storage building. The place was otherwise deserted, so I took the first empty spot and put the car into "Park." I turned off the ignition and started to get out of the car.

"What are you doing?" Luca said.

"I'm taking a break from driving so we can talk face-to-face."

Before she could object, I walked around to the passenger side of the car and opened her door. Extending a hand, I helped her out and told her to stretch her legs for a minute. When she was done, I led us around to the back of the vehicle next to the trunk and lifted her up onto it so that we were eye to eye.

"Okay. Let's talk now."

Luca looked down at her hands. "I . . . You're in such a great place in your life and—"

I stopped her. "Look at me, Luca. If you're about to say what I think you're about to say, I want you to at least look into my eyes while you speak."

She swallowed, took a deep breath, and raised her eyes to meet mine with a nod. "We're just so different, Griff. You're a round hole, and I'm a square peg. We don't fit."

I started to get angry. She was feeling vulnerable and scared; I understood that. But I didn't care. She needed to fight harder for us. "Just say it, Luca."

She looked down again. This time for a solid minute before looking back up at me. A fat tear rolled down her cheek. "Sometimes when love isn't enough to make things right, we need to let it go."

I looked back and forth between her eyes. "Are you finished?"

She looked confused but nodded.

"Fine. Then it's my turn to speak."

"Okay . . ."

"I only have one thing to say, but I want to make sure you hear it loud and clear, Luca."

She looked at me and waited.

I leaned in close so that our noses were touching and spoke directly into her eyes with one stern word. *"No."*

Apparently she thought I had more to add. But I didn't. After thirty seconds of silence, she wrinkled her nose. "No?"

"That's right. *No.*"

"But I don't understand . . ."

"What part of the word *no* don't you understand?"

"What are you saying no to?"

"Everything. You dumping me. You thinking I'm better off without you. You thinking you can just walk away from what we have and I'll let you. The answer is just no. *One big giant fucking no.*"

She still seemed confused when I thought I'd been crystal clear. "But . . ."

"But nothing, Luca."

"Griffin . . ."

I walked away to cool down, leaving her sitting on the car for a few minutes. When I came back, I held out my hand. "Are you ready to go now?"

Again her face wrinkled. I took a deep breath and lifted her from the car, setting her feet on the ground. Then I leaned in and kissed her lips. "When you're ready to discuss *how* we're going to make things work, I'll be ready to have that conversation. But I'm done having this one, and I want to go home. I'm tired and I want to go home." I started to walk back to my side of the car and then realized she might have gotten a mixed message from my last sentence. So I walked back to where she still stood at the back of the car and cleared that shit up. "So there's no confusion, when I say 'home'—I don't mean my house in California. Because that isn't where home is anymore, Luca. Home is wherever you are."

The house was so quiet. I could hear Luca's breaths but wasn't sure if she was sleeping or not. After we arrived in Vermont, she'd busied herself with mundane tasks—going through mail, picking up Hortencia, cleaning out some expired food from the fridge—anything to avoid having a meaningful conversation. We were both wiped out from the drive home, so we ordered some dinner and turned in pretty early. It was clear from Luca's body language that sex wasn't on the menu for tonight. Not that I'd wanted stimulation, but I'd thought that maybe us getting lost in the physical might help her remember the connection we shared. But she'd come to bed in an oversize sweatshirt and joggers and given me her back.

I'd spent the last hour staring at the ceiling in the dark, trying to figure out what the fuck to do. I knew I'd never be able to sleep with so much on my mind, so I decided to get what I needed to say off my chest—whether she heard me or not.

"I don't know if you're awake, but I need to say a few things."

Luca didn't budge, and I didn't hear any change in her breathing pattern, so I assumed she must've really fallen asleep. I didn't let that stop me.

"We all have light and dark inside us, love. We try to hide the darkness from others because we're afraid it will scare them away. But your dark doesn't scare me, Luca. It only makes me want to hold your hand and be your light until you can find your own again. That's what people do when they're in love. I won't always be able to give you your light back, because sometimes you need to find that within yourself, but I'll stand by your side and hold your hand in the dark so things aren't so scary."

Luca took a big croaky breath in, and I still wasn't certain she was awake. Until the next sound came—a raw, agonizing, painful cry that rang out like it was being viciously ripped from her body. It was horrible. She sobbed—long, throaty, sad cries that made my own tears start flowing. So much anguish came out of her, I knew in my heart that this cry wasn't only about what had happened yesterday. It felt like years of pent-up sadness, loneliness, and grief that had found its way out of a long tunnel after years of being stuck in darkness.

I wrapped my arms around her and held on tight, both of us crying for the longest time. Eventually, when every painful sob had racked its way through her body, she started to calm down.

"The concert was my idea," she choked out.

Oh God. The inside of my chest felt like someone had reached in, torn out my still-beating heart, and squeezed it into an angry fist. "It might have been your idea, but what happened wasn't your fault. Millions of teenagers go to concerts every weekend, Luca."

"She always had a smile on her face."

I tightened my grip around her. "I'm sure she was incredible."

"I . . . I miss her so much."

"I know, sweetheart."

"I loved her."

"You love hard. I know you did."

"I couldn't find her." Her voice cracked and shook. "The crowd. It just pushed me toward the door, and I tried to look around, but all I could see was people everywhere."

I'd been to enough concerts to imagine how a horde of panicked teenagers would act during an emergency evacuation. Mass chaos with everyone pushing and pulling. If I hadn't understood the basis of Luca's fears before now, the visual of her little body being pushed through a crowd while she frantically tried to look for her friend really explained her feeling of having no control. I shut my eyes. I'd basically done the same thing to her—pushing her out of the hotel, down the stairs, and through the crowd.

"Shh . . . you're safe now. We're both safe, sweetheart."

Eventually Luca's crying exhausted her so much that she literally cried herself to sleep. One minute she'd been whimpering through a painful breath in, and then the next she breathed out a snore. I stayed awake until after the sun rose, holding her tight and listening for any change in her breathing. Visions of the night she described kept playing over and over in my head, and I was so angry with myself that I hadn't been with her—even though I knew logically that made no sense. We were just kids and had lived an ocean apart. Still, that didn't make what I felt any less real.

Somehow I finally fell asleep, and when I woke up in the early afternoon, the first thing I did was reach for my girl. A feeling of panic hit me, finding nothing but a cold bed where she'd been sleeping. And a note.

Be back later. I emptied your suitcase and did your laundry so you can pack for your flight.

-Luca

At least she'd left out what she'd really been thinking: *Don't let the door hit you on the ass on your way out.*

CHAPTER 26

LUCA

"I just don't see how it could possibly work. A long-distance relationship is hard enough, but one that basically involves Griffin coming to visit me in my little sheltered bubble whenever he has time off from being a rock star isn't realistic."

"What does Griffin have to say about all of this?"

Doc and I had been walking for at least two hours. When he arrived this morning without binoculars, I knew today was going to be a long and hard session. We'd talked for more than an hour and a half about what had happened at the hotel and how I reacted and felt. That conversation led to what was going on with Griffin and me, and now we'd moved on to the subject that gave me physical chest pains. *Saying goodbye to Griffin later.*

"He doesn't understand how being with someone like me will drag him down. He's worked so hard to get where he is, and I can't tie a noose around his neck. His heart is in the right place; he definitely means well, but he deserves so much more. He should have a woman who stands on the side of the stage while he plays to sold-out stadiums and goes to charity balls with him."

"Griffin doesn't seem like a charity-ball type of man. He seems more like he'd write a check and make an anonymous donation to something that's important to him and then come home to chill."

Doc's use of the word *chill* made me smile. "You know what I mean. It's not the event that's important; it's him being able to share all his successes with a real partner. What if he won a Grammy award? I would never be able to even go to an event like that."

"And you believe the only way you can share that success is by standing next to him physically? Can't a person stand by someone's side in a figurative sense? What about a woman who chooses to stay home and raise the children while a man goes off to work every day? Isn't she standing by her man's side?"

"That's not the same thing."

Doc shook his head. "Explain to me how it's different."

"Well, those are choices that a couple makes together. They have one big pool of responsibilities, and they're divvying them up—one person doing the job of child-rearing and the other of supporting the family financially. But in my case—no one gets to make a choice because I'm so screwed up."

Doc stopped walking and waited until I turned back and gave him my full attention. "You're wrong, Luca. Someone is making a choice about this relationship and how it will work—and that's *you*. You're not giving Griffin any choices at all."

◆ ◆ ◆

Doc had left me with a lot to think about. It wasn't that I didn't understand what he was trying to convey; I just wasn't sure I believed it, that Griffin knew what was right for him, that he would be able to work around my issues forever. He might be willing to accommodate my limitations *now*, while things were still fresh and exciting with us, but being with someone who couldn't truly have his back would get old real fast. I *wanted* things to work out with him more than I wanted to breathe. I just didn't think the reality of our lives would allow it. Losing him later might be harder than letting him go now. But the thought of truly letting him go was painful. I was still so confused—that was all I was sure about.

Griffin was sitting at the foot of my bed with his hands on his temples when I returned home. His hair was a mess. It looked like he'd been raking his fingers through it in frustration. He didn't see me at the doorway. Observing him like this, seeing how frustrated he looked, really brought home how serious this situation was—what I'd done to him. He was doing everything in his power to make things right for me. But it shouldn't have to be this hard. It wasn't fair for him to have to constantly walk on eggshells just to make me feel safe and happy. I cared about him so much, and I honestly wondered if that meant I needed to let him go.

The suitcase was upright. He was all packed. My needing to talk to Doc had cost me valuable hours with Griffin. Now it was nearly time for him to leave to catch his flight back to Chicago. While there, he would finish the video shoot he'd abruptly had to abandon because of me. Then he'd fly back to LA before leaving with his bandmates for the tour. It was going to be quite some time before I saw Griffin again—if ever. My stomach was in knots.

He'd ended up returning the rental car and had insisted on calling an Uber rather than have me drive him to the airport. I hated the fact that I was relieved about that, since navigating the airport always stressed me out. It was so congested. A "normal" person would have insisted on driving him.

When Griffin finally noticed me standing there, he remained silent. The look of melancholy on his face was evident. I just couldn't be sure whether it was disappointment in the way our trip had turned out or the fact that he had to leave. As much as I'd ruined things, I just wanted him to stay—forever. I wanted to cuddle with him on the couch tonight, order a pineapple pizza, and fall asleep in his arms. I wasn't ready to share him with the world again.

"I'm sorry that you have to go when things are so up in the air between us," I finally said.

He stood from the bed and walked toward me.

His eyes looked tired when he said, "Nothing is up in the air from my point of view. I've got a lot of fight in me, Luca. I'm here for the long haul if you want me to be. But in the end, regardless of what I might have said about not letting you leave me, I can't *force* you to do anything. That's the one thing I can't do." He wiped a tear from my cheek. "It will never be perfect. It will never *not* be scary. So if you're waiting for this to not feel terrifying, it never will. There will be hard times. But there will be amazing ones, too. You have to decide whether we're worth the hardships. In the end, it's going to come down to one thing: whether love is enough."

"I do love you so much," I blurted through my tears.

"I know you do." Griffin kissed the top of my head and repeated, "I know you do."

The sound of a car beeping resonated.

He closed his eyes. "Shit. That's my ride."

I gripped his shirt. "Damn it. Not yet."

"Figures the bloody Uber would be right on time."

Griffin brought me into him and squeezed me hard. I felt the weight of a thousand words in that hug.

"Please call me when you land," I said.

"I will."

He finally planted a long kiss on my lips before ripping himself away. "I can't do long goodbyes. They suck. So I'm gonna slip out."

"Me neither. I hate them."

Rolling his suitcase, he started walking toward the door when he stopped and turned around to face me. "In case I wasn't clear, love *is* enough for me, Luca. But you have to *let* me love you."

The days after Griffin left felt strange to say the least. My life seemed emptier than it ever had. Having him with me for that extended period of time had made me realize how alone I'd really been for so long. It had felt so good to have him around, to feel so protected.

I'd finally made it to the grocery store for my first overnight shopping trip since the time Griffin had accompanied me. This place now reminded me of him. As I perused the aisles, I'd remember things we spoke about the one time we were here together or remember items he'd dumped into the cart as I spotted them on the shelves.

Melons: Griffin.

Fruity Pebbles: Griffin.

Doritos: Griffin.

Daydreaming, I leaned against the cart and pushed it slowly, nearly missing a broken jar of tomato sauce by my feet in aisle eleven.

It took longer than usual to make it around the entire market. I finally arrived at the register.

Doris beamed when she spotted me. "Well, well, well. I've been waiting to see you. Someone has a lot of explaining to do!"

I cringed, not wanting to get into Griffin right now.

"Hey, Doris," I said, beginning to unload my cart.

"Long time no see." She started to scan my items while shaking her head. "You and Cole Archer. I still can't wrap my head around it."

"Believe me, even *I* haven't fully wrapped my head around it."

"Is he still staying with you? Where is he?" she asked, eyes wide.

"He's on tour, actually. A dozen cities around the United States."

"When will you see him again?"

"I'm not sure," I answered truthfully.

"I want you to know that I didn't tell a soul he was in Vermont. I didn't want to make trouble for you."

"Thank you. I appreciate that."

"My niece would have shit a brick if she knew. I didn't risk it, because she has a big mouth. Someday I'll tell her." She snickered. "She's gonna kill me."

I nodded silently.

She picked up on my worried vibe. "Is everything okay with you two?"

Should I be honest with her? Heck, there were so few people I even talked to on a regular basis. Doc and Doris were pretty much it. I decided to open up a little.

"I'm not sure if it's going to work out. You know about . . . my issues . . . Well, some things happened while I went away with him, and let's just say . . . it really brought home how difficult it would be to make it work."

She stopped scanning. "Wait a second . . . you're not considering breaking up with him?" When I didn't say anything, she drew her own conclusion. "Luca . . . that boy loves you. He *loves* you. You can't do this to me."

To *her*? Was I hearing her correctly?

"To *you*?"

"Yes. I haven't been able to stop thinking about that speech he gave the night he was here with you. It gave me hope that dreams really can come true, things beyond our wildest imagination. I mean, how does sheltered little Luca living in the boonies of Vermont end up with a superstar? And he turns out to be her childhood pen pal? That is the stuff fairy tales are made of, Luca. And it's your life. Your freaking life! Please don't throw this away because of fear. You'll never get it back. And it's . . . magic. Pure magic."

Magic. That was exactly what I needed at this point. I wished I had a magic wand to erase all of my fears.

Doris had stars in her eyes. I didn't want to burst her bubble any further. At the same time, I couldn't take her advice seriously. She was too starstruck and blinded by her awe of the whole situation.

"I appreciate the advice, Doris. I promise to take it into consideration."

"I'll be pushing for ya. Don't you let that boy go and make beautiful babies with someone else."

That comment really hit me where it hurt. It upset me for multiple reasons. The thought of Griffin with anyone else, let alone "making babies" with that person, was a tough pill to swallow. But that would be the reality if I chose to let him go. I'd have to see it all play out in the media, and it would kill me. The other thing was . . . what kind of mother would I make if I couldn't take my child all the places they wanted to go? What if my kid wanted to see Disney or attend some event held in an arena? I wouldn't be able to take him. I shook my head to rid myself of the thoughts.

As I helped Doris bag my groceries, my mood lightened, and I took a moment to reflect on Griffin's declaration of love that had taken place right here at this very register. It had to easily be the most romantic thing ever to happen at a supermarket in the middle of the night.

CHAPTER 27

LUCA

The following day, I went to check my PO box and found the last thing I ever expected: a letter from Griffin.

He wrote me a letter?

To say I was perplexed would be an understatement. I thought the days of receiving his letters were over. He'd called me every day whenever he could from the road, so this was definitely a surprise.

As I held the envelope in my hands, that old familiar excitement ran through me. I'd forgotten how much I missed this feeling of anticipation. It took me aback to realize it was still there. After all, this whole thing with Griffin had been a whirlwind. Everything had happened so fast since California. It still seemed like just yesterday that all we had were the letters.

I raced back to my car to open it.

Dear Luca,
Greetings from a dark tour bus somewhere off I-95 in Bumfuck, Virginia. The guys are off doing what they do, and I've locked myself in a bunk for some peace. You'd think it would be miserable in this tiny space, but it's bigger than you'd think—they call it a "condo"

bunk. And it's nice and quiet in here. It's perfect for working on new lyrics. The movement of the bus actually rocks me to sleep most nights.

I have a bed and a telly in here and oddly, that's all I really need. Wait. No. Far from all I need. The one thing I'm missing is you. I know we've been talking to each other every day, but those calls are too rushed. And that's my fault. It's usually too late to call by the time things have calmed down for me. But such is tour life.

Today's performance in DC was exhausting. It's amazing how I can look out into the audience at thousands of adoring faces screaming my name and not have it faze me in the least. I've become so jaded in that respect, and it's a little disappointing. Not to mention, it's fucking hard to sing "Luca" now. And it's always the one everyone wants to hear. I keep wanting to change the words. Because there's just so much more to the story now, isn't there? If they only knew. Anyway, I need to stop complaining about my job, because I'm really fucking lucky to have it, and I know that. I don't mean to sound ungrateful.

I just wish you were here. That's all. I told myself this letter was going to be light and fun—bring back the old vibe. Guess I already ruined that one, eh? I miss our pizza nights. I miss food shopping with you. Fuck, I even miss Hortencia. (I refused bacon at breakfast yesterday. Now that's true love.)

Anyway . . . I miss you.

I heard an ABBA song today and thought of you. It was fucking depressing. "One of Us," it was called. Listen to the words. You'll know what I mean.

Also, "Knowing Me, Knowing You," this letter will hopefully lead to more correspondence. I can only hope that my "Dancing Queen" takes a hint and writes me back. The only question is . . . how the fuck will you get a letter to me? "Mamma Mia," what a conundrum. Take it as a challenge. How does one receive letters on the road? I don't care how you do it, just "Gimme! Gimme! Gimme!" Figure out how to get me your letter. You have my schedule. I challenge you. "I Have a Dream" that you'll find a way to do it.

Could I BE any more annoying using ABBA songs to communicate with you? (There's our friend Chandler Bing again.)

God, I'm tired. And wired. And have I mentioned that I miss you?

Later, gator,
Griff
Actually . . .

LOVE,
Griffin

P.S. "I Do, I Do, I Do, I Do, I Do" is the answer. The question is, does Griffin love Luca very much?

P.P.S. I dare you to correspond in your next letter incorporating the ABBA songs I didn't use. Let's see who does it better. "The Winner Takes It All." (Another one you can't use.)

P.P.P.S. A little ABBA trivia for you. What's the song "Super Trouper" about? I looked it up and it's eerie how much it mirrors my life right now.

Well, he'd done it. He'd managed to make me smile. Leave it to Griffin.

I clutched the letter to my chest before reading it a couple of more times.

Griffin had given me his entire tour schedule with a special number for the tour manager in case I needed to reach him in an emergency. If I planned this wisely, I could have my letter delivered to one of the venues. That's what I'd do. I'd call the manager and figure out how to get a letter to Griffin like he'd asked. That meant I had to accept his ABBA challenge, too.

◆ ◆ ◆

It felt like old times as I settled into my couch later that night and started to write back to him. Talk about déjà vu.

> Dear Griffin,
> Wow. I learn something new from you every day. I'd never really paid attention to the lyrics of "Super Trouper." Some believe that song is about how challenging stardom is. The part that really got to me is when they sing about loneliness despite having all those fans. And how stardom doesn't take away the longing for that one person. Shit. It's like it mirrored exactly what you said in your letter to me.
> I have this fantasy of cuddling next to you at night in your little bunk. In my dreams, there's no light, but we don't need it. It's just you and me and the sound of the road. I think about that a lot. My heart is on that bus with you. Please know that.
> Anyway, "Honey Honey," I'm trying to catch myself before this letter gets too emotional or sad.

Because our letters have always been about lifting each other up. (Even when we're letting each other down.) Lifting each other up should be "The Name of the Game," but I guess I can't help it. The emotional side of things is winning out tonight.

"The Day Before You Came" to stay with me, I couldn't have imagined how much having you here would change the way I see my world without you in it. Now that you've come and gone, I see how much brighter things really are when you're by my side. "When All Is Said and Done," I am finding it really hard to live without you. But I'm no closer to a conclusion on how this could possibly work between us long-term. I don't know if it's too much to ask you to "Take a Chance on Me" when I might fail you. I just don't have the right answer. All I really want is for you to continue to "Lay All Your Love on Me," but I'm scared and sending out an "SOS" to the universe to help lead me in the right direction.

God, I totally flubbed up making that fun. It turned out to be a rambling, depressing diatribe about my insecurities mixed in with a bunch of ABBA songs. But do I at least get points for incorporating them like you asked?

Anyway, I miss you, too. So much. Which was the city that you said would have a live feed of the concert I'd be able to watch? I think you mentioned it was toward the end of the tour? I can't wait to watch you live, Griffin. Even though I should be there in person, please know that I'm so proud of you, how you get up there and perform even when you're feeling down. That takes a lot. And I know I'm the cause of some of the thoughts that might be bringing you down lately. I want to change that so badly. But I have to change *me*. And that's always been hard.

I love you.
Luca
P.S. "Hasta Mañana." (Figured I'd get one more in.)

◆ ◆ ◆

A few days later, the phone rang in the middle of the afternoon. My heart sped up upon recognizing it was Griffin.

I picked up. "Hey!"

"You did good, baby. They delivered the letter to my dressing room at The Palladium. I knew you'd come through."

My heart fluttered. "I'm so glad it got to you. I was really worried that it would get lost or just miss you, and then I'd have to figure out a way to get it to the next place."

"Nope, it was perfect." He hesitated. "Listen, I don't have that much time, because they're calling me for a sound check, but I wanted to give you a heads-up about something. I figured you wouldn't know about it if you're still following through on your vow not to Google me."

My stomach dropped. *What do I not know about?*

"Okay . . ."

"They posted some photos on a celebrity website of us vacating the hotel in Chicago during the fire alarm."

I breathed out a sigh of relief. "I see."

"I know you sometimes read the tabloids in the supermarket, and I don't yet know if any of those photos ended up in any of the magazines as well, but I wanted to warn you in case you happened to see it."

"It's okay . . . Believe it or not, it doesn't really bother me to be photographed. I mean, it's intrusive and not ideal, but it doesn't make me panic or anything."

"Well, that's a relief, because that trip was hard enough without that moment having to live in infamy."

"It's okay. Don't worry about the photos."

He sighed into the phone, and I could sense his own relief. I had to pick my battles. With enough going against me when it came to our relationship, the least I could do was let the photos slide.

"I'm still shocked they haven't figured out your identity. If they were to find out your name was Luca, all hell would break loose. I could only imagine the headlines." He fell silent for a moment before he changed the subject. "Speaking of tabloids, I called my father today."

That surprised me. "Really . . . ?"

"Yes. I don't know what possessed me. I guess I felt like it was time. He wants me to come to London for a visit. He seemed apologetic about what he'd done and wants to make amends."

"That's great, Griff."

"Yeah. I have to tread lightly, though. I don't want to get hurt again."

"I understand."

Hearing him say that broke my heart a little. I didn't want to *be* the one to hurt him.

I heard someone call his name, and then he finally said, "Shit. I have to go."

"Go. Get ready for the show. Thank you for calling."

"I love you, Luca."

"I love you, too."

CHAPTER 28

GRIFFIN

A little girl caught my attention as I walked to the stadium door. I backed up and motioned to my security that I needed a minute. They hated when I ventured into the crowd, but I couldn't resist going over to say hello. A few dozen fans yelled from behind wooden barricades that lined the walkway between where we'd pulled up and the entrance to tonight's venue. One little angelic face happened to look a hell of a lot like Luca.

I bent down to her level. "Hey there. What's your name?"

She was probably only six or seven years old and really could have passed for Luca's daughter with her long, dark hair; giant green eyes; and thick black eyelashes.

"Frankie."

"Frankie, huh? That's a cool name. Is it short for something?"

She nodded. "Francine."

Her mum interrupted. "She knows every word of all your songs. Seriously, we thought of writing to you to ask you to sing the multiplication tables for her."

I smiled. "Is that so, Frankie? You like my music, huh?"

She nodded her adorable little head rapidly.

"Do you think you can sing me something? What's your favorite?"

"'I Stand Still.'"

Wow. That was sort of a heavy song for a little girl. Most people assumed I'd written it for a girl I'd been hung up on, but in actuality it was written for my mum. It was a slow solo ballad, and the lyrics talked about how I didn't realize how important she was in my life until she was gone. "Can you sing me a little bit?"

The little girl looked at her mum, who prompted her. "Go ahead, sweetheart. It's okay."

Frankie looked nervous, so I figured I'd help her out. "I'll tell you what . . . how about if I start, and you can join in when you're ready?"

She nodded.

Softly, I began to sing the first verse. By the end of the first sentence, little Frankie started to rock back and forth with the biggest smile plastered on her face. She was really freaking adorable. I could easily imagine Luca and I might have a little girl who looked a lot like her. So I just kept singing. When I got to the end of the first verse, I stopped. "You ready to join me yet?"

Frankie nodded again. This time, when I started singing, she joined right in. My brows jumped hearing how pretty her voice was. I didn't know why, but I hadn't expected she could really sing. Her voice was tiny, but she sang in perfect pitch and had the sweetest sound I'd heard in a long time. I lowered my own voice to hear more of hers, and she kept going. Eventually, I stopped singing altogether and just watched her take it away.

The resemblance to Luca was really uncanny, and I thought my girl might get a kick out of seeing Frankie sing, too. So I dug my phone out of my pocket and motioned to her mum that I'd like to record and got her blessing. I seriously couldn't have conjured up a better part of any song to capture on video to send to Luca than what unfolded as I pressed "Record."

Since the day that you left

I felt a hole in my heart.
Going through the motions
Through the window I thrive
But behind the curtain I only survive

I hit the button to turn the camera around to face me and leaned in to join little Frankie for the chorus while holding my arm out to keep recording.

The world keeps spinning without you.
The world keeps spinning round and round.
The world keeps spinning, but I stand still
I stand still
I stand still

When I was done, the crowd around us started to applaud. I put out my hand to shake little Frankie's and then kissed the top of her hand before kissing her mum's cheek.

"You stay right here," I said. "I'm going to send my manager back out in a few minutes to get you some backstage passes so you can meet the rest of my mates and see the concert from the first row."

"Oh my God!" Frankie's mum covered her mouth. "Thank you so much."

"No, thank you for sharing your daughter with me today."

I signed a few autographs on my way to the entrance and then located my manager to go run out and make sure Frankie got some VIP treatment. Since the sound check I'd come early to run through wasn't ready for me yet, I headed to my dressing room and sat down to play back the video I'd recorded.

Watching it made me realize how much being with Luca had really changed things for me. I used to get a high walking into a concert venue filled with screaming fans, but now I got that same feeling thinking about having a little girl with Luca someday. Money and fame couldn't buy happiness, and I was starting to think I'd trade thousands of women wearing my face on their chests for one woman resting *her face* on my chest at night. That was pretty fucked up.

But my Luca had had a tough few days. She and Doc had ventured out to get Hortencia some food, and she'd had a meltdown in the store. Apparently she'd had an easier time with little outings like that before our incident in Chicago, so she'd been feeling particularly defeated lately. The video was the perfect message to cheer her up.

Or so I thought.

I typed a text out before attaching the video.

Griffin: This little beauty's name is Frankie. She looks just like I picture our own little girl might look. Frankie picked the song to sing, but the words couldn't be more fitting for how I feel without you by my side, love. I stand still. The world keeps spinning, but I stand still without you. XO Call you after the show tonight.

I hit "Send" just as the sound tech knocked on my door. "Ready when you are, Cole."

"Sounds good. Be out in a minute. Just waiting to hear back from my girl."

I watched as the message went from "Sent" to "Delivered" to "Read."

The video was probably a minute or two long, so I didn't expect an immediate response. Though after ten minutes, I didn't want to keep the team waiting too much longer. So I headed out to the stage. I checked my phone one last time before we started.

Still nothing.

Luca must've been busy writing. I knew how I got when I was in the middle of composing a song. Sometimes I'd go into my own little bubble, and making any outside contact would pop it. I figured I'd hear back from her by the time the sound check was done.

Though I figured wrong.

◆ ◆ ◆

"What the fuck, Luca?"

I paced back and forth in my hotel room after hitting "Redial" for the tenth time. Luca hadn't written back by the time my sound check ended. She also hadn't written back by the time the concert had started, either. When I still hadn't heard from her after the show ended, I started to worry. So I'd sent her a text to check in. Just like the video I'd sent, she'd read it but sent nothing in response. I also left her a few voice messages.

Could I have upset her with that video I'd sent earlier? Was there something on there that would have made her get angry or sad? I didn't think so, but just to be sure, I played it back twice and reread the text that I'd sent along with it. As far as I could see, the messages were only a sweet reminder to Luca that I'd been thinking about her.

Since nothing should have upset her, it made my mind wander to even worse scenarios. I started to get nervous that something might've happened to her. Of course the worst shit ran through my mind.

Someone broke in and she's lying there unconscious.

Yet my texts were being read. I supposed the intruder could be reading them. Though that seemed ridiculous for even my vivid imagination.

She fell and hit her head.

Again, was she lying there reading her texts while gushing blood?

Unfortunately, there was only one thing that made sense.

Her last few tough days were weighing heavily on her, and she didn't want to talk to me.

A sense of déjà vu hit me. I knew this feeling. Eight years ago I'd felt an overwhelming sense of dread when I went to the mailbox every day and found no letter from Luca. We might've changed our mode of communication, but my gut told me the same shit was about to go down—my girl was starting to pull away from me.

The next morning, we had to leave by eight in order to get to our next stop. I was exhausted as shit, because when I finally fell asleep last night, I woke up every half hour to check my phone for a text from Luca. None ever came.

Clinging to a last-ditch hope that maybe she'd fallen asleep early yesterday and then slept in today, I waited until we stopped for our first gas fill-up, and the guys hopped off the bus to get some breakfast, to call in the big guns.

"Hello."

"Hey. It's Griffin. I'm sorry to bother you, Doc. But I'm worried about Luca. She's not answering her cell—not text or calls."

Doc sighed into the phone. "This is a difficult situation for me, son. I have doctor-patient confidentiality with Luca. Yet I care about her."

Fuck, I was afraid he'd say that. "Can you just tell me if she's okay? When was the last time you saw her?"

"I was with her this morning for an hour."

I felt relieved she was okay, but my chest physically ached confirming she just didn't want to talk to me. "She's okay? She's not physically harmed or anything?"

"She's physically okay. You shouldn't worry about that."

I felt so damn helpless this far away. "I know you can't talk about her issues. But I don't know what to do. I'm on the road, and I can't get there right now. Can you tell me how I should handle someone who has some extreme fears? What would you tell a husband or a wife who came to you for advice on how to manage someone with extreme anxiety who's distancing themselves?"

"I'd tell them that it's not possible to manage someone with extreme anxiety. You can support them and love them, but you're going to need lots of patience if you're in this for the long haul. When someone cuts open a leg, the doctor stitches it up—but it still takes a long time for it to fully heal. Even after months pass, there's a scar. And long after that scar fades, if you hit that skin where the wound was, it will break open easier than other areas. Anxiety is no different."

I exhaled. "Yeah. Okay."

"Have patience, Griffin. I know that's easier said than done, but I don't think I'm breaking doctor-patient confidentiality when I say that Luca loves you. They say that time heals all wounds, but I think when the wound stems from a broken heart, love is equally as important."

I nodded and swallowed. "Thanks, Doc."

After hanging up, I sat around thinking for a while. Luca was physically okay and had Doc. I knew she was struggling and wished there was something I could do to make her better. But if time was what she needed, then I had no choice but to give her a little space and let her know I wasn't going anywhere.

She'd been reading all my texts, so I composed one more.

Griffin: Hey, beautiful. I just wanted you to know I'm thinking of you today. I'm going to give you a little breathing space, rather than call and text a million times and add stress to everything you're going through. I'm here if you need me, and I have faith in what we have. Take care of yourself, baby.

I tossed the phone on my cubby bed and lay back with one arm covering my eyes. I was shocked to hear my phone ding a minute later.

Luca: Thank you. You take care, too, Griffin.

CHAPTER 29

LUCA

I picked up the framed photo on my nightstand, the one I'd taken out of my drawer a few days ago, and ran my finger along Isabella's face.

"Hey, Izzy. I'm sorry I put you away for so long. It's not that I didn't want to see you. Trust me. I love your smiling face. It's just . . . it's hard, you know? Remember when you went out with Tommy Nystrom our sophomore year? You guys were so cute together. Then his dad got relocated for work, and he moved to Arizona. You had pictures of you two together all over your room. And you were so sad for months after he left. I talked you into taking them down and within two weeks you met Andrew Harding. It wasn't that you didn't like Tommy anymore—he just wasn't there, and the constant reminder was making you sad. Well, that's sort of like why I had to put away your pictures. I didn't put them away so that I can meet a new best friend, just the same as you didn't put Tommy's photo away looking for a new boyfriend. But sometimes we need to stop living in the past to allow ourselves to be happy."

I didn't realize tears had been rolling down my face until one hit the glass of the frame in my hand. Wiping them away, I set the photo back onto my nightstand. The last week had been brutal. When we first got back home from Chicago, I was okay. Sad because I didn't think Griffin and I would make it, but the situation I'd experienced with the fire alarm really hadn't hit me. *Until it did.* A few days later, I woke up in the middle of the night hyperventilating. I'd heard fire alarms blaring so vividly that I ran out of the house in a panic at two in the morning. It took a solid twenty minutes to talk myself into going back inside, even after I realized that no alarm had really gone off. Things started to spiral out of control after that—a meltdown in the pet store, profuse sweating while trying to write, and a constant feeling that something bad was looming. On top of that, fear of having another vivid nightmare had turned me into an insomniac.

Doc said my delayed physiological response was a form of post-traumatic stress disorder. We spent a few days talking about the night of the concert, something we hadn't actually done in a few years. Yesterday he'd had me write down the details of what happened that night. The process was supposed to help examine the way I thought about the trauma so that we could come up with a new way to live with it. Basically, I'd taken a step back in my therapy—and it felt about *three years* back in time.

The one good thing was that writing about the events of the fire made me want to remember the good times with Izzy, too. So today I'd dug out my storage box from the attic and gone through some of my keepsakes. There were birthday cards, photos, videos of us acting silly together, and even a sketch of a tattoo that Isabella had wanted us both to get of the sun, moon, and stars.

I took my yearbook out from the box and turned the pages until I got to her photo. She was so pretty and smiling so brightly. The universe hadn't given her an inkling of what was coming when that photo was taken. I was just about to put the book back into the box when it slipped from my hands and landed upside down with the inside cover open. Isabella's handwriting was splashed all over the pages. I'd forgotten about the long letter she'd written inside my yearbook.

Dear Luca,

They say your two best friends are supposed to write inside the front and back covers of your yearbooks. I want you to know that my back cover will remain blank. Because I only have one very best friend in the world and that's you, Luca Vinetti.

It feels like yesterday that it was the first day of kindergarten and we met. I stood at the bus stop waiting for the school bus to come. Man, was I shitting a pickle. I mean, what if everyone hated me? What if I couldn't make any friends? What if everyone thought I was a weirdo?

Now, granted, that summer I'd been very frustrated with the big cowlick that always stuck up on the right side of the front of my hair, and I'd had the bright idea that if I cut it off at the base of the roots, no one would notice. So I was waiting for that bus while missing a good chunk of hair on one side of my head. Basically, I was a weirdo, so any of our classmates would have had a damn good reason to keep away.

Anyway, I got on that bus wearing a big cowboy hat, thinking no one would notice my hair if I rocked my cool new style. The only problem was, cowboy hats were totally uncool and all the kids started making fun of me. Telling them my father was a farmer—in Manhattan—didn't exactly help my situation. But you got up from your seat and walked over and sat down next to me. You told me to ignore them, though I couldn't. That day was absolutely horrible, and I dreaded going back on Tuesday. Until I got on the bus and saw you sitting there with an ear-to-ear smile—wearing a big old cowboy hat. That's when I realized that I was a weirdo, but my new best friend loved me anyway.

Yearbooks are supposed to be about reminding people of all the good times you've shared. Since there aren't enough pages in this book to begin to put a dent in our memories, I'm going to tell you the reasons I love you, instead.

You always laugh at my bad jokes.

You're the kindest person I know.

You taught me to follow my dreams by watching you chase your own down.

You can't wait to wake up tomorrow to experience life.

You always have a smile on your face.

You're fearless.

The last twelve years were a blast, but it's only the beginning for us. You're going to conquer the world, Luca Vinetti. We may be going off to college a thousand miles apart, but no matter how much distance life puts between us, I'll always be rooting for you.

Your BF Forever,

Izzy

Griffin: Morning, my beautiful girl. Why did the sperm cross the road?

A few seconds later, a second text came in.

Griffin: Because I put on the wrong sock this morning.

I don't know why, but the joke sent me into a fit of laughter. Maybe it was maniacal, I'm not sure, but it felt like I needed it. Griffin had been texting me twice daily over the last week, since I'd been avoiding him. Each morning he'd send me a joke, and each evening he'd let me know the various ways he'd thought of me throughout the day. I sometimes texted back, but it was nothing more than a gratuitous thank-you or lame smiley face. It wasn't because I didn't want to have contact with him; it was because I didn't know what to say. I was ashamed of how I'd spiraled into a dark place, and I also didn't know how to talk to him about us—where we were. So I'd done the immature thing and pulled away without explanation.

I reread his text and couldn't help but laugh at the joke a second time. In my head, I pictured him *actually* putting on a crusty sock. Then I remembered Izzy's letter from the yearbook that I'd read yesterday.

You always laugh at my bad jokes.

I did have a penchant for really bad jokes. She was right about that. But the rest of the stuff, I wasn't so sure.

You're fearless.

God, had I really been fearless once? Because I couldn't remember a time when I lived without fear.

You can't wait to wake up tomorrow to experience life.

Experience *life.* I'd created a world that was just about as far away from real *life* as it could be. I lived in the middle of nowhere, wrote about characters who were figments of my imagination, and often the only person I spoke to during the day was Hortencia.

We may be going off to college a thousand miles apart, but no matter how much distance life puts between us, I'll always be rooting for you.

She couldn't possibly have known just how much distance would wind up between us, but for some reason, today I felt like she *was* rooting for me. I felt her presence more than ever, only today, it gave me a little courage. So I decided to type back to Griff.

Luca: What do tofu and a dildo have in common?

He responded two seconds later.

Griffin: What?

Luca: They're both meat substitutes.

Griffin: LOL. What do you call a twenty-five-year-old rock star who doesn't masturbate when he hasn't seen his girl for two full weeks?

Luca: What?

Griffin: A liar.

I laughed out loud again.

Luca: What do you call a truck full of dildos?

Griffin: What?

Luca: Toys for Twats.

Griffin: Okay, that one just made me spit water through my nose.

It was the first time I'd had a smile on my face in two weeks. I looked over at the photo still on my nightstand. "Thanks, Izzy."

Taking a deep breath, I moved my finger up over Griffin's name and hit "Call" instead of texting him.

He answered on the first ring.

"Hey."

"Hey. Are you busy? I needed to hear your voice."

"I'm never too busy for you, love."

CHAPTER 30

GRIFFIN

The light mood of our conversation quickly changed. "I'm sorry I've been so distant lately," she said. "I feel like I've taken a few steps back since you left."

I hated that she felt guilty for anything. "You never have to apologize for how you feel. You know I accept you as you are. You're not required to act or feel a certain way. But I *do* need you to respond at some point to my messages so that I know you're okay."

"I'm sorry if I worried you at all."

An inexplicable feeling of dread filled me.

"Luca . . . ," I said, "tell me what's on your mind. Please."

After the longest moment of silence ever, she finally said, "I don't want to hold you back anymore, Griffin."

"You're not holding me back . . . I—"

"You say that because you love me, but the truth is . . . I *am* and I just . . . I can't . . ."

She can't.

My heart began to race. "Can't what? Say it, Luca. I need to hear it." My tone was bordering on angry. "You need to be very clear here. *Very* clear."

"I can't be the person you need," she finally said. "At least not right now. I feel this pressure to get over my fears at a pace that's just not realistic. I keep feeling like I'm holding up your life . . . and I feel like that pressure is too much to bear. It's weighing me down and I . . . can't breathe anymore."

Fuck. This was really happening.

I was really losing her.

I felt helpless.

How could I even attempt to fight for her if she was telling me that the fight was suffocating her? I always told myself I'd know if I needed to let her go—if it ever got to that point where it felt like being together was doing her more harm than good. Even though ending things didn't feel natural, it felt like I had no choice but to listen to her.

"You want to break up? Is that what you're telling me, Luca? I need you to be clear with me."

Her voice was shaky. "I think that's for the best right now. I *do* think we should break up." She let out a breath that sounded like she'd been holding it in.

Well, it couldn't get any clearer than that. I *heard* the words, but I still couldn't believe them.

"Okay." I swallowed. "How do we handle things? Does this mean we don't talk anymore?"

I could hear her crying on the other end, and I suspected that was because the reality of what she'd just done had hit her. Me, on the other hand? I was just numb . . . still not wanting to believe what she was telling me.

"I don't know," she answered. "I don't know what would be best. Because hearing from you would be painful and not hearing from you would be even more painful."

More anger was slowly creeping in. I was so disappointed at life—at her. At everything.

"Why don't we just take it one day at a time. I haven't even begun to process this. But I heard you loud and clear, Luca. Okay? I heard you loud and clear."

Things went quiet again, and then she muttered, "I'm so sorry, Griffin."

"I'm sorry, too, love. I really am. More than you could ever know."

◆ ◆ ◆

I'd never canceled a show in my entire career. But I just couldn't perform that night in Minneapolis. I'd faked a flu-like illness and created a shit storm of a logistical nightmare for my tour manager and publicist. But it didn't matter. Nothing mattered. Tomorrow I knew I would somehow pick myself up to perform in the next city, but I needed tonight to mourn. This was my first time playing the sick card; I'd earned this breakdown.

It took everything in me not to call Luca and check on her. Every hour, I found my finger hovering over her name in my text messages. Eventually, I opted to call Doc instead. At least, through him, I could make sure she was okay without upsetting her. I wasn't even certain she'd told him that she'd broken up with me.

He answered. "Hello?"

"Doc. It's Griffin."

"Oh . . . Griffin. Is everything okay?"

The words just wouldn't come out. For the first time since I could remember, perhaps when Mum died, I felt tears forming in my eyes. It was bound to happen, I supposed. Even though I wasn't saying anything, he could clearly surmise that something was wrong.

"Tell me what happened, son. Is it Luca?"

"She ended things earlier today."

His breath hitched.

Wiping my eyes and fighting the damn tears, I continued. "I wanted to let you know in case she hadn't told you yet, so that you can look out for her and make sure she's okay. Because I know it wasn't easy for her."

"I'm sorry to hear this. I really am. I know how hard you've tried to make her happy and to make things work."

"It wasn't hard enough, apparently."

"I've never witnessed anyone work harder to save a relationship, Griffin. You did everything you could. Luca is just not ready, as much as she wishes she could be—as much as I know she truly loves you."

"I know she loves me . . . as much as she could love anyone. That's why it hurts to have to accept this. I'm hurting not only for myself but because I somehow know she's hurting even more. I know this wasn't easy for her . . . to let me go."

"No, I can only imagine," he said. "I'm glad you told me, because I hadn't heard from her all day, and now I know why."

"I canceled my show tonight, Doc. Thousands of people paid to come see me, and I stood them up because I couldn't bear to sing when I feel so destroyed inside." I exhaled. "You know I wrote a song about her, back when I was angry at her before we reunited. Did she ever tell you that?"

"Oh yes. I've listened to it several times."

I don't know why that made me laugh a little. I couldn't picture Doc listening to my music for some reason.

"Yeah. That song is always hard to sing, but I don't think the words would even be able to come out tonight. They'd better somehow find their way out in the next city, because I can't afford to cancel again."

"It's perfectly acceptable to exercise self-care from time to time. Don't worry about the fans you're letting down. Allow yourself this time to recuperate."

"Jesus. Now I'm wondering if I called you for her . . . or for me."

"Either way is okay by me. You're a good man, Griffin. There's no one else I would rather see my Luca with. I'll let you in on a secret. I may be her doctor . . . but in truth, if I'm being honest . . . she's really like a daughter to me. Our relationship goes far beyond doctor-patient. I wanted nothing more than to see things work out between the two of you, and my heart is heavy knowing both of you are in pain."

"You're a good man, too, Doc. Please take care of her." I raked my fingers through my hair.

"You can count on that." He paused. "Griffin?"

"Yeah . . ."

"Maybe you can put some of the feelings you're experiencing to good use. Perhaps it's time for a new song. I can imagine expressing yourself through your music would be therapeutic for you. Just a thought."

Dismissing his suggestion, I said, "I can't imagine writing music right now. My heart is broken."

"My gut is telling me that you shouldn't count Luca out. I have every confidence that someday she will realize her mistake, but that could be a very long time from now. I don't expect it's fair to ask you to wait."

"I'd wait forever for her if I really felt she'd come around. Right now? I'm too shattered to believe that. Because I never thought she'd actually let me go, Doc. If I'm honest . . . I'm fucking floored."

"Trust in fate, Griffin. Look how far it's gotten you both thus far. Go on with your life, but trust in the fact that if you and Luca are meant to be . . . then someday the same universe that brought you together will work its magic again."

"You've been a good friend, Doc. Not just to Luca, but to me. If there's anything I can ever do for you, please let me know."

◆ ◆ ◆

My original assumption about not being able to write music was wrong. The following two days as we traveled to our next destination—Des Moines—I wrote lyrics and the accompanying music like a madman. It ended up being therapeutic for me, and although much of it was unusable, I had made progress on a song that I planned to perform at our final show if my bandmates could pick it up fast enough.

It was really hard not to call or text Luca, but I just didn't think opening the lines of communication right now would make this any easier. Honestly, a part of me was just still so damn angry that she'd given up on us. I didn't want to take that anger out on her. I'd call her eventually to check in, but I needed more time to let this set in. I'd not only lost my lover, but I'd lost my best friend. Again.

After a dinner break, I reentered the tour bus before we were set to hit the road again. To my shock, there was a girl lying in my bunk, dressed in nothing but lacy panties and a bra.

"Uh . . . what are you doing in here?" I asked.

"Buddy said you might want some company tonight?"

Fuck.

Where had she even come from? Had she been on the bus since Minneapolis? Buddy was my guitarist and the only bandmate I typically confided in. He'd confronted me after the show cancellation, and I eventually admitted what happened. He must have thought that fucking Luca out of my system was the way to go tonight. That wasn't going to be happening. It was way too soon. Maybe there would come a time when it didn't feel like cheating. But at this point in time, my body still felt like it belonged to Luca. And that was fucked up.

"Well, Buddy was wrong. I'd actually really like to be alone, but thank you for thinking of me."

She looked disappointed. "Are you sure?"

"Yeah."

She rolled off the bed and disappeared down into another section of the bus. After she left, we started moving. I shut off the interior light and just crashed.

CHAPTER 31

LUCA

I hadn't gotten a single good night's sleep since ending things with Griffin. I'd have painful thoughts about him drowning his sorrows in women or alcohol. And who could blame him after what I'd done to him? The breakup had put me in a constantly strange mood, one of overall apathy. Without being able to look forward to Griffin's calls, his letters, his voice, his touch, it was as if I didn't care about anything at all anymore, didn't care if the world crumbled around me.

In the midst of it all, though, I'd done something I'd been putting off for years. I'd driven to the nearest tattoo shop and had the sun, moon, and stars tattoo that Isabella had wanted us to get permanently etched onto the inside of my forearm. I'd been "talking" to Izzy more lately and had felt like it was time to finally make that ink a reality.

Doc had just arrived at my house and would be seeing it for the first time.

"I have something to show you," I said as he sat down at the kitchen table.

"Did you finally get around to painting the Atlantic puffin?"

"No. He's still on the back burner, as is all painting at the moment." I rolled up my sleeve and displayed my new skin art. "I got a tattoo."

His eyes widened. "Oh wow."

"Isabella and I designed this together. We'd planned to get matching ones. I hadn't even been able to look at the design, let alone think about getting it, up until recently. I went and had it done a couple of days ago."

Doc tilted his head to examine it. "It's very beautiful. Why do you think you were suddenly able to do it?"

"Everything has felt different since letting Griffin go; maybe it's a side effect of a broken heart. It almost feels like . . . I have nothing to lose anymore."

"Well, permanently marking your skin with a reminder of Isabella is certainly a huge step toward healing and acceptance. I'm quite proud of you."

"Yeah. I agree. I'm proud of me, too." I smiled.

"As for your new outlook after ending things with Griffin, I don't think we ever know how traumatic events will impact us until they happen."

"It's seriously like I just don't care about anything anymore, like I don't care if I live or die."

His expression dampened. "You're not feeling suicidal at all, right? Because, Luca, you need to tell me if that ever happens."

"No. Not suicidal. I could never take my own life. I'd be too scared. It's just a feeling of overall numbness."

"Have you spoken to him?"

"No. I haven't contacted him, and he hasn't contacted me, either. Pretty sure he might hate me right now."

Doc's eyes moved from side to side. He looked a little guilty, like there was something he wasn't telling me.

"What's that look?"

"He doesn't hate you."

"And you know this because?"

"He's called a few times to check on you. He's concerned about you."

"You've spoken to Griffin?"

"He never exactly told me not to tell you. Though I was never sure if I should. But I'm telling you now. Seeing as though you've drawn the wrong conclusion regarding his current attitude toward you, I felt it was necessary."

"Did he say anything else?"

"He mainly just wants to know if you're okay. I tell him what I can without violating our confidentiality."

I didn't know whether Griffin contacting Doc made me feel worse or not. I missed him so incredibly much, but at the same time, a part of me hoped he wasn't hung up on me, that he could move on with his life like he deserved. Yet the bigger part of me was relieved that he didn't hate me, and that he cared enough to check on me. Even in our absence, Griffin *knew* me; he knew contacting me would send me into an emotional tailspin.

"Thank you for keeping him posted. I'm sorry you're stuck in the middle."

"It's no problem, Luca. I consider Griffin a friend. Of course, my allegiance will always be to you, so if you tell me not to speak to him, I won't."

"No. I would never do that."

A part of me wanted to say, "Tell him I love him." But I couldn't.

I don't know what possessed me to check Archer's website that night. I knew the tour would be winding down soon. The site listed all the past locations, and I couldn't help but notice that next to Minneapolis, it said: Canceled. I looked at the date and realized that it was the day I'd ended things. My heart clenched. I wouldn't know for sure, but my gut told me that Griffin was too upset to perform. Given that he was the quintessential professional, that really spoke volumes about what I'd done to him.

I noticed that tomorrow night was the Los Angeles concert. I remembered Griffin saying that there would be a live feed available of that show that could be viewed on the band's website. It was a gift to their fans around the world who couldn't attend one of their concerts. I knew it would be incredibly painful to watch, but a part of me needed to know he was okay. I needed to hear his voice and see his face, even if it killed me. I looked down at the tattoo on my inner forearm. I could hear Izzy's words from her yearbook message. *"You're fearless."* That was her impression of me and had nothing to do with the current reality . . . but I could at least *try* to live up to it occasionally. Watching Griffin tomorrow would be a true test of strength for sure.

◆ ◆ ◆

The following night, my heart had never beat so fast. I wasn't ready for this, but I would never be ready. A message on the site prompted me to click on a box to watch the Los Angeles concert live. I must have been early. It said it was set to start at 8:00 Pacific time, so that meant there were still ten minutes or so to go. My hands were clammy and my knees were bobbing up and down.

The wait seemed like forever until the screen suddenly changed. My heart sped up. The show was about to start. I heard the sound of thousands of people screaming as the lighting changed. Then a camera slowly zoomed in on the stage. There was Griffin sitting on a stool with a spotlight on him. He began to sing a cappella, and it immediately gave me chills. My heart came alive at the sound of his crooning. Then the instruments eventually joined in. It was a song I recognized as being one of their more popular tunes.

An enormous amount of pride built in my chest. *God, you're amazing, Griffin.* His gritty voice never sounded all that much different from the recorded versions of their songs; he was so good live. I found myself totally glued to the screen, captivated by him, as if I were merely a member of the audience. How I longed to be there. How I longed to feel the energy of that room, the heat, the vibration of the music. How I longed to be watching it all from just backstage, to leap into his arms and tell him how proud I was of him when the show was over. My eyes welled with tears. The longer I watched, the more that inexplicable feeling that had been whispering to me lately grew louder. I had described it to Doc as apathy, not caring whether I was living or dead, but now it seemed I understood exactly what it was. *Nothing matters without him.* If someone had asked me a year ago what the worst thing that could happen to me was . . . I would have told them it was having a panic attack and dying. If someone asked me today, my answer would be different. The worst thing to happen to me *had happened.* It was having to live every day knowing Griffin was out there and not being able to experience this life with him. He'd asked me if I believed love was enough, if I would be willing to experience all of the negative things in order to have him in my life. At the time, I truly didn't know the answer. Now . . . it seemed clear to me. Love *is* everything. It matters more than fear, more than death. It transcends time. I would literally do anything to have him back in my life, even if it killed me.

Even if it kills me.

That realization was huge.

To truly overcome any fear, you had to be, at least on some level, willing to die for what was on the other side. I was most definitely willing to die for Griffin.

I didn't know what to do with this revelation.

The beginning notes of "Luca" began to play, and I remembered Griffin telling me how strange it was to sing it after we reunited, since the song had been written out of anger. I was sure it had even more painful feelings associated with it now. The camera focused in on his face, and I noticed him shut his eyes tightly before he began to sing. It was as if he had to gear up for it, to prepare himself to utter those first words and start. I could only imagine what it felt like to have to sing about me over and over when I'd hurt him so much.

He made it through the song, and the crowd went wild. It was evident by how long the applause lasted that "Luca" was their most popular song. He'd always said that, but now I truly got it. He'd often told me that they ended the shows on that one. But it seemed it wasn't the last song tonight.

Griffin returned to the microphone amid the cheers of the crowd and the chanting of "Cole."

His voice echoed through the arena. "I was wondering if you'd be okay with one more song tonight . . ."

The crowd responded by erupting into an even louder series of applause and screaming.

"This one is new . . . never before recorded . . . and possibly never to be sung again. It's called 'You're in Me,' and it's dedicated to my one true love. You know who you are."

My eyes watered.

The crowd went wild.

I struggled to listen to the words as he started to sing.

The day you walked away,
You never really left.
You may not know it.
But you're still here.

You say you're scared . . .
But I'm scared, too,
To live in this world without you.

You can leave, but you'll always be here.
In my heart and soul . . . everywhere.

You're in me.
Till the end,
It will always be you, my friend.

They tell me to move on.
But if I do,
When I look at her, I'll only see you.
You're in me.
Till the end,
It will always be you, my friend.

Even though you've left scars . . .
You're still my sun, moon, and stars.

What?

I didn't hear anything else once he'd sung those words. *My sun, moon, and stars.* The rest of the song was a blur as I sat there frozen, so overcome with emotion. I'd never once mentioned the sun, moon, and stars tattoo to Griffin. He couldn't have known anything, and yet those words were somehow in his heart. I was pretty sure it was because on some level, *he* lived inside mine. Looking down at my tattoo, I knew beyond the shadow of a doubt that this was Izzy sending me the ultimate message of all.

CHAPTER 32

LUCA

Day five and nothing.

I didn't know what I'd expected, but each day I went to my mailbox, finding it empty, made me feel a little more hopeless.

Griffin had poured his heart out in song, so I'd decided to do the same thing in my own way, doing what I did best—writing. I'd stayed up the entire night after the LA concert and let my heart bleed onto paper. I told him I'd been scared and thought it was the right thing to do to let him go, but that I'd finally realized I was more afraid of losing him than any single fear I could possibly have. I feared being trapped in a physical place, but that was nothing compared to living life with my *heart* trapped.

Starting around page fourteen of my rambling letter, I'd also laid out some thoughts on how we might be able to make it work. I'd researched possible places I could live not too far from LA. There were some really nice rural communities within a fifty-mile radius of Los Angeles. I hated to leave Doc, but he'd said we could do video therapy and promised that if I did decide to relocate, that he would visit a few times a year. Last night, he'd even come over with a list of birds recently spotted in the Topanga Canyon area—one of the places I'd mentioned might be a good fit for me out in California. And he and Martha had been chatting about him stopping by again at some point.

But now it was starting to feel like I'd jumped the gun with my planning. I still had Griffin's travel schedule and confirmed that the letter I'd overnighted to his hotel had been personally delivered to him three days ago. When he didn't call or text right away, I refused to believe that he was done with me. So I'd convinced myself that the reason it was taking so long to hear from him was because he wanted to write back to me in a letter. *Talk about clinging to false hopes.* Though now realization had begun to set in that the true reason it was taking so long might actually be because he wasn't planning on responding at all.

And I couldn't blame him. All my mental health issues were enough trouble, but then I'd gone and broken things off. How many times could a man be expected to offer his heart just to have the woman he loved stomp on it? At some point, he'd smarten up and move on, and, unfortunately, I might've driven him to that point the last time I'd pushed him away.

A feeling of melancholy settled in that evening. I didn't have the energy to write or pretty much do anything productive at all, so I ordered Chinese takeout and plopped myself on the couch with a set of chopsticks and a cardboard container in my hands. Hortencia was lying on her bed across the room and looked over at my unshowered ass and seemed to shake her head and sigh.

"Yeah. I know. But what can I tell you? There are days you don't smell so pretty yourself."

Great. Now I was talking to a dead girl and arguing with a pig.

Flicking on the television, I mindlessly pushed the "Channel" button, looking for something to watch. Where were all the tearjerker movies when you needed them? *Dear John*, *A Dog's Purpose*, maybe *Me Before You*. Nothing seemed to be on but the news and reality TV. Giving up, I tossed the remote on the couch next to me and dug into my container to wallow in food.

My mouth was stuffed so full that I nearly choked hearing the name Cole Archer on the television. I looked up and my stomach did a flip seeing Griffin's handsome face on the screen.

"It's good to see you," the reporter said.

"Good to see you, too, Maryanne."

Griffin and some pretty dark-haired reporter with big eyes were standing in front of a stadium. A bunch of teenage girls and women were in the background shouting his name. Maryanne glanced back at them. "Looks like your fans are excited for the last show of your tour tonight."

He flashed a dimpled grin at the crowd and waved. "I'm just as excited as they are for tonight."

God, so much emotion came over me seeing his smile—excitement, sadness, *longing*.

"So Cole . . . you unveiled a new song to the world a few nights ago. Can you tell us about it? Who is this mystery woman, and how long have you two been together?"

I held my breath and stared at the TV. My heart started to hammer inside my chest but then stopped when the smile on Griff's face fell. "There is no woman, really. She was just a figment of my imagination."

"So you're not in a relationship with someone named Luca, then?"

Griff looked away. He shook his head. "Sometimes when you want to believe someone exists badly enough, you make up an entire fantasy about a relationship in your head. That's all it was."

It felt like someone had kicked me in the stomach. *Oh God, Griffin. What we have is real. I swear.*

Maryanne looked at the camera and smiled. "You heard it here first, ladies. There is *no Luca*. Which means we still have one very eligible bachelor, Seattle."

The woman kissed Griff on the cheek, and he walked toward the entrance to the stadium without looking back.

I stared at the television as the enormity of what had just transpired kicked in. Tears started to stream down my face. I'd really lost him.

Accepting that Griffin and I were over was a lot like losing Izzy. I went through the different stages of loss. I'd wake up each morning thinking it was a bad dream—*denial*. Then it would hit me that I'd really lost him, and the pain would come back with a vengeance. I knew I'd wavered back and forth about our relationship, but by midafternoon the fact that he hadn't answered my letter made me *angry*. I'd believed him when he said he loved me—that he'd give me time and would be there waiting if things changed. I guess I hadn't realized that *time . . .* was limited to two weeks. By evening, I was scooping mint–chocolate chip ice cream directly from the half-gallon container to eat away my sadness—*depression*. Then when I couldn't fall asleep, I'd lie in bed staring up at the ceiling for hours cooking up a crazy scheme to get him to change his mind—*bargaining*. The last stage—*acceptance*—had taken me eight years to arrive at for Izzy, and I felt like this one could take longer.

Doc came over for our morning therapy session, and my tired ass was dragging. I had to force myself to get dressed for our walk in the woods but figured some fresh air would do me good. "Have you heard from Griff?" I asked, unable to hide the hopefulness in my voice.

He frowned and shook his head. "I'm sorry, Luca, I haven't."

"But you'd tell me if you had, right?"

"Yes, I'd tell you."

It wasn't like I was sitting around waiting for Griff to call or return my letter anymore—eight days had now passed since he'd received my heart on a platter, and three since he'd told the world there was no Luca. Yet I still held out some sort of stupid hope that he at least wanted to check on me, that he at least cared.

"Let me ask you something, Doc. Would you think I was ridiculous if I went out to LA to talk to him, even though he's made it pretty clear that he doesn't want to have contact with me?"

"I think sometimes in life we have to go for the gusto, and if people don't think we're acting ridiculous, then we're not trying hard enough."

I nodded. "I just feel like I need closure. I spent the last eight years obsessing over what would have happened if I hadn't bought Izzy and me the tickets to that concert. I can't spend the next eight years wondering what might have happened if I'd gone to talk to him one last time."

"Our fears are temporary—they come and go throughout life. But regret is permanent—we carry it with us forever. If you go and it doesn't turn out the way you wanted it to, you'll be sad, but you'll be able to move on knowing you tried to win his heart back."

"You're right. I need to do it. Even if he slams the door in my face, I need to shout through it and give it everything I have."

Doc smiled. "My sister is in New Mexico with her daughter for the rest of the summer, so I still have the RV. I could gas it up, and we could leave tonight."

I appreciated the offer, I really did. And having a road companion for that long haul made the trip so much more bearable. But yet, it felt like this was something I needed to do on my own. I'd just have to take double the time and go slow. I'd relied on Doc enough. This trip was something I needed to do for Griffin and me, but it was also something I needed to do just for myself.

"Thank you so much for the offer, Doc. I appreciate it more than you'll ever know. But do you think your sister would mind if I borrowed the RV myself?"

Doc stopped in place. "Yourself? You want to drive three thousand miles alone?"

I hoped I hadn't hurt his feelings. "Yes. I can't explain it, but I feel like it's something I really need to do alone."

Doc took a deep breath in and out and smiled. "Now you're talking. Go for the gusto, Luca."

◆ ◆ ◆

I couldn't believe I was doing this. I'd spent the last day and a half preparing. I had the same route Doc and I had taken last time mapped out on my phone and also on printed maps. Because I'd be traveling all alone, I reduced my driving schedule each day to three hundred miles. I'd researched safe spots to park each night—RV places with security and good ratings—and I'd stocked the camper with all the essentials I'd need for two weeks. The gas tank was full, the oil was changed, and Doc had disassembled the passenger seat and removed it so that Hortencia's bed could sit on the floor in the front with me.

The sun had just started to go down, and I walked around my house double-checking I had turned everything off and unplugged any potential fire hazards. I stopped in my bedroom and had my hand on the light switch, about to turn it off, when the framed photo of Isabella and me caught my eye from the nightstand. I walked over and picked it up.

"It feels like you should be coming with me. But in my heart I know I need to do this on my own. Though that's not true, is it, Izzy? I don't need the photo to have you with me, because you'll always be in my heart." I took a deep breath and ran my finger over her face. "I'm going to go be *fearless*. I'll see you in a few weeks."

I set the frame back down on my nightstand and this time smiled looking back before closing the door. In the kitchen, I grabbed Hortencia's leash and bent to get her water bowl. As I stood, a flash of light hit me in the eyes through the blinds. The window over the sink faced the front of the house, and I leaned forward and separated two of the slats to peer out. Finding headlights, I smiled and shook my head. Doc had wanted to come see me off for my trip, but I'd told him it would be late and he didn't have to. I should've known he'd show up anyway. I grabbed my purse and a few last-minute things and headed outside.

The second I opened the screen door, Hortencia took off running and *groink*ing toward the headlights. She loved Doc. I locked up the door and shielded my eyes as I turned. He must've had his brights on the entire drive over, because it looked like a floodlight was beaming at me. "Doc . . . turn off your headlights!" I walked a few steps forward and the lights went out.

It took my eyes a solid ten seconds to adjust to the darkness, but when they did, I froze. It wasn't Doc's car in my driveway, and it definitely wasn't Doc.

Griffin hopped down from the driver's seat of a giant RV and slammed the door shut. We both stood there just staring for the longest time.

"What . . . what are you doing here?" I finally said.

He nodded to Doc's sister's RV parked next to the one he'd come out of. I had it running to warm it up. "Going somewhere?"

I swallowed. "I was . . . going to drive to California to see you."

Neither of us moved. "Is Doc in the RV already?"

I shook my head. "I was driving alone."

Griffin's brows rose. "You were going to drive three thousand miles by yourself?"

I nodded. "I needed to see you."

He shoved his hands into his pockets. "Well, here I am. Got something you need to say?"

I'd spent days thinking about what I would say when I showed up at his front door, yet now that I was standing twenty feet away from him, I didn't know where to even begin.

Griffin took a few steps toward me, the gravel crunching under his feet as he walked. He pulled something out of his pocket and held it up. "I got your letter."

"I know. I tracked it and saw that you signed for it."

He shook his head. "Styx signed for it. Not me."

"Your drummer?"

"I'd gotten drunk and passed out in my room. Styx's room was next door, and he heard the hotel manager knocking and took the letter for me. When he saw the return address, he decided the last thing I needed was more communication from you." He paused. "You fucked me up pretty good, Luca."

It felt like a tennis ball was stuck in my throat, and no matter how many times I tried to swallow, I couldn't get rid of it.

Griffin closed the distance between us and extended the letter I'd written back to me. It was still sealed.

"You . . . you didn't open it?"

Griff shook his head back and forth slowly. "I was on my way to the airport when Styx finally decided to give it to me. I didn't want anything you'd written inside to change my mind about coming, so I didn't read it."

My forehead wrinkled. I'd fucked him up, yet he was here without having read my letter. "Where were you going when he gave you the envelope?"

"Here."

"But . . . but why?"

"I'm angry at you. I'm pissed off. I'm tired from not sleeping. I don't want to sing another goddamn song with your name in it. I'm irritated as hell. But the fact remains that I still want to spend every angry, pissed-off, tired, irritated moment with you. So I don't give a flying shit what's in this letter. I'm here, and I'm not leaving until we figure this out. I don't have anywhere to be for three months, so if you won't let me stay, then my new tricked-out RV that cost me more than my house in California is going to be parked outside your house for a long-ass time."

Oh my God. We'd come full circle. I'd stopped reading his letters so many years ago, and here he was today handing me my unopened one in person. I'd taken a crazy chance and parked my RV in front of his house, and here he was today ready to park in front of mine for a chance at us.

I took the letter from Griffin's hand and opened the seal. My voice was low and shaky when I started to read.

"Dear Griffin,

"For eight years, I've been afraid of the dark.

"For eight years, I've been afraid of letting go.

"For eight years, I've been afraid of being trapped.

"For eight years, I've been afraid of fire.

"For eight years, I've been afraid of trying.

"Your love made me realize I wasn't really ever afraid of the dark, I was afraid of what lurked inside the darkness.

"I wasn't afraid of letting go, I was afraid to accept what was already gone.

"I wasn't afraid of being trapped, I was afraid to be free.

"I wasn't afraid of fire, I was afraid to be burned.

"I wasn't afraid of trying, I was afraid of getting hurt."

I knew the next few lines by heart, so I lowered my letter and spoke into Griffin's eyes.

"I'm not saying I'm better, because I have a long road ahead of me. But I'm tired of letting fear rule my life. I'm terrified of loving you, Griffin. I'm terrified of what would happen if I let myself love you and then lost you."

I looked up and saw Griffin's eyes filled with tears.

"But I'm more terrified of living my life without your love than I am of taking a chance. So please forgive me. I screwed up. And I'm probably going to screw up some more." I reached out my hand. "Please take me back, Griffin. Because I love you more than the total of all my fears put together."

Griffin's eyes went back and forth between mine. "What do you call a twenty-five-year-old British rock star who meets the girl of his dreams through a letter in second grade and drives to her house after she dumps him?"

I laughed. "I don't know. Impetuous?"

Griff took both my cheeks into his hands. "Home. You call him finally home."

CHAPTER 33

GRIFFIN

I dumped my keys on the table as I entered the house. "I'm back and I've got the magazine, love."

Luca had been getting some writing in while I spent the morning out running errands. For several months, I'd been hibernating with her until I had to leave for the European leg of the tour.

The plan was that she would stay here in Vermont while I was gone. When I returned, we would venture out west together in the mansion on wheels I'd purchased. Then we'd divide our time among California, Vermont, and the open road.

I threw the magazine on the bed. Luca grabbed it and examined the cover. It was a photo of us where my arms were wrapped around Luca as we both smiled for the camera. The title was: *Cole Archer: Meet the Real Luca.*

"Oh my God. I look so Photoshopped." She ran her hand over her face on the cover. "I kind of like it." She laughed.

"You look beautiful, Photoshopped or not. I, on the other hand, look like Hortencia's arsehole."

"Do you think we did the right thing? I mean, there's no going back now."

"This was the only choice we had. If you want the press to leave you alone somewhat, you have to nip things in the bud, take control of the situation. You give them what they want on *your* terms so they have nothing left to chase after."

She fanned through the pages. "Did you read it?"

"I did. I had to make sure there were no surprises before I let you see it. They did a good job on it. I suppose my threatening legal action if they so much as altered one word of our verbiage helped."

We'd sold the rights to our entire love story, told from start to finish, to a reputable national magazine. The cover feature rendered us $3 million, which we donated in Isabella's name to a hospital that treated burn victims.

If Luca was truly going to be in my day-to-day life, I knew I couldn't hide her. People were going to find out who she was whether I liked it or not. If there was one thing I'd learned about the press over the years, it was not to run away from them. Run toward them. Give them what they wanted before they even knew they wanted it.

"You want to read it now?" I asked.

"Maybe in a bit. I have to gear myself up for it."

"Okay, good, because I want to show you something first."

Her eyes widened. "What?"

I rolled up my sleeve to reveal the fresh ink I'd just gotten tattooed onto my inner forearm. I'd gone to the same artist who had tattooed the sun, moon, and stars design onto Luca's arm and asked him to replicate it on mine.

She gasped and covered her mouth.

I examined her face. "I can't tell if you love it or if you're thoroughly freaked out."

She laughed. "Oh my God. No, I love it. It's perfect. It's identical to mine. He really did a great job."

"I truly feel like your Izzy has been instrumental in guiding us back together. I wanted to honor her. I know it was supposed to be her getting the matching tattoo with you, but I hope I can stand in her place . . . in her honor."

"She would have loved you, Griff."

"Yeah?"

"You know . . . I used to talk to her about you a lot. And she'd say, 'I think that British boy is your soul mate.' I didn't see it so clearly then, never imagined I would ever even have a chance to meet you. I knew you and I had a connection for sure but never thought of you as being my soul mate. But now I know she was right. She had a sense about it that I didn't."

"Thank you for sharing that. I love her even more now."

She ran her finger over the clear bandage, looking pensive.

"What are you thinking about?"

Her question threw me for a loop. "When we were apart . . . did you ever . . . ?"

She hesitated to finish her question. But I knew what she was asking.

"Did I ever fuck anyone else?"

She nodded.

I'd had opportunities to sleep with other women while Luca and I were apart. I couldn't lie and say there weren't times when I'd thought about getting it over with in an attempt to try to forget the pain of her breaking up with me. But in the end, I didn't want anyone else, and my gut told me I'd regret it.

"A part of me just *knew*, Luca. I knew that somehow we'd end up back together. I didn't want to have to look you in the eyes and tell you that I had slept with someone else. If you'd taken years to come around, I'm not sure I could have been alone for that amount of time, but I'm so glad you didn't make me wait too long. It honestly never felt like you weren't a part of me, even when we were separated. I never had the desire for anyone but you. And no, I wasn't with anyone. I'm glad I was true to you."

A breath of relief escaped her. "I'd been so afraid to bring it up. But it was bothering me, and I just had to know."

"I'm glad you finally asked." I was curious. "Would it have changed things between us if I had been with someone else?"

"No. I would have understood, although it would have been upsetting. But I'm relieved."

"What about you?" I asked. "Anyone I have to murder?"

"Not unless it's a Furby."

Luca was making me so proud lately. The other day, she'd come with me to the pet store in the middle of the afternoon, and today we'd ventured to the supermarket for the first time during the day.

What seemed like a simple thing for most people was in fact a huge step for her. But ever since we got back together, she was more determined than ever to challenge her fears. I hoped that one day she'd be able to fly in planes and attend one of my concerts, but one step at a time. I knew I'd never force her to do anything she wasn't ready for.

"How are you doing?" I asked as we approached the grocery store from the parking lot.

She blew out a breath. "Anxious. But even if I poop my pants, I'm not running away."

"If you poop your pants, love, *I'll* be the one running away." I winked.

She managed a laugh despite her nerves.

Squeezing her hand, I held on to her as we made our way through the sliding glass doors. The bright fluorescent lights greeted us. It was the afternoon, so while more crowded than the middle of the night, the market wasn't mobbed by any means.

"You okay?"

She nodded and let out a shaky breath. "Yeah."

"Good."

"What now?" she asked.

"Now? We put one foot in front of the other and we shop."

This was what it was all about. One step at a time. I was thrilled when she'd told Doc not to come, that she would be okay with just me. It wasn't that I didn't appreciate all that he'd done for her, but she'd be leaving Vermont soon enough and needed to learn to lean on me—until she didn't need to lean on anyone at all.

We came upon the watermelons.

"What was that trick, babe? Show me again how you pick the best one."

I didn't really want to know, but it was a good way to get her mind off her nerves.

She lifted one of them and demonstrated. "You have to hold it up to your ear and tap it with your finger. If it's hollow, it's perfect."

I pulled her toward me and nestled my head in her neck, taking in a long whiff of her scent. My cheek landed on her chest, and I could feel her heart beating against me. Then I tapped gently on her breast and placed my ear on her heart.

She laughed. "What are you doing?"

"Yup. I've found the one for me. I've most definitely picked the best."

EPILOGUE

LUCA

Two Years Later

Dear Luca,
You would think after all these years . . . after all the
letters I've written you, this one would come easily.
But somehow, I feel like a thirteen-year-old boy again,
afraid to tell the girl he's falling in love with how he
feels. A lot has changed since then. I've been inside of
you. I've gotten to love you in ways I never thought
possible. And yet . . . it feels like yesterday that I was
just that boy in London waiting for the next letter
to come. I could have never imagined the journey
life would take us on to get to where we are today.
Your bravery in pushing through your fears not only
inspires me but proves every day just how much you
love me. You letting me hold your hand while you
white-knuckle your way through life with me, letting

the fear do its worst so that we can be together, is the ultimate proof of your love.

Before Mum died, she told me that her greatest wish for me was that I would someday find someone who loved me as much as she did. It brings me great joy knowing that she's looking down at me right now and seeing that I have. She can rest in peace knowing I'm loved and cared for. And I hope your father and Doc are looking down right now and thinking the same thing—knowing that their girl is cherished. I'm so happy to be the man who gets to love you. Over the past couple of years, you've proven that you would do anything for me. And I want you to know that I would do anything for you. I'd die for you, Luca. You're the only person I can honestly say that about. Bloody hell, could this letter BE any sappier? (I had to bring Chandler Bing from *Friends* back for the occasion.) Sappy or not . . . there is just no other way to convey it. Luca Vinetti, my love for you is greater than the sun, the moon, and the stars. It knows no bounds. Our story is not one that fairy tales are made of . . . it's raw and real but the truest kind of love nevertheless. I was wondering if you would do me the honor of becoming my wife. Marry me, Luca. When you're done reading this letter, you're going to look up at me, and then I'm going to drop to one knee. I'm going to ask you again to marry me. If you say yes, you'll make me the happiest guy on earth. If you say no, I'll love you anyway, and it won't matter whether there's a ring on your finger to prove it. I love you, Luca. From now until eternity.

Your love,
Griffin

P.S. Please say yes.
P.P.S. Marry Mee-Mee.

I folded the letter and closed my eyes, remembering the day Griffin had proposed a year ago. We'd been roaming the country in the RV after he'd returned from his European tour. While Griffin was away in Europe, Doc died suddenly of a heart attack. I'd gone to check on him in his tiny house and found him in bed unconscious. It was the second most difficult moment of my life and really proved just how much strength I had. Because I never would have thought I could have survived finding him like that. But I just *knew* I had to be strong for him, that he would never want to be the source of my grief. I owed it to Doc to put his own teachings to good use when it came to losing him.

Right after Doc died, Griffin flew back from Europe to be with me, citing a family emergency. The tour was put on hold until we had some time to properly grieve. After he returned to Europe and finished the last couple of postponed shows, he came back to Vermont. That was when our new life began as we took to the open road with Hortencia in tow. It was during that trip, parked somewhere in Florida, that Griffin had handed me his proposal letter before getting down on one knee. Of course, I said yes.

Now, one year later, we were home in Los Angeles on the morning of our wedding day. Griff had agreed to get ready in the RV so that I could have some privacy. We planned to do photos before the ceremony. So he'd be seeing me soon.

With the entire second floor of our home to myself, I was taking this time to enjoy the peace and quiet—aside from Hortencia's occasional oinking. While I'd made a few friends out here, I chose not to have any bridesmaids. There was no one who could replace Izzy today;

she was here in spirit as my maid of honor. The ceremony would be small, just some of our closest friends. Griffin's dad flew in from London with his new wife. I knew that was stressful for Griff, but I was proud of him for taking that step in inviting him.

Our wedding would be taking place at the Dr. Chester Maxwell Aviary here in Los Angeles. Griffin had given them a sizable donation, and they'd renamed it in Doc's memory. This was a very emotional day for me, far more than I'd ever imagined. The two men who I would have wanted to walk me down the aisle—my father and Doc—were both gone. So Griffin would be doing the honors.

I opened the window to let some fresh air in before I would have to put on my dress. In my silk robe, I stared up at the clear California sky and took a deep breath in.

It was then that I noticed a red cardinal perched on the wrought iron balcony. Of course, any time a bird would so much as fly by me, it would make me think of Doc. But there was something different about this one. It wasn't flitting around or chirping like the other birds that roamed around the garden. It was *stoic*. This one just seemed to be staring at me.

"Hello," I said.

It tilted its head in response.

I specifically remembered Doc saying something about the red cardinal, how people often believed they were messengers from lost loved ones.

I'd expected it to fly away, but instead it flew toward me and landed on the windowsill right next to me. My eyes began to well up with tears, mainly for how pathetic I was in hoping that this was somehow Doc sending me a message—or Doc himself. I wanted to believe more than anything that this little bird was him. But I would never know. I just started to cry.

I imagined where my life would be without Doc and without Griffin. It was ironic, because were it not for Doc, I might never have reconnected with Griffin, because the California trip wouldn't have happened. And without Griffin, I couldn't imagine how I would have dealt with losing Doc—the only family I had left. I was so lucky to have had such important men in my life who'd impacted me in profound ways.

"Hello, friend," I said to the bird. "I'm going to pretend that it's you. Because it makes me happy to think that you might have transformed into one of the creatures that were so beloved to you. But most of all, I want to believe that you're here with me today, where you should be. You would have walked me down the aisle, you know." I wiped my eyes. "I'm sorry I never got to say goodbye to you. But I know you're here with me still. When I'm scared, I still hear your voice cheering me on. I carry you everywhere. Because of you I am, Chester Maxwell."

The bird suddenly flew away. No goodbye. No warning. Nothing. Then again, that's how it went, didn't it?

There was a knock at the door. "Yes?" I wiped my eyes.

"Hi, Miss Vinetti. Is it safe to come in?"

It was the photographer, Leah.

I opened the door. "Hi. Yes. I just have to touch up my eye makeup and slip into my dress. Would you mind helping me?"

"Not at all."

While I would have much rather had my mother or Izzy here to zip up the back of my gown instead of Leah, I took solace in the fact that I would be with Griffin soon, and these feelings of loneliness would then be replaced by the joy of our wedding day.

After I was dressed, Leah took some photos of me looking in the mirror as I redid my makeup.

It was now time to meet Griffin outside.

"Mr. Archer asked for you and him to have some privacy in the courtyard before pictures start. So I'll capture the moment he sees you and then disappear for about ten minutes before coming back to take your outdoor photos."

"Okay. Thank you."

When I emerged from the house into the yard, Griffin's back was facing me as he stood under a jacaranda tree.

"Griffin?"

When he turned around and got a look at me, he immediately started crying. I'd rarely seen Griffin cry—not happy tears, at least. But there was certainly no bigger proof of his love for me than to witness them falling from his eyes right now.

"You look even more beautiful than I could have ever imagined."

"Thank you. And you look so handsome." I adjusted his boutonniere and patted his chest. "I love that vest." I felt like I should have been crying, but I think I was all cried out. That didn't mean I wasn't happy beyond belief right now.

I noticed that Griffin was holding a small gift bag.

"What's in the bag?"

"I wasn't sure if you had something old, something borrowed, something blue . . ."

"I hadn't even remembered that tradition." I smiled. "I don't, actually. You got me covered?"

"I got you covered." He winked, then took the first item out of the bag. "Something old," he said as he took out a silver locket. "This belonged to my mother. When I inherited it after she died, it was empty. So I took the photo you have of Izzy and had a copy made of it that was just the right size to fit inside."

Okay, now I was crying.

As he placed it around my neck, I said, "My makeup is going to be ruined."

"We'll fix it."

There was nothing Griffin couldn't fix or make better.

My heart raced in anticipation as he pulled out the next item.

"Something borrowed," he said before opening a velvet box. In it were the most stunning diamond earrings from Harry Winston. Those had to have cost a fortune.

"Oh my God. These are exquisite."

"I hope you really like them. You don't have to wear them if you don't."

"I do." I smiled. "I really do. Thank you."

I took out the smaller diamond studs I'd been wearing before he helped me put the new earrings on. They were gorgeous, dangling chandelier-style and likely cost as much as this wedding.

"Something blue." He flashed a wicked smile before taking out a tiny Furby key chain. It was the one I'd left behind at his house during my first trip out to see him. It happened to be a royal-blue color. He'd added a little safety pin to the end. Bending down, he pinned it to the underside of my dress.

"That's perfect." I beamed.

"And we can use it until the battery runs out later." He winked.

After he put the bag aside, I realized he'd skipped over "something new."

"Isn't one missing? Something new?"

"Yes, my love. But it's not in the bag. It's inside of *you*."

Griffin knelt down and kissed my stomach.

The greatest reward for facing my fears was that he and I had made a little human. Four months along, I wasn't showing enough to have to wear a maternity dress. Thankfully, the cut of the gown I'd chosen hid what small bump I had pretty well. But in only a matter of months, we would be welcoming a baby boy, who we planned to name Griffin Chester Marchese. And my life once again would be changed forever.

Was I terrified of becoming a mother? Absolutely. But I would dive headfirst into it and take everything as it came just as I had been trying to do with everything else. That approach had gotten me far. It had gotten me *here* to the most important day of my life.

Griffin took my hand as we walked through his garden, relishing this calm before the wedding.

"Best thing I ever did was answer your first letter, you know," he said.

I squeezed his hand. "Best thing I ever did was send it."

"Speaking of your first letter, I recently went through all my boxes and came across it. I'm holding it in my pocket today as my own 'something old.'"

"Really?"

He reached inside and took it out before unfolding it.

Shock crossed his face. "My God."

"What?"

"I never noticed this. Look at the date, Luca. Holy shit. Look at the date!"

It was *today's* date—exactly twenty years ago.

My mouth hung open. "We're getting married two decades to the day of the very first time I ever wrote you."

"And we had no idea when we picked this date for our wedding. I'd say that's pretty damn amazing."

I had no recollection of what I'd written that very first time. I looked down at that fateful letter and smiled as I read it.

Dear Griffin,

You don't know me, but my teacher gave me your name. I'm Luca. I think you're looking for a pen pal? Would you want to be mine?

I'm seven, live in New York, love black licorice and dancing.

I would love to know what it's like in England. Do you have black licorice there? I heard people drive on the opposite side of the road. That is so weird!

Your pen pal (?),
Luca

P.S. Mrs. Ryan showed me a list of kids, and I picked your name, Griffin Quinn. I don't know why. Maybe because my mom watches that show *Dr. Quinn, Medicine Woman*. But you stuck out. It was just a feeling I had that you were it—my pen pal. My dad always says to trust your gut. My gut loves black licorice. And my gut tells me we're going to be friends, Griffin. I really hope you write back.

SURPRISE!

Dear Readers,

We have a BIG SURPRISE for you! How would you like to HEAR Griffin sing the song he wrote to Luca in the book? Just click to sign up for our newsletter and grab a free download of Griff singing his heart out for the woman he loves!

We hope you love it as much as we do!

https://www.subscribepage.com/DirtyLetters

Much love,
Vi and Penelope

ACKNOWLEDGMENTS

Thank you to all of the amazing bloggers who spread the news about our books. Without you, so many readers would never discover us. We are so grateful for all your hard work and support.

To Julie—thank you for your friendship, daily support, and encouragement. Looking forward to seeing what you have in store for us next!

To Luna—thank you for blessing us with your incredible creative talent and for being there for us each and every day.

To our super agent, Kimberly Brower—thank you for being our partner and guiding us to find the right partners in publishing. You're so much more than our agent, and we appreciate you always being there for us—even at six in the morning.

To our amazing editor at Montlake, Lindsey Faber, and to Lauren Plude and the entire Montlake team—not many authors are lucky enough to say the editing process was a pleasure, but it truly was. Thank you for trusting us and making *Dirty Letters* the best it could be.

Last but never least, to our readers—thank you for letting us into your hearts. We know that there are so many choices for you out there, and we are honored that you stick with us. Thank you for your loyalty and love. Without you, there would be no success!

Much love,
Penelope and Vi

ABOUT THE AUTHORS

Photo © 2017 Irene Bella Photography

Vi Keeland is a #1 *New York Times*, #1 *Wall Street Journal*, and *USA Today* bestselling author. With millions of books sold, her titles have appeared on over a hundred bestseller lists and are currently translated into more than twenty-five languages. She resides in New York with her husband and their three children, where she is living out her own happily ever after with the boy she met at age six.

Connect with Vi Keeland

Facebook Fan Group:

https://www.facebook.com/groups/ViKeelandFanGroup/

Facebook

https://www.facebook.com/pages/Author-Vi-Keeland-/435952616513958

Website
http://www.vikeeland.com
Twitter
@vikeeland
https://twitter.com/ViKeeland
Instagram
@Vi_Keeland
http://instagram.com/Vi_Keeland/

Photo © 2016 Angela Rowlings

Penelope Ward is a *New York Times*, *USA Today*, and #1 *Wall Street Journal* bestselling author. With more than two million books sold, she's a twenty-one-time *New York Times* bestseller. Her novels are published in more than a dozen languages and can be found in bookstores around the world. Having grown up in Boston with five older brothers, she spent most of her twenties as a television news anchor before switching to a more family-friendly career. She is the proud mother of a beautiful fifteen-year-old girl with autism and a thirteen-year-old boy. Penelope and her family reside in Rhode Island.

Connect with Penelope Ward:
Facebook Private Fan Group:
https://www.facebook.com/groups/PenelopesPeeps/

Facebook:
https://www.facebook.com/penelopewardauthor
Website:
http://www.penelopewardauthor.com
Twitter:
@PenelopeAuthor
https://twitter.com/PenelopeAuthor
Instagram:
@penelopewardauthor
http://instagram.com/PenelopeWardAuthor/